Vinegar Hill

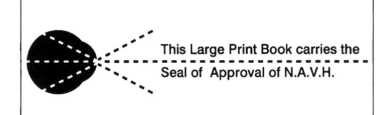
This Large Print Book carries the
Seal of Approval of N.A.V.H.

VINEGAR HILL

A. Manette Ansay

Thorndike Press • Thorndike, Maine

Selections one and three of this book first appeared in slightly different form in *Willow Springs*. Section seven was originally published in slightly different form in *Quarterly West*.

Grateful acknowledgment is made for permission to reprint excerpts from the following copyrighted works: "Winter Haven" from *In the Walled City* by Stewart O'Nan. Reprinted by the University of Pittsburgh Press © 1993 by Stewart O'Nan. *Between the Acts* by Virginia Woolf. Copyright 1941 by Harcourt Brace & Company and renewed by Leonard Woolf. Reprinted by permission of the publisher.

Published in 2000 by arrangement with
William Morrow and Co., Inc.

Thorndike Press Large Print Basic Series.

The tree indicium is a trademark of Thorndike Press.

The text of this Large Print edition is unabridged.
Other aspects of the book may vary from the original edition.

Set in 16 pt. Plantin by Rick Gundberg.

Printed in the United States on permanent paper.

ISBN 0-7862-2511-4 (lg. print : hc : alk. paper)
ISBN 0-7862-2512-2 (lg. print : sc : alk. paper)

For Sylvia J. Ansay

Acknowledgments

Thanks to the Stonecoast Writers Conference, where I took my very first story for repair. Thanks to the MacDowell Colony, where *Vinegar Hill* was completed. Thanks to Claire Wachtel, who always loved this book, and to Tia Maggini and the good folks at Avon Books for keeping it in print. Thanks to Deborah Schneider, who never lost faith; to my wonderfully tireless and creative father and "personal publicist" Dick Ansay; to my gifted mother and first reader, Sylvia J. Ansay; and to Jake Smith — still crazy after all these years.

Contents

Pendant from her chain her cross swung as she leant out and the sun struck it. How could she weight herself down by that sleek symbol? How stamp herself so volatile, so vagrant, with that image?

—Virginia Woolf
Between the Acts

God isn't like a star that can go out.

—Stewart O'Nan
In the Walled City

Braid

1

In the gray light of the kitchen, Ellen sets the table for supper, keeping the chipped plate back for herself before lowering the rest in turn. The plates are pink with yellow flowers twisting around the edges, and they glow between the pale frosted glasses, the stainless steel knives and forks, the plastic pitcher of milk. In the center of the table, the roast platter steams between the bowl of wrinkled peas, the loaf of sliced bread. Ellen wipes a water stain from the cupped palm of a spoon. Soon all the bright plates and glasses and flatware will be soiled, and she finds herself imagining how it must be to wait for that first hot splash of meat, the cold dribble of milk.

"Time to eat," she calls down the narrow hallway to the living room, where the children and her husband and his parents are all watching TV. She gets the cloth napkins from the drawer and folds them into tall, peaked hats, something her mother always did when she wanted the table to look nice. The napkins are also pink, and they match the plates and the tablecloth, and come very close to matching the curtains, which are drawn tightly closed. The yard beyond stretches plain and white into the next yard and the next, the single scrawny pine along the lot line stiff with ice. When Ellen walks home from work late in the afternoon, that tree reminds her of an animal, the way it stands without the slightest movement, corralled by the neat rows of houses lining the block.

The children straggle in and sit twisting in their chairs, raising the cloth napkin hats to their heads, giggling at their game. James and his parents shake out the hats, and James smooths his across his lap, his shoulders firm against the back of his chair. Ellen sets a saucer of margarine beside him, and abruptly the color seems too bright, like cheddar cheese or sweet acorn squash. She fights a vague queasy feeling; when James's father begins Grace, she closes her eyes, speaking each word clearly in her mind, trying to concentrate. It's one of the first prayers she ever learned, chanting along with her mother and sisters in the cozy heat of their farmhouse kitchen, the family cats brushing their ankles like silk. She remembers the rich odors of *mustripen* and sausage and thick bread pudding, the eager edge of hunger a deepening crease that ran from her chest to her stomach.

Bless us O Lord. These thy gifts.

By the time she has finished praying, the serving bowls have already begun their slow start and stop around the table. The children look at her curiously; she quickly takes a piece of bread. James ladles peas onto his plate with a clatter that lets her know she has embarrassed him in front of his parents, in his parents' home. They eat without speaking, and it's hard to swallow without the gravy of conversation, the children's playful bickering, James's questions about her day, her own questions and his responses, the hollow overlappings of their words.

She watches his jaw as he chews his roast, the roast she has prepared for him, dry, the way he likes it. The motion of his jaw is steady and unconcerned; his lips are pinched tight over his teeth. She thinks, *I have kissed those lips, I have pushed my tongue against those teeth,* and this thought fascinates and repels her. Amy asks for milk and Ellen fills her glass. Herbert's napkin slides to the floor and she tells him to pick it up. But her eyes are fixed to James's jaw, and she thinks about how strange it is that one small thing like a jaw or a look or a brush of a hand can become so much larger than it actually is, so large that it closes itself around you and squeezes until it is hard to find air.

It is November, and she can hear the wind moving over the walls of the house, stroking the windows, trying to coax its way past the curtains to blow the flowers from the napkins and plates, to muss the perfect leaves of the plastic plants that hang side by side above the sink. The house is filled with knickknacks — china angels, statues of saints, small glass animals with beady eyes — and each of them has to be dusted and the surface beneath polished with lemon oil, and then each has to be set back down precisely as it was before, the beady eyes staring in the same direction, the dust settling about it in the same design. The copper duck and goose Jell-O molds have hung for so long above the stove that the paint behind them has kept its color, and when Ellen takes them down for polishing, a perfect bright shape of a duck or goose remains. *A place for everything; everything in its place.* The house is as rigid, as precise as a church, and there was nothing to disturb its ways until three months ago, when Ellen and James and the children moved in because they had no place and nowhere else to go.

James had been laid off just as the lilacs in the yard of their rented house bloomed, open-eyed and fragrant, trusting the Illinois winter

14

had passed. The next day, an ice storm trapped the world in crystal. The school where Ellen taught closed for the day, and she spent the morning playing cards with Amy and Herbert — their school had closed as well — and mourning the lilacs, and the budding trees, and most of all the colorful heads of the tulips, which were frozen to the ground. James watched TV on the couch, bundled in a quilt, his body tucked close against itself as if he wanted to disappear. *Talk to me,* Ellen said, but he listened to her the way you'd listen to a faucet drip, not assigning any particular meaning to the sound.

He refused to look for work. He read the paper in the morning and napped in the afternoon. She came home with the children one evening to find him pawing through a shoe box of old photographs. Most were of his older brother, Mitch, who had died in 1957, fifteen years before.

"If we lived closer to home," James said, "I could tend to Mitchie's grave. Pa doesn't care about things like that, and Mother isn't able to do it anymore."

Ellen could see Amy and Herbert tasting the word *grave* with their tongues. She tried not to notice that James was still in his bathrobe. Bits of egg were caught on one sleeve; dandruff lightened his eyebrows. "*This* is our home," she began, but James shook his head as if he were clearing away a brief spell of dizziness, shaking free of an unpleasant thought. Yet he had been the one to choose the house, just before Amy was born: a bungalow with two bedrooms, a porch, and a sunny, modern kitchen. The first night after they'd moved in, a thunderstorm startled them out of their sleep and it was James who raced through the rooms closing windows, already protective of the woodwork, the carpet, the neatly painted walls that cradled the beginning of their lives together. Since then, they had brought two children into this house, penciling lines on the kitchen wall to mark each year of their growth. James had repapered the bathroom; Ellen had sewn curtains for the living room windows. The furniture was arranged to cover the marks on the carpet from the time Amy broke open a pen. The ivy hanging in the kitchen window had woven itself into the blinds. The house had become a diary of their lives, and Ellen could not imagine leaving it.

But they couldn't live on her salary alone, and when the bulk of their savings was gone it was the excuse that James was looking for. They would live with his parents, he said, to save money. They would get back on their feet. After all, where else could they go? And as each day passed and he did not look for work and the money dwindled and disappeared, Ellen could feel his excitement building until, at the end of the summer, they left Illinois, the rented house, the stunted lilacs. They moved back to Holly's Field, Wisconsin, the town where they had both grown up and their parents had grown up too.

James's parents are not old — Fritz is just sixty, Mary-Margaret is sixty-four — but the house is thick with the smell of old age, of pale gray skin and Ben-Gay and many dry roasts and silent suppers. *My whole life I worked hard,* Fritz likes to say, *now all I want is some peace.* Ellen watches him take yet another slice of bread; he sweeps it across his plate, and the bread picks up the juices and the colors and the shattered bits of food until he raises it, dripping, to his mouth. He chews ferociously, but without pleasure. Meals, like everything else in life, are just another task to complete. Everyone must wait quietly until his food is eaten and his plate wiped clean with bread. *Children should be seen and not heard,* he says, when Amy and Herbert complain. Then he leads after-dinner Grace, even the children staring briefly at their hands, even James's restlessness steadied by the drone of his father's voice.

"Salt," Mary-Margaret says, peering around the table. Ellen finds it behind the milk jug and passes it down, but Mary-Margaret doesn't want it for herself; she sets it in front of James and smiles, proud to have anticipated his needs. James is his mother's boy again; under her care, he sleeps less, he has even managed to put on weight. In Illinois, he'd sit down to dinner, apologize, push his plate aside. Now his throat bulges as he swallows another chunk of meat, jaws grinding steadily.

The first time Ellen sat at this table she was twenty years old, bright-cheeked after a spring afternoon spent walking along the lakefront with James, planning their upcoming wedding. It was 1959, and she was eager to make a good impression. She didn't know then that Mary-Margaret disliked her, that she was considered *Jimmy's mistake.* They had dinner: dry pot roast, canned peas, and, for dessert, blue-frosted angel food cake, which Mary-Margaret pinched into cubes and ate with her fingers like bread. Mary-Margaret asked James, *How long does she intend to go to school? Ain't high school good enough?* and Ellen said, *I'm going to be a primary school teacher, and for that I need a college degree.* Mary-Margaret asked James, *Do her parents speak High or Low German?* and Ellen said, *My mother speaks Luxembourg and German.* *Low German,* Mary-Margaret said, *and her father, too. He's dead but I remember him coming into the church in a stocking cap!* Then she and Fritz spoke in German about Ellen's father while Ellen chewed on a mouthful of that dry roast, trying to swallow it down. Thirteen years later the roast has not changed, but now Mary-Margaret won't tolerate guests, family or otherwise. Even Ellen's mother and sisters may not visit because of Mary-Margaret's poor nerves.

And now Mary-Margaret dresses only in pink. Pink stretch pants and pink polyester blouses, pink hose, pink shoes. She puts on her long pink rayon nighties and pink chenille robes by four in the afternoon, because she has to be careful of her heart. Then she goes into the living room and plays the piano until supper. The big color television is in the living room also; Fritz turns the TV volume louder and she strikes the piano keys harder, pounding out hymns and singing along in a cracked, dry voice until Fritz says, *What's that? Did somebody bring in a cat?* Then he shakes with the sort of laughter that is angry, bitter, taunting, not amused. *A cat would've made me a better wife.* Their arguments fill the house like an odor, clinging to the sofa and seeping between the bedsheets, lingering in Ellen's hair.

Each night, before she goes to bed, Mary-Margaret calls Ellen into the bathroom to rub

Ben-Gay on her shoulders and to watch her take her pills so she won't forget and take the same ones twice. Biting her cheek, Ellen obeys; to refuse means James's cold back stretched like a wall down the middle of the bed. *She's old, she's unwell. You couldn't do her that one favor?* The bathroom is also pink; the shelves are lined with powders, oils, creams, perfumes. Some of the bottles are so old Ellen wonders if they are valuable. Certainly they are beautiful. Many are in the shape of the Virgin, but there are also birds and buildings and flowers, and high up on the top shelf is an empty bottle shaped like a ballerina, dressed in a full-skirted pink gauze dress. Beside it stands a tiny upright piano, still filled with perfume, which Amy particularly loves. Would you ask her if I could hold it? she asked Ellen once. You have to ask her that yourself, Ellen told her, although they both knew what the answer would be. Mary-Margaret doesn't care for little girls; it is boys who mean the future, the family blood, the family name. Ellen rubs Mary-Margaret's pale gray shoulders and her fingers sink into the softness past skin, past thin span of muscle, until they jar against bone. Taped to the mirror is a prayer card, a picture of Christ on the cross. His eyes are closed, His lips half-parted. The caption reads, *Lord, Help Me to Accept What I Cannot*

Change, and Ellen finds herself reading these words, without meaning to, over and over.

Nights, she goes in to James smelling like his mother, like the house, like the dry pot roast from the kitchen. She strips down to her panties which are not pink but white; cotton panties, practical panties, with blood stains at the crotch, perhaps, or the elastic sagging at the waist. James wears boxer shorts with flies that are stained the pale yellow of daisies, and he watches the portable black-and-white television on the low table at the foot of the bed. Television, like prayer, is soothing to James, and he watches until he falls asleep. It is Ellen who jolts awake later on and gets up to turn it off, filled with a loneliness as dense as clay inside her. Some nights she doesn't wake up until after the programming has ended. The shrill held note of the dead airtime is twisted through her dreams, which are of police sirens and fire alarms and running and climbing and seeking escape.

James finishes his roast, and Mary-Margaret is quick to pass the serving dish. "You should have more," she says to him, pleased as if she has cooked it. But Ellen cooks the meals and cleans the house, as part of their payment for shelter, for warmth, for dry pot roast and peas. Mary-Margaret makes out the shopping list; on weekends Ellen shops and on weeknights after work she cooks the meals the way Mary-Margaret tells her to. And now Mary-Margaret offers to James what Ellen has made, the roast that she has prepared.

"This is good," he says.

He does not say it to Ellen. He takes the center of the roast, his favorite part; the children beg for the round bone but Fritz tells them to be quiet. Three months ago James would have given them the bone, he might even have smiled and teased them; now he is at home with his parents and their rules, and himself and his rules, which have all become the same.

"Here," Mary-Margaret says to Herbert. "Here is a nice bone for you."

The bone is a long straight bone, not the kind of bone he wants.

"Daddy," Herbert says. But James can't look at a straight bone and see why it isn't as good as a round one, why the marrow in a round bone will be sweeter because of the feel of its shape upon the tongue. In fact James does not eat his marrow; he has remembered over the last three months that bones are to be left on the plate in neat piles, and that chewing on them is disgusting. Herbert gets his love of marrow from Ellen, from her Low German blood, from her country ways.

"If you had a bone, you would give it to

me," Herbert says against Ellen's ear, and abruptly he is happy. He drinks his milk and neatly wipes his face with the back of his hand.

"Use your napkin," James says. His hair sticks up at the top of his head; crumbs are scattered on his chin. He has finally found a job, but it is at the same place he worked after high school, selling farm machinery for Travis Manufacturer. He travels out of state and is gone for weeks at a time. When he comes home his eyes move over Ellen and the children without stopping. She shows him ads for apartments, and though he makes deposits at the bank each month, he says *Money, money* in a way that she knows means there will never be enough.

"Can I be excused?" Herbert asks Ellen.

"There's Grace still," Mary-Margaret says.

"Children should be seen and not heard," says Fritz.

Ellen says to Herbert, "There's Grace."

And she helps him to lay his knife, fork, and spoon at four o'clock on his plate. She helps him to fold his napkin neatly. But she is lost in her husband's jaw, the dry meat churning behind his lips, that one small thing so much larger than it is and her own self getting smaller and more far away. She takes a deep breath, expels it, moves her food around on her plate. She feels the children watching, and she smiles at them until the anxious looks that have sharpened their faces fade.

"You don't eat your food?" Mary-Margaret scolds. "Fussy, fussy!"

"I'm just not hungry," Ellen says. The queasiness in her stomach spreads to her chest, a sudden dizzy warmth. But she spears the first lump of meat with her fork, places it in her mouth, tries not to think about its slow descent into her body.

2

After the dishes are washed and put away, Ellen bundles up in James's coat, because it is warmer than her own, and goes into the living room, where he and Fritz and Mary-Margaret are watching TV. It's a comfortable room with moss-colored carpet, Fritz's La-Z-Boy, Mary-Margaret's embroidered parlor chair, and a long rectangular picture of the Last Supper, done in somber golds and greens. Beside the TV, Mary-Margaret's piano shines with lemon oil. Amy and Herbert are sitting on the floor, pretending to do their homework with their books spread out in front of them. But their eyes are wide and glassy. They are staring at the screen. They look down quickly when Ellen appears, shapeless as a boulder, the coat sleeves so long that just her fingertips show.

"I'm going for a walk," she says.

"Why?" Herbert says.

"I need the exercise," she says, although that is not the only reason. She kisses him, and then Amy. Their skin feels warm against her lips. "If I'm not back by eight-thirty, put yourselves to bed."

"But you'll be back by eight-thirty, won't you?" Herbert says.

"I'll try." She leans over to kiss James good-bye and accidentally blocks the screen. He looks at her irritably, then controls himself.

"Have a nice walk," he says, and he lets himself be kissed. Amy looks from Ellen to Mary-Margaret, then back at Ellen. She is built like her grandmother, tall and thin, with long willowy arms and legs she hasn't grown into yet. Over the summer, she shot up three inches; her face lengthened; her freckles lightened to match the color of her skin. Now her braid reaches down to where her waist dips inward, the first suggestion of a woman's graceful shape. Her eyes are James's dark, worried eyes.

"What?" Ellen says. She is sweating in the heavy coat, edging toward the door.

Amy tosses her head and her long braid swings. "Herbert gets scared when you're gone."

"Mama's boy," Mary-Margaret says. *"Hasenfuss."*

"I'll be back soon," Ellen says to Amy. They both ignore Mary-Margaret, who speaks in rapid German to Fritz, beginning a

26

long complaint that needs no translation.

Ellen almost trips on the threshold in her hurry to get outside. The cold air tastes sweet; she closes the door and breathes deeply, chasing the sour smell of the house from her lungs. These after-dinner walks are the only time she can take for herself, but even so, as she walks down the steep, narrow driveway, she feels terrible, as though she's stealing. By walking, she's not making sure the kids finish their homework; by walking, she's not available to James if he needs her. And she has papers to grade, one stack of them on the dresser at home, another waiting on her desk at school. Her classroom has three tall windows, each with a chip of stained glass crowning the top. She loves to work there in the late afternoons, composing lesson plans as the sun drizzles gold between the hanging plants, the last echoey voices of the children fading toward home. But grading papers depresses her: this far into the year, she doesn't need to see them to know what grade each student will receive. It seems so unfair, so hopeless. Sometimes she buys brightly colored stars and pastes them on each of the papers *just because you're all nice people*. But the kids don't buy it: nice doesn't get you anywhere, nice doesn't count. Looks count, and the right kind of clothes counts.

Two plus two equals four counts.

From the street the house looks peaceful: 512 Vinegar Hill, a pale brick ranch set too close to the street. The lamp in the living room window glows red; an eye peering back at her, curious but calm. The heads of Fritz and Mary-Margaret are just visible, and they could be the heads of any older couple, sitting side by side. They could be very much in love. They could be talking instead of watching TV, discussing Nixon's re-election, the situation in Vietnam, the weather, the supper they have eaten.

That was a good roast, the man might say. *Delicious.*

Oh no, it was much too dry.

No, really, it was good.

Or maybe the woman wouldn't answer the man. Maybe she would smile, just a bit, just enough for him to see that she was pleased. There would be history in that smile, and he might reach out to touch her hand, to twist the gold band on her finger, and the feeling between them would be so strong that a stranger walking by would notice the pale brick house set too close to the street and, inside it, the backs of two gray heads, and perhaps would imagine the woman's smile.

But there is nothing between Fritz and Mary-Margaret that might cause a stranger to notice, to slow and watch and wonder without really knowing why. At night they sleep in narrow twin beds as neatly as dolls, flat on their backs, chins raised in the air. Often, before they go to sleep, their voices rise and fall in the sing-song way of a prayer. Fritz knows something terrible about Mary-Margaret that he ultimately threatens to reveal, and this threat ends the fight instantly, with Mary-Margaret saying *No, no.* There are secrets everywhere in this house. Ellen walks around them, passes through them, sensing things without understanding what they mean.

She heads toward the downtown past other ranch-style houses, each centered primly on its rectangular lot. The doors and windows, the chimneys and driveways are all rectangular too, and the quiet streets cut larger rectangles that cover the town like the neat lines on a piece of graph paper. The most easterly line is formed by Lake Michigan; the coast curves gently until it reaches the downtown, where it juts inland to form the harbor. Perched on the bluff, Saint Michael's Church overlooks it all — the harbor, the downtown shops and businesses, the rows of rectangular houses that sprawl to the west for a quarter of a mile — the clock in the steeple like a huge, patient eye.

As a child, Ellen was afraid of that clock,

that steeple, the gaunt cross at its peak. Strings of smoke from the electric company rippled behind it like the shadows of large birds, and she was always relieved to go inside, to sit between her mother and her sisters in their usual pew down front. The altar shone like a holiday table, decorated with flowers and white linen; the air was scented with incense, shoe polish, the sweet odor of women's perfume. Often she'd sleep with her head on her mother's purse, lulled by the murmur of the congregation's responses and the slow, steady thrum of the hymns. The church was no less familiar than any room in the house where she, like all of her sisters, had been born, fifteen miles north of Holly's Field. They came to Saint Michael's for Mass on Sundays, for Wednesday night Devotions whenever they could, for plays and recitals and long days of school, for holiday celebrations. Every Christmas Eve, their mother drove them up and down the streets of Holly's Field to see the Christmas lights, ending the tour at Saint Michael's parking lot — the grand finale — where a twenty-foot wreath opened the darkness like an astonished red mouth. This was a treat they waited for all year, talked about for weeks afterward. And yet, Ellen always felt a sweet, secret relief at folding back into the blackness of the countryside, heading for home, the quietly lit farmhouses spread out from one another as if they'd fallen to earth, a shower of meteorites, each still faintly burning.

Now, though it's less than a week since Thanksgiving, Holly's Field is already strung with decorations. Plastic Santa Clauses wave from front lawns; nativity scenes glow between the bushes. Looking back, Ellen notices that only the house at 512 is dim, giving off the frail light of an ordinary table lamp. Fritz refuses to pay for the extra electricity; he doesn't want the bother of putting up a Christmas tree. Other years, visiting for a few days at Christmas, Ellen didn't mind. After all, there were lights and decorations and a fresh-cut tree at her mother's house for the children to enjoy. But this year it was different because 512 Vinegar Hill was home.

"Lights?" Fritz said to James, when Ellen mentioned it at the table one evening. "Is this where your money goes, Jimmy? Lights!"

"It's my money too," Ellen said. "I work too," but Fritz ignored her.

"Gals, they are quick with our wallets," he said, and he thumped the table next to James, laughing. Ellen looked at her plate because she was afraid that, if she looked up, she would see James laughing too. Then she got up and began to clear the table, lifting the

31

fried potatoes away just as Fritz reached out to take some more. He stared at her. His eyes were bright and small. Pigs' eyes. *You expect me to be afraid of you?* she thought. The potato dish burned in her palms.

When she'd first seen the scars on James's back, she hadn't known what they were. She traced one with her finger as he sat on the bed. It was several days after their wedding, and the first time she had seen his upper body in the light. She took her finger away when she realized he could not feel it.

"Pa was good with his belt," James said, and it was several years before Ellen saw him without his T-shirt again.

Now she stood in front of Fritz, hating him as James would not. *Weak old man,* she thought, dizzy with contempt.

James wiped his mouth on his napkin. "Pa's not finished," he said quietly.

"We're on a budget, remember?" Ellen said, and she put the potatoes on the counter.

You know I'm right. Fight him. Don't fight me.

But James got up and brought the potatoes back to the table, back to his father. Then he sat down and all of them, even the children, continued the meal without her.

Later, as they got into bed, James said, "We never had Christmas lights."

"What do you mean?" Ellen said. "We l
lights last year, and the year before that, in tι
crab apple tree outside the . . ."

Then she realized the *we* was *them*.

"I am your family," she said.

She could feel the weight of his body in the bed, and she wanted to stretch out her leg, kick that weight far away. "I am your family," she said again, so angry she did not know what else to say. She snapped off the lights and rolled to the far edge of the bed, imagining long dialogues that left James overwhelmed by her devastating arguments, her cool distance, her glib responses to his apologies. She woke to the alarm in the morning feeling as though she hadn't slept. Still, she knew that she had; James was pressed against her, an arm flung over her stomach. She tried to get up but the arm tightened, and they cuddled up then the way they had on weekend mornings in Illinois, dozing and waking, discussing the week's small misunderstandings, laughing over meaningless things. *If we just had some time to ourselves,* she thinks, *we could talk to each other the way we used to. Maybe about nothing in particular at first, but even that would be a start.*

Turning on to Main Street, she wants so much to have a good Christmas, a Christmas that will be the way they remember them-

selves, she and James, when they look back and remember the children as children, and themselves as young; when they sit in a lighted window at night with only the backs of their gray heads showing while strangers pass by and wonder who they are and who they were. So far, there have been few memories they can actually share. When Amy was born, James was in Ann Arbor. When Bert was born, he was north of La Crosse. Christmases and Easters, birthdays and anniversaries, James is usually on the road. Ellen never used to mind. He'd call from motel rooms, from gas stations and restaurants. *What's new?* he would say, and she'd bring him up to date. But lately she's realized that he doesn't listen, or if he does, he quickly forgets. It is a lonely thing, remembering for someone else, and she's grown to envy her sisters, whose husbands come home every night for supper and sit down in the same places, their own places, at their tables to eat.

Ellen's father died when she was five, and for several years his place at the table was left respectfully empty. But the table was small and soon Heidi's elbow jutted where his cup once stood; Gert switched her chair with his to accommodate her new, wide hips. One night, Ellen realized she couldn't tell where Daddy used to sit. Everyone except Miriam,

who had married, was spread evenly around the table; Mom, Gert, Ketty, Heidi, Julia, and herself. Without the space there, she could not remember what her father looked like, and she cried while Mom tried to console her; her sisters, all much older, said she was too young to remember him anyway. Ellen thinks now that she should be used to absence, that James's long trips shouldn't bother her because at least she knows he will come home. But his place at the table disappears as soon as he's gone, casually, as if he'd never really existed.

This year he missed Thanksgiving; he was somewhere in South Dakota. Ellen left Fritz and Mary-Margaret watching the Macy's parade on TV, and drove the children to her mother's for Thanksgiving dinner. The barns and the house were strung with lights; a blinking gold turkey sat on top of the purple martin house in the courtyard. Ellen's sisters were already in the house with their husbands and most of their children and grandchildren. Miriam beckoned to Ellen from the kitchen radiator; Ellen sat beside her on the warm metal bars. A tangle of children fought over dominoes at their feet as Mom's dog barked and spun in circles like a bobbin.

"How are you, Sputzie?" Miriam said, using Ellen's old nickname. Her gray hair was tucked up in a bun at the back of her head, and she wore the hearing aid her husband and grown-up children had chipped in for.

"Okay," Ellen said. It always took her a while to shake off the quiet of Mary-Margaret's house, to reorient herself to the commotion of her family. Her voice felt cramped and thin beside the voices of her sisters, and she wondered if, once, she had talked in the same expressive way, her hands slicing the air as she spoke instead of pinning her arms to her sides. Julia came over with her baby and kissed Ellen wetly on the cheek. Ellen and Miriam made room for her, and they laughed at the tight fit, remembering how, once, there had been room for all six of them to sit on the radiator together.

"So how's life with the in-laws?" Julia asked.

"It's awful," Ellen began, relieved to be asked, but Miriam started to laugh.

"I remember when me and Henry were living with his folks," she said. "It was after George and Petey were born. We all stayed together in the guest room; me and Henry got the top of the bed, and George and Petey got the bottom. Henry's ma had cancer, and everywhere I turned, there was somebody giving me orders. . . ."

She spoke as if she were telling a funny story, something she had overheard or was making up on the spot. *This really happened to you,* Ellen wanted to say. *How did you feel? How did you cope?* But she did not ask; it would be wrong to encourage Miriam to complain, un-Christian, perhaps unwomanly. Even Ketty, whose husband drinks, never complains about her marriage. "Remember that you love him," was the advice she had given Ellen when she married James. "Sometimes you'll forget, but you do."

Thirteen years ago, Ellen thought marriage meant love. Now she believes that marriage means need, and when the need isn't there, what comes next? On her wedding day, she had looked across the street from the church to the cemetery and imagined all the women who had come before her, who had married and borne children and died. *Some day,* she thought, *that same peace will be mine.* But perhaps what she saw was not peace, but silence. Perhaps those women entered the ground because they were tired and had nowhere else to go. Peace and exhaustion would look the same from where she had stood at age twenty, at the top of the church steps, high above the cold ground.

At the crosswalk, she stops and waits for a slow line of cars to pass. The downtown is larger than it was years ago when she and James drove around on restless spring nights, turning right, then right, then right again, making bigger and bigger squares, Chinese boxes swallowing the space where they'd just been. Snow begins to fall, smoothing away the cracks and wrinkles of the sidewalks and streets, re-creating a world without sharp edges, without color, without sound. Ellen crosses to the other side and finds a perfect trail of footprints from a woman's neat boot. She places her own feet carefully, following in the footsteps of this stranger so that she herself leaves no tracks, no trace, no sign that she has ever been here.

"Anything might happen to her," Mary-Margaret says, and though Amy feels her stomach tighten, she keeps her expression the same.

When nobody looks away from the TV, Mary-Margaret says, "You know, she walks down by the lake. That's where they found that girl. I told you about that, Jimmy, and I told her about it too. That girl, she'd been strangled with her own hair, and it was weeks before they found her. For all you know, there might be more girls going to be killed, and then Ellen, she don't listen, she goes walking down there at night without a brain in her head when there's men out there who would wrap a sweet girl's braid around her throat."

She strokes her own throat, her fingers pushing deep beneath the pink collar.

"Mom's hair isn't long enough," Amy says, making her voice deliberately calm. "Mom's hair is shorter than Dad's. How are they going to strangle her with that?"

"You just listen to her," Mary-Margaret says. "Jimmy, you just listen to your daughter."

James glances at Amy but he doesn't say anything. Amy does not expect him to.

"Out walking in the dark where anything might grab her. She don't think, she don't use her head. And that girl, she didn't have a stitch of clothes on either. *Schrecklich*. It was weeks before they found her."

"Is Mom okay?" Herbert says. He sucks his thumb; saliva leaks down the side of his hand.

"Don't listen to her," Amy tells him. "She wants to scare you, that's all."

"Jimmy, just listen to your daughter."

"She wants to scare you."

"Enough," Fritz says. "You kids don't want to watch the TV, you go in the other room."

"Walking down there in the dark. There's dogs down there too, dogs gone wild. They say them dogs will attack anything, half of them sick with the rabies, and then Ellen goes down there without a brain in her head."

Herbert starts crying; Amy shoves him hard.

"She's teasing you," she says, though she isn't always absolutely sure. She knows that bad things can happen to anyone at any time, but wouldn't they happen easier in the dark when you can't see them coming? "Dad, tell him," Amy says.

James does not say anything.

"So thoughtless of her to go out in the dark. Anything might happen, but she can't think of her children, no, not her husband either. She goes down to the lake front without a brain in her head and they don't find what's left of her for weeks."

Herbert screams.

"Jesus Christ," Fritz says. "You kids get in the other room!"

"She's teasing you, Herbert, she's being mean."

"Jimmy!" Mary-Margaret says.

James looks at Mary-Margaret uncomfortably. "Mother, he believes everything you say."

"Well, so do I," Mary-Margaret says. "All that damp night air. She'll come down with pneumonia, you wait and see. For all we know she's lying there dead right now."

Herbert screams again, and Fritz gets up. "Enough!" he says, and he grabs Herbert roughly. But suddenly Mary-Margaret is there; she pulls Herbert away from Fritz and leads him back to her chair. Her voice is smooth, coaxing.

"He'll be quiet now, won't you, Bertie? You'll sit on Grandma's lap and be Grandma's little boy. Grandma will take care of you."

"Jesus H. Christ," Fritz says, but he slumps back into his chair.

"Herbert, you're so stupid," Amy says. Sometimes she hates her brother.

"Jimmy, listen to your daughter!"

"Quiet!" Fritz bellows, and they all are silent, staring at the TV.

The downtown is crisp with light from the window decorations and the street lamps hung with wreaths. Ellen walks past the grocery store, the bank, the Fashion Depot, and several tiny gift shops selling Holly's Field souvenirs. Each summer, people swarm up from Chicago to stay at the Fisherman's Inn, to eat at the Fish Wish or the Seafood International, to hike the stone walkway out to the lighthouse and take pictures of the view. Ellen stops at the town's only stoplight and waits for the WALK signal to flash. The fine for jaywalking is two hundred dollars. Only tourists learn the hard way.

High on the hill, the steeple of Saint Michael's is outlined in lights: an arm reaching toward God. Every Wednesday morning, Ellen walks her students from the school to the church for Mass. The inside is just as beautiful to Ellen now as it was when she was a child, with its carved wooden pews and reaching windows shining with stained glass. She marvels at how easy it is to believe in God when you sit in a church like St. Michael's, breathing the smell of incense and wood, and the light warped a lovely color. Her sisters attend whenever they can; Ellen nods to them across the pews, and she smiles at her nieces and nephews, who are sitting with their own grades. Sometimes, she sees Amy and Herbert too, and then she feels that everything is as it should be. *These are my children, I am their mother.* But the feeling doesn't last.

She folds up the collar on James's coat; she is walking hard now, swinging her arms. It feels good to move her body, to break into a sweat and flush with bright heat, her heart a steady song inside her. She spent most of her childhood working outdoors with her sisters, pulling thistles in the fields, shoveling stalls in the cow barn, carrying heavy pails of milk. Even now, her shoulders are rounded from the weight of those pails; her legs and upper arms brim with muscle. As she turns toward the lake, gusts of wind pinch her cheeks and she squints to see the moon rippling between the clouds, following beside her like a curious eye. The lake is rough, so she chooses the higher path that winds its way past the courthouse, past the band shell, past the water treatment plant, until it reaches the upper bluff park.

Many years ago, a woman was found dead somewhere along this trail. She'd been killed by her husband, strangled with her own braided hair. People have seen her ghost here, but Ellen is not afraid. If she appears, Ellen will show her the outcropping of rock that looks like a cow, and the shadowy sumac with its soft, deer fur, and the moon's odd dance through the clouds. She will remind her how there are so many things on the earth that are beautiful and good. Even a ghost must remember some happiness. Even in the midst of that terrible marriage, there must have been moments when she slipped away and swam naked in a nearby creek or walked along the lakefront picking up stones. The ghost will remember those quiet times; she'll lead Ellen up the path, saying, *This is where the wild strawberries grow thickest; this is where I came to braid my hair.*

But the ghost does not appear; soon Ellen has reached the upper bluff park. The trail ends beneath a clump of pines that overlooks Holly's Field. Ellen feels the way she thinks God must feel, powerful and strong. The town below seems like a toy town: there is the fire department with its large, circular drive; there is the police station, the church, the tavern, the grocery store, and the mill. Tiny cars line the streets, tucked nose to tail, and the green paper trees are capped in white. The rows of houses twinkle with lights; each of them looks the same. If she reaches down and swings open the hinged walls, there will be the mothers and fathers, the brothers and sisters, the cats and dogs, all with red-paint smiles. Ellen can almost believe this, standing beneath the pines.

When she gets home, it is after nine. The house is dark; she lets herself in with James's key from his coat pocket. The stale smell of the house swallows her in. She turns on the lights, hangs up her coat, takes off her shoes, all by rote. A toy house, she thinks, with toy children and toy mothers and fathers. She feels deliciously calm, self-centered. Her glasses fog and she takes them off, wipes them with a corner of her shirt. Without them, the room is softly blurred. She puts them back on and shapes snap into focus: couch, chair, coffee table, television, the Last Supper framed in

44

mock gold. Jesus is stretching a hand out to Judas, who has already turned away. Ellen has often wondered what it was that Judas intended to buy with the thirty pieces of silver. Thirty pieces of silver must have been a lot of money. You could go away on thirty pieces of silver, far away, and never come back.

But there is nowhere Ellen wants to go. James and the children are here; her mother and sisters are close by, and even though she doesn't get to visit them often, she likes knowing that they are near. As soon as she and James have their own apartment, things will get better between them. And they'll have visitors: Ellen's sisters, old friends she lost track of when she moved to Illinois, new friends she and James will make together, friends of the children. She looks around the living room, realizing it won't be difficult to move: nothing here belongs to either of them. Before they left Illinois, they'd had a huge rummage sale. After they'd sold what they could not fit in the car or send by mail, they found themselves with seven hundred dollars.

"Think what we could do with this money," James had said their last night in the house. They had sold their wedding bed and were lying on a pallet of blankets with the children. "We could take a trip. To Florida maybe. No snow; they say it's cheap to live.

We could get jobs —"

"They say they need teachers in the South," Ellen said eagerly.

James looked at her and laughed. "You sound like you're serious," he said.

"Aren't you?"

James stopped laughing. "Of course I'm not serious," he said. "What could you possibly be thinking of?"

She parts the curtains and cups her hand to the window, trying to replace the snowy pines with palm trees and hibiscus. She cannot imagine the neighbor's Santa glowing in the warm, moist Florida night, the children growing up with tanned skin and soft southern drawls. Saint Michael's chimes ten o'clock; she smooths the curtains closed and goes down the hall to make sure the children are sleeping. Inside their room, the air is sour. Herbert is curled up in Amy's bed. When he hears Ellen, he sits bolt upright and turns on the small lamp beside the bed.

"I thought you were dead," he says. His eyes are wide and terrible.

"I told you she wasn't," Amy says. Her face is in her pillow; she doesn't move.

Ellen picks Herbert up and carries him to his own bed. "What made you think I was dead?" she says.

"You went out in the dark."

"There's nothing in the dark that isn't there in the light. There's nothing to be afraid of." She kisses him, tucks the blankets around his shoulders. "See?" She points to the lamp shade, which is decorated with angels. "Your guardian angel is watching over you, just like my guardian angel watches over me. Your guardian angel will follow you into your dreams and make them beautiful." Her voice is low and soft, a lullaby. Already his eyes are closing.

"What is he so afraid of?" she whispers to Amy. Amy still hasn't moved; now she rolls over and stares at Ellen angrily. This child is no toy.

"*I'm* not afraid," Amy says.

"Of what?" Ellen says. "How can I know if you won't tell me?"

Amy closes her eyes and does not say anything. She pulls away when Ellen kisses her good night. It is probably nothing. It is probably everything. It has been a difficult year for them all. Ellen watches her as she pretends to sleep, clutching her long braid in her fists.

Memory

3

Mary-Margaret's sister, Salome, has a marvelous way with hair. *I wouldn't dare go out of the house if it weren't for Salome,* Mary-Margaret says. Salome is a large woman, barrel-shaped and drum-hipped, with a pleasant face wrinkled as the leaves of a plant. Her swollen fingers flash and twirl through Mary-Margaret's curls, scissoring split ends, pulling out loose hair. "It's a gift you got," Mary-Margaret says. "You've had it ever since we was girls."

They do not look anything like sisters. It's a wintry Saturday afternoon, and they are in Mary-Margaret's small kitchen, with Mary-Margaret sitting at the table and Salome standing behind her. The yellow-flowered curtains are drawn tightly closed; when the wind gusts particularly hard, they lift slightly, as if they were breathing. Salome sneaks looks at the portable TV on the counter while she divides Mary-Margaret's hair into two crookedy sections, then divides those sections. The show on TV is a western, and the men all talk the same, look the same. *Cowboys*. It is difficult to find the plot, and as Salome studies the screen her wrinkled-plant face furrows deeper. She breathes heavily; she walked all the way from her apartment downtown and still hasn't caught her breath.

"I don't know how you can do this right staring at the TV that way," Mary-Margaret says. The yellow-flowered tablecloth is spread with combs, scissors, curlers, clips and bobby pins, setting solutions, a chipped hand mirror. Salome dumps a handful of tiny gray curlers into Mary-Margaret's lap, where they whisper against one another. She rubs her swollen knuckles with Ben-Gay, flexes, begins to roll the first curl. She is sixty-nine, five years older than Mary-Margaret. There is no plot to the cowboy show that she can see.

"You were always the talented one," Mary-Margaret says. "You were always the one to remember things. And strong! You were healthy as a horse," Mary-Margaret says, and she shakes her head. "I was always frail."

"Hold still," Salome says. She watches the TV, Ben-Gay chilling her fingers, its smell mixing with the smell of the setting solution waiting on the table, and Mary-Margaret's gardenia perfume, and the underlying smell of the kitchen, which is stale and thick in the air. Her ankles are beginning to swell and she shifts, foot to foot.

"I had no appetite. I would eat a chicken wing maybe, a piece of butter-bread. You ate more than the boys put together, and Mama would say how no man would want a wife bigger than he was. I was just a scrap of a thing. My health was always poor. Mama said I was slender as a willow, she called me her little willow tree."

"Hold still."

"I got colds, and flus and pleurisy. I got the chicken pox twice and I got measles and German measles and pneumonia and rheumatic fever. That's what damaged my heart. I got to be careful of my heart, that's what they told Mama, they said, For the rest of her life she will have to be careful. And they told God's truth — the littlest thing and my heart does a flip-flop. Now Fritz, he has got a heart like a mule. Forty years together and there ain't nothing I know to disturb that man. You were the same way, I remember you. Mama used to say how you had got a heart like a mule. Forty years together and there ain't nothing I know to disturb the man. You were the same way, I remember you. Mama used to say how you had got a heart like a mule. She'd say, How's that gal going to find herself a man with a heart like the one she's got? I remember you, Salome, you never once got sick, you never cried, you were strong as a horse. Me, I was the sickly one, and when they told Mama I was going to live, that's when she gave me her ring. She said, I always meant for you to get this when you were grown, but I want you to have it now."

Mary-Margaret fingers the ring, a gold band with a diamond chip. For all Salome can do with hair, she isn't much for company, and the burden of conversation falls on Mary-Margaret alone. Fritz is at the Senior Citizens' Center playing cards, Ellen has taken the kids to the supermarket, James is out of town. Mary-Margaret and Salome are alone in the house, in the yellow-flowered kitchen that Mary-Margaret has set up as best she can to resemble her mother's kitchen. The silver is in the drawer to the left of the sink; the garbage is kept in a sealed green bucket. And the small yellow flowers are everywhere, on the curtains and tablecloth, on the crisp dish towels hanging from the oven door.

"Remember how Mama loved buttercups?" Mary-Margaret says. "She had buttercups on her aprons and stenciled high up the walls and she stitched buttercups onto her pockets. In spring she'd fill the house with buttercups, and when I was sick she'd put buttercups in a jar of water by my bed. Or if there weren't no buttercups, some other yellow flowers. Dandelions or paintbrush. When I got nervous upsets she dipped a buttercup in water and rubbed it under my chin and across my forehead and it made me feel cool and clean. You never got nervous upsets, you never cared about nothing, but my nerves were already frenzied when I was just a little thing. *Willow tree,* Mama used to say, *You may bend but you won't break,* but when you and the boys and Pa slaughtered, I spent the week in bed. In winter Mama'd serve up pork pie and bacon and chops, but all I could think of was the squealing and the blood and I couldn't eat a thing," Mary-Margaret says.

A gunfight breaks out on TV as Salome begins to roll the second section of curls. She pauses, mouth open. If there is a plot, she cannot find it. The two fighting are the ones she had thought were on the same side. But who can tell nowadays what side anybody's on? Salome's ankles are swollen over the edges of her sneakers. She shifts painfully, foot to foot.

"I hope you got your mind on your business instead of on that TV," Mary-Margaret says. "Do you want a chair? Those ankles look sore. I got a lady's ankle; they haven't swelled up on me either. The only times they swelled up was the times I carried children, and let me tell you that was something awful. I swear, my ankles were swollen as melons and the color of melons too. You're lucky you never married, you don't know how it feels, but I tell you I don't know how I got through it. And look, it's almost Christmas, and Jimmy ain't even here with me. Leaves me his wife and kids and drives away to who-knows-where. Well, let me tell you something, these here are my golden years. I don't intend to spend my golden years baby-sitting Jimmy's wife and kids."

"Hold still," Salome says. She finishes wrapping the curls. She remembers the morning Mitch was born, the afternoon James was born. She remembers the night the others were born, twin boys, the ones who have not been mentioned since.

"And that gal he married! She leaves him and the kids alone, and you know who has to take care of those kids? It's yours truly, that's who. Salome, she is like a child, now everything is *Christmas, Christmas, it's gonna be Christmas*" — Mary-Margaret makes her voice pinched and high — "like a two-year-old. She goes and hangs tinsel on the TV set. You can't see to watch with tinsel hanging there. She said it was a joke, but Fritz, he ripped it down and told her keep your jokes to yourself. I warned Jimmy what kind she was, but that's how they reward you for all the grief you've gone through to raise them. They turn you a deaf ear after everything you've done."

Salome nods, intent on the TV.

"You're talkative today," Mary-Margaret says. "You are about as talkative as this chair. How long do these stay in?"

"One half hour," Salome says. "How come you got to ask me that every time? How come you can't remember one half hour?"

"I never was good at remembering things," Mary-Margaret says. "You were the one who could remember things. At school you were the smart one. Remember how you could recite the psalms? You were such a funny-looking thing, and they got you up there in front of the church to recite, I will never forget it. You had hair like a wild mare, and it stuck straight up no matter what Mama put in it. Mama said, I can't let you up there looking like a cyclone, and she greased it down good with bacon fat. Don't let nobody close enough to smell you, she said, but we smelled you in the wagon and it was sweet."

"Tilt back your head," Salome says. She squirts setting solution on Mary-Margaret's hair from a small plastic bottle and checks the time.

"The towel," Mary-Margaret says. "I need the towel, it's going to get in my eyes."

"Tilt back your head."

"I can't breathe! It burns in my nose."

"I can't breathe either. Keep your head back."

The cowboys are riding hard through the rolling hills of a prairie. In the distance is a dark speck that could be a bush or a rock or a bit of dirt on the screen but that turns out to be another cowboy. How do they know which one to chase? Fool cowboys all look the same, but this one is holding a girl, and her thin legs are like wings stuck out of the horse's side. Salome cannot remember ever having seen a horse with wings. She has never seen a cowboy either, but they are not so different from the boys she grew up with. All of them spoke with the same flat voices. All of them looked the same way the cowboys do; there was no telling any of them apart. Hard stooped shoulders. Mean mouths.

"You're lucky that didn't go in my eyes," Mary-Margaret says. Setting solution runs down her neck; Salome blots at it with her apron. "What was that psalm you recited in front of church?"

"Psalm sixty-nine."

"How did it go?"

Salome wraps Mary-Margaret's head in plastic. The lone cowboy is dead now, shot by the others. His chest is dark with blood that on a color screen would be red. But the color of the blood doesn't matter; blood is blood, just like dead is dead. Salome can see on a black-and-white screen as good as on a color.

"Save me, O God," she says in a high school-girl voice, careful to smother her thick German accent, to pronounce her word endings and *th*'s, *"for the waters are come into my soul. I sink in deep mire, where there is no standing: I am come into deep waters, where the floods overflow me. I am weary of my crying: my throat is dried: mine eyes fail while I wait for my God."*

"How long does this plastic stay on?"

"Five minutes. The plastic stays for five minutes, how come you can't remember that?"

"I have always had a poor memory for things. You are the one with the memory. You were always the smart one. You were the one they stood up in front of the church to recite, and then half way through your hair lifted up off your head. All that bacon fat and it still wouldn't lie flat. There you were with your hair stuck straight up and shining with grease."

"They that hate me without a cause are more than the hairs of mine head: they that would destroy me, being mine enemies wrongfully, are mighty."

"You always had the good memory," Mary-Margaret says, but Salome isn't listening. The cowboys are weeping over the dead cowboy. It seems there has been a mistake; the girl cries too, and her blond hair whips the wind like a flag as a cowboy minister prays over the body. Even on TV you can see how the Bible speaks the truth. Even a cowboy who looks like all the others will be counted by God and recognized.

"Deliver me out of the mire, and let me not sink: let me be delivered from them that hate me, and out of the deep waters."

"There's no call to show off, that's what Mama always said too. There's nothing worse than a show-off, she said, and that afternoon, when we got home from church, she let you have it good. Putting on airs in the house of God, waving your arms like you was acting. We'd hoped you would marry that Federmier boy, but no one would have you after that. Everybody remembered you waving your arms and your hair shining with that stinky grease. Everybody remembers a show-off!" Mary-Margaret shouts.

"Five minutes is up," Salome says. "Go over by the sink, I'll wash it out."

"That was no five minutes."

"Five minutes."

"Turn off the TV. If you'd pay some attention to me you would know when it was five minutes, but you've been watching that thing all along. Turn it off, turn it off!" Mary-Margaret says. Salome turns off the TV and stares at the yellow-flowered curtains drawn tightly closed. She remembers the recitation: the dress she borrowed from her cousin, white like a bride's, with a plain scooped collar and full skirt, and the flickering candles, and the solemn, weighted feeling of her feet as she approached the altar, step by step, stopping before she reached the red carpet, which girls were not allowed to touch. Outside it was a brilliant May day; inside the church was blurred and dim with shadow. The faces in the congregation were like faces she had never seen before, and even now she remembers it: the wonderful feeling of knowing no one and no one knowing you; the wide open space of all that.

"*Now* it's been five minutes," Mary-Margaret says. Salome leads her to the sink and bends her head beneath the faucet. Mary-Margaret's neck is tender as a bird's beneath Salome's thick hand. "Oh, it hurts my back," Mary-Margaret says. "Wash it out, wash it out, hurry."

Salome adjusts the water temperature and rinses Mary-Margaret's hair, the way she did when she was a child and Mary-Margaret was always younger, always more helpless, always more frail.

61

Your sister isn't strong, Mama told her again and again. *Versprich mir. Promise you'll take care of your sister.* Salome coaxed Mary-Margaret to eat and helped her with chores. She rinsed her hair with chamomile and wrapped it up in rags so she would have curls for Mass each Sunday. She sewed Mary-Margaret's wedding dress and assisted Mama at the birth of Mary-Margaret's children. All her life, Salome has kept her promise.

Versprich mir.

"I'll put in some of that blue rinse you like," Salome murmurs. "Here, I'm almost done." But the psalm is singing inside her; she can remember every word, spread out before her clear as on any printed page, and feel the suck of her breath, the cold stare of the congregation. *Let not the water-flood overflow me, neither let the deep swallow me up, and let not the pit shut her mouth upon me.* She finishes the blue rinse and wraps a towel around Mary-Margaret's head, helps her to stand straight.

"I'm dizzy," Mary-Margaret says. "I think I'm going to faint."

Salome guides her back to the chair and begins to towel the thin mat of pale blue curls, taking half-breaths to avoid the ammonia smell. "Now ain't this nice?" she says, making her voice penny bright. "I believe this is the nicest one yet. You got curls like a *schönes*

Mädchen," but Mary-Margaret will not be comforted.

"There are times I still miss Mama," she says, and she twists her mother's ring round and round on her finger. "Oh, don't you miss Mama sometimes?"

The hands toweling Mary-Margaret's hair freeze for a brittle moment. Salome keeps no yellow flowers in her own lonely kitchen. She has emptied her mind of everything but God, who does not let a sparrow fall from the sky unnoticed, who mourns a cowboy who looked just like the rest, who will certainly remember Salome on the Day of Judgment and welcome her home. *Reproach hath broken my heart, and I am full of heaviness: and I looked for some to take pity, but there was none, and for comforters, but I found none.*

"Hold still," Salome says.

4

Ellen comes through the front door with a crash, carrying two grocery bags and clutching a jug of milk. Amy trails behind with a box of laundry soap; she holds the door for Herbert, who is dreamily swinging a loaf of bread. All of them pause when they see Mary-Margaret. She sits in her chair beside the window, crowned by a halo of wispy blue curls. Salome is bundled up in a tattered coat, her big black purse hanging from her shoulder.

"Auntie Salome," Ellen says, looking studiously away from Mary-Margaret. The room smells of ammonia. "If you give me a minute to unload these groceries, I'll take you home."

"Powdered milk is cheaper," Mary-Margaret says, looking at the milk jug. Her eyes are red behind her bifocals, and the veins in her forehead stand out in a pattern that reminds Ellen of stained glass. "How come you took so long?"

Ellen shrugs. She has been at her mother's,

but she does not tell Mary-Margaret this and neither do the kids. When James is traveling, Ellen has to borrow Fritz and Mary-Margaret's car, and they complain whenever she uses it for something more than the usual household errands. Everything else is frivolous.

Wasting gas. Money doesn't grow on trees.

"It stinks in here," Amy says.

"Beauty has its price," Ellen says, and she herds them quickly into the kitchen, leaving her coat on. She is busy putting away the perishables when she feels Salome's finger against her neck. She jumps; Salome has always made her nervous, the way she moves, silent as a cat, the way she will stare directly at you saying nothing. *Senile old bat,* Fritz calls her, and Mary-Margaret does not object. Ellen tries not to look at her ankles, which have swollen over the edges of her sneakers. She wonders how Salome manages to walk all the way from her apartment downtown, which she does faithfully, every other month, to give Mary-Margaret her permanent wave.

"I don't need the ride," Salome murmurs. "I wouldn't trouble you."

"No, really, it's no trouble." Ellen searches for a lie. "I have another errand to run." She closes the refrigerator to find Salome emptying out the remaining grocery bag. She uses two hands to lower each can unsteadily to the counter. "You don't have to do that," Ellen says. A can slips away, thumps to the floor just inches from Bert's foot. He picks it up, studies it carefully.

"Green beans," he says. "Mom, look. I can read it."

Amy says, "You didn't read it, you just looked at the picture."

"Green beans," Ellen says, watching Salome.

"Read this word," Amy tells Bert, grabbing the can. "This one word right here."

Salome is putting cans of peas and kidney beans into the sink. She opens the oven door, loads the racks with fruit cocktail, tomato paste, rolls of toilet tissue. She sniffs the bars of Ivory and slips them into the silverware drawer.

"Beans!" Herbert shouts.

"How quickly this goes with someone to help me," Ellen says to Salome, grateful that the kids haven't noticed. Salome's heavy face is perspiring, and Ellen sees that she has been paid for the extra trip downtown. For years, Salome worked as a domestic, keeping house for a doctor in Whitefish Bay. Now she lives by herself on Social Security, with no family left except Mary-Margaret. Ellen realizes she must be lonely, and she makes up her mind to stop over for a visit now and then on her evening walks. Odd Auntie Salome. Mary-

Margaret's sister. It's hard to imagine either of them as children, wide-eyed and sturdy, bending over some game with their heads nearly touching, the way Amy and Herbert do. But perhaps that's what Ellen needs most: glimpses of Mary-Margaret as a child, a sister, a teenage girl, a young woman with two children and a husband already angry, distant, beginning to stoop from seasons of hard work. There must be a way to pass through Mary-Margaret's bitter cloud and grasp hold, a clumsy embrace, if only for a moment. "Thank you for your help," she tells Salome.

"You are welcome." Salome's stern voice is a warning; the collar of her house dress flops loose like the ear of a dog that has been in a fight. Ellen wonders what to talk about on the drive back to Salome's apartment. The children, maybe? Cutting hair? The science project Ellen is helping her class set up at school? She folds up the empty grocery bags and tucks them under the sink. What she wants is a real conversation, one adult to another, and it occurs to her that she is the one who is lonely. The days end and begin again without a seam, a wrinkle, a welcome dropped stitch. She keeps the house, shops, cooks, goes to work, takes care of the children, reasons with Mary-Margaret and Fritz, worries over James's increasingly silent moods. There's no time left over for renewing high school friendships or chatting with the other teachers in the lounge after school. Sometimes she phones her sisters on weekends, and it's good to laugh with them for a while, but when she tries to explain how she's feeling, they simply assure her that things will get better. And perhaps they're right; after all, they're older, they've been married longer, they've lived through their own empty times. Certainly, women like Salome have survived worse, caring for families that are not their own, raising children they'll never see again, all for minimum wage and, perhaps, a small bonus for the holidays.

Outside, Ellen hovers next to Salome as they cross the icy driveway to the car, wanting to hold her elbow, but knowing it would only hurt Salome's fierce pride. Today at her mother's, she helped clean the pantry from the floor to the very top shelves. Mom noticed how quickly Ellen claimed the ladder. "You think I'm too old to climb up there?" she said. She is seventy-two. "Get down from there," she said, and for the rest of the afternoon she played the acrobat while Ellen cleaned the cupboards down below. This had always been the chore of the youngest child, the one not yet trusted with heights, still forbidden to touch the china cups peering down from the top shelf. The pantry was a small, windowless room off the kitchen, cool in summer, warm in winter, smelling of vanilla and soft cooking lard, a favorite place to hide with a doll or a diary. A child crouched on the floor could imagine herself in a secret passage, each irregular cupboard a false door, an intriguing deception filled with possibility. There was sugar to lick from the tip of a wet finger pecked into the bin behind the door. There were dried apples, prunes, sour-skinned pears; sometimes there was a bundt cake, untouchable yellow moon, or a tall white-frosted angel food gleaming from the top shelf like a star.

Once, during a summer visit home from Illinois, Amy disappeared for almost an hour. Ellen and James searched the house, the barn, the chicken coop; they called out into the fields, double-checked the wooden seal on the old well. "Where could that child have slipped to?" Mom said, coming up from checking the cold cellar, and hearing the old phrase, *slipped to*, Ellen suddenly knew. There in the pantry, tucked into the same narrow cupboard that had been Ellen's secret place, was Amy, fast asleep beside a burlap bag of cat chow. "James," Ellen hissed toward the kitchen, wanting someone else to confirm that this was a flesh-and-blood child and not a ghost, the shadow of her own childhood self preserved by a trick of light, a modern-day miracle.

Sneaking glances at Salome, Ellen wonders what ghosts have been left behind in the house she and Mary-Margaret grew up in, the only daughters in a family made up of six brothers, a father known for his skill at farming, a mother who had once taught school. Sometimes Mary-Margaret speaks of her mother with such longing that it's hard to believe she's been dead since James was small. Yet Ellen has never heard Salome talk about anything more personal than the weather, the homily at last Sunday's Mass, her sister's fresh-curled hair.

They arrive safely at the car and Ellen gets in, relieved. She starts to put on her seat belt but Salome shakes her head, fixing her gaze on Ellen, who realizes, shocked, that Salome's eyes are a beautiful marbled blue, like the pictures of the world in the children's science books. "If it is your time to die," Salome says solemnly, "these things here won't help you."

Ellen's hand automatically releases the seat belt; this is something her mother might say. Out at the farm this afternoon, she noticed a crisp blue sticker pressed to the old Fridgidaire: *God Is My Pilot.* Then were are you, Mom? Ellen thought to herself as she wrestled the children out of their coats, trying not to imagine the empty cockpit, the long plummet down to earth. No matter how hard she might try to believe, doubt would tear her from the sky in a fiery scream. The thought felt hollow in the pit of her stomach. How could she even think that she didn't trust God? Perhaps this was a test of her faith. Perhaps this was the same sort of temptation the saints felt so long ago — an odd thought that quickly took root, burning with poisonous flowers.

"Where did you get the sticker?" Ellen asked her mother, piling the coats on the radiator.

"I won it at Bingo." Mom kissed the children hello and they clung to her possessively until she thumped into a hard-backed kitchen chair, pulling them along into her lap, a gesture as fluid, as easy as breathing. "My snickle-britches," she told them over their chatter, and when Ellen looked back at the sticker it suddenly seemed reasonable. Only God knew what was in store for her. Only God could make decisions based on all the facts.

Yet lately God seemed so far removed. While the children were playing out in the barn, she had tried once more to explain to Mom about James, how badly things had been going.

"I don't know what to do," she told her,

71

flushing, because even as she was speaking, she knew she would wish she had not. "I work full-time plus take care of the kids and his parents too, but when I ask him to help me, he won't."

"If you'd quit your job, you wouldn't need to ask for help. And you'd have more time to spend with him. It's not like you need the money to pay rent." Mom had never approved of Ellen working after the children were born.

"But he doesn't want to spend time with me. The other night, I suggested we go out to dinner, just the two of us, and he said, *Money doesn't grow on trees.* That's exactly what he says to the kids when they ask for something. It's as if he doesn't see me anymore, Mom. It's like I'm invisible."

Mom got increasingly busy polishing the flour canisters. She restacked the cups and saucers. She worked a stray toothpick from between the shelf and the wall. "Are you doing your wifely duty?" she said. It took a minute for Ellen to realize what she meant. It had been almost a year since James had been interested in wifely duties of any kind. Once, she'd slipped naked into bed beside him, nuzzled her chin against his neck. *I'm too tired for this foolishness,* he had said in the voice he used with the children whenever they made too much noise. It was hard to approach him after that; in fact, her body did seem foolish to her: doughy lumps for breasts, dark raisin navel — a cookie doll the children might make at school, decorate with sweet sprinkles, and crumble into their mouths.

"He's . . . not willing," Ellen said. She was lining the cupboards with fresh paper, and her voice sounded hollow, caught deep in the wooden bins.

"Lose some weight," Mom said gruffly. "Or gain some. Find out what he likes."

And Ellen had agreed, wanting so much to be close to her mother the way her older, more traditional sisters were. The advice she got from them was the same: *"Disguise yourself. Don't say what you feel."* This was the key to a happy marriage, the key to a strong faith in God.

Driving home, she had stared out across the empty fields. Clouds formed a low, drifting ceiling above them, gray and white and darker gray; the distant farmhouses were also gray, the occasional sunflower shape of a windmill sprouting beside them. She passed a weathered barn, a herd of black-and-white Holsteins exhaling somber, smoky puffs. Frost heaves slashed dark lines across the road, some so neatly parallel that they looked like painted cattle guards, but Ellen drove across them without flinching, watching for the clumps of pines that marked the boundaries of each field, hungry for that deep dull green that seemed like a promise somehow, a wish, a prayer. Summers, working in the fields with her sisters picking stones, driving tractor, casting down each new, fine web of seed, she would squint into the distance at the next cool clump of pines where they might break to rest and drink clear jars of sweetened water. They sang as they worked, their skirts knotted high between their legs, moving from north to south so that the sun was never directly in their eyes, and the cows in the neighboring pastures moved with them, bells tolling like voices. There is no bitterness in her memories of these fields, the long hours spent inching over the land, the same life that James re-members with such distaste. His children will never put their hands into dirt. His children will never know sunburn, chilblains, the numbing repetition of the hoe.

"I suppose you're right," she tells Salome, and she leaves her seat belt dangling loose at her side. Salome leans back in her seat, trusting and contented, one hand caressing her throat. But Ellen is distracted as she guides the car through the snowy streets, waiting for the patch of black ice, the speeding car, the drunken driver blaring his horn.

5

Mary-Margaret shoos the children away and lies down on the daybed. She twists Mama's ring round and round on her pinky finger. There is magic in this ring, she knows, even though Father Bork refuses to bless it, warning of superstition. But once, she stopped by the church at midday when she knew it would be empty. She dipped the ring into the holy-water font and wore it on her finger as it dried. When she knelt to light a candle, the flame flared high, and Mary-Margaret saw Mama's face as clearly as if she were standing there. There were no signs of torture in Mama's eyes; her hair was unsinged, her lips moist and pink. Even though she knows Mama must be burning in Hell, Mary-Margaret takes comfort from that image.

She gets up and goes to sit at the piano, places her fingers on the keys. Arthritis has stiffened her hands; they are bulbous, ugly, she does not recognize them. As a girl, she had the most beautiful hands. Winter nights, she rubbed them with butter to keep them supple and strong. In the warm summer months, she walked three and a half miles into Holly's Field to sit in the organ loft at Saint Michael's, where she closed her eyes and played whatever her mind could hear, the world around her tumbling from her shoulders like a robe.

The piano had been a gift from Mama the year after Salome left home for good, when Mary-Margaret turned fifteen. Mama bought it used from a family in Cedarton, and though the pedals stuck, all the keys worked except for three. Mornings, after she finished helping in the kitchen, Mary-Margaret carried her little gray cat into the living room, settled her warmly into her lap, and played the piano until it was time to fetch dinner to her father and older brothers in the field. She hated reading music and memorized things quickly — the notes looked ugly and hard, like goat droppings. Nothing Mary-Margaret saw on the page looked anything like the way the music really felt. When she played, she saw past the ragged landscapes that were the lives of her mother and sister and the neighboring women; she peered into a world of color and sound, of finishing schools and glorious cathedrals, a world where Mama promised her that one day she would go. She would not be the wife of a farmer, bound to his whims and the whims of God's seasons, the random disasters and strokes of good luck that brought children and drought, sickness and the occasional windfall of cash from a bumper crop. She would not lose her teeth to childbirth, her eyesight to the summer sun's glare. She would not lose her music to a man's desire for land and sons.

Now, she plays a few minor chords, hums the beginning of a melody. But she has no ear for the music anymore; her soul is wide and plain as a field of winter wheat. The Lord giveth and He taketh away. For many years, Fritz kept the piano stored in the barn, and by the time he allowed it into the house, Mama was dead and Mary-Margaret's fingers had forgotten how to play beyond the simple notes, the movement of her fingers.

Goddamn caterwauling. Cat in heat.

Cat would make a better mother than you.

She has imagined Fritz's death many times. Sometimes at night, she lies awake, staring at him across the space between their beds, thinking of how it would be to fetch the straight razor from beside the bathroom sink, the scissors from Mama's old sewing basket. After Mama died Mary-Margaret chopped up a panful of iris leaves and simmered them on the wood stove until all that was left was a caramel-colored liquid. It would have been easy, then, to pour it into his coffee. It would be easy, even now, to cradle the razor in her hand, sweep it hard across his throat as if she were slicing the sour thick skin of a rutabaga.

Frightened, she slides her mother-of-pearl pillbox out of the pocket of her housecoat. Thinking about something can make it happen, which is why having such thoughts is a sin. She taps out two pills, swallows them dry, then closes her eyes. She is not brave the way Mama was brave. She cannot defy God's law. When Mary-Margaret dies, her unsoiled soul will go up to Heaven, kept from Mama's soul forever.

"Talk to me, Mary-May," Father Bork says when he stops by on his monthly visit. He uses the name Mama used when he'd come to Mama's house for tea and Mary-Margaret, wearing her nicest dress, would carry it to him in a pink china cup. *Mary-May, get Father his sugar. Mary-May, tell Father your kitty-cat's name.* "There's been something troubling your mind for years. I'm your confessor, child. I'm here to help." But Mary-Margaret never talks about Ann, although she sometimes cries and clutches Father Bork's hand. It embarrasses her to have him see her come to this. She wonders what he thinks when he looks at her now, an old woman weeping into a crumpled pink handkerchief. She wonders what James thinks, what Mitch thinks when he looks down from Heaven. She does not let herself wonder about the other two, who are floating in limbo between the saved and the banished, unbaptized, without the slightest hope of rest, comfort, home.

It was Pa who forced her to marry in 1932, the year she turned twenty-four. *I ain't keeping no old maids,* he said. Francis Grier was a hired man's son, the youngest of fourteen children. He was known as a hard, strong worker, and when Pa offered him Mary-Margaret, he said he'd agree if she came with forty acres of good land. *We got ourselves a fella knows what he wants,* Pa told Mama. *Best kind of man you can find.* It was the only time in her life that Mary-Margaret saw her mother cry.

She was married two months later, and after the brief wedding service, Mama slipped a prayer card into her hand. *Pray this tonight, when you need to,* she said, and during the long, silent ride in the wagon back to Fritz's shanty, Mary-Margaret kept it pressed to her heart. When they arrived she went into the tiny bedroom and put on the white lace nightgown Mama and Salome had made for her. *You do what he tells you,* Mama had said, but when Fritz came in, his hands dark with wagon grease, he ripped the pretty gown from

her chest to her knees. *I don't like none of that,*
he said. That night, she chanted Mama's
prayer so deep inside herself that Fritz, no
matter what he might do, couldn't truly find
her.

Lord, help me to accept what I cannot change.
Lord, help me to accept this.

Three weeks later, Pa was gored by a neighbor's bull, and before he died he willed the
farm and everything else he owned to Fritz.
Fritz and Mary-Margaret moved into the big
stone farmhouse, and Fritz told Mama she
could stay if she did not interfere. *You raised*
up a goddamn lady, he told her, *now I got to fix*
her for a wife. And Mama held back, though
her face flushed when Mary-Margaret appeared in the morning for breakfast with an
eye swollen shut, an arm in a makeshift sling.
Nights, Mary-Margaret prayed silently as the
hands moved over her body, forcing open her
jaws, squeezing her breasts until she gasped,
but, praise to God, she never made a sound
that might have trickled through the walls to
the narrow room where Mama slept. Sometimes, though, she was unable to hide her
shame. *Get out,* he'd tell Mama, lifting Mary-
Margaret's skirts as she stood washing laundry in the galvanized tub. At times like that,
he liked to look into Mama's face and see all
the things there that she wished to do to him,

but, he thought, dared not. Over the years, the color of Mama's hatred turned red as blood; Mary-Margaret could see it like a haze around her head, but Fritz, like his sons, could not see color, could not understand what it might mean.

When she opens her eyes, Jimmy's little girl is standing there, one foot stepping on the other. The pills Mary-Margaret swallowed make her feel soft and warm, as though a hand were trailing down her spine. She sees herself at Amy's age, with lovely slim hands and hair in curls. Mama taught Salome how to make those curls by wrapping Mary-Margaret's hair in bits of rags. Salome herself had stringy hair, no good for curling. Now Mary-Margaret sees Salome in this girl's straight hair, in her close-together eyes and stubby lashes. She feels repulsed by this little girl the way she always felt repulsed by Salome. The smell of Salome when they slept side by side in the tiny bed Pa made for them; the dribbling sound of her snores. *Common* Salome, yet it was Salome the teachers admired. It was Salome who dreamed dreams that always came true, mystifying even Mama. But Mary-Margaret was the beautiful one, the one who heard music in everything, the one who had made up her mind she would be different from Salome and her mother and

81

any other woman she had ever known.

"Can we have some bread and butter if we eat it at the counter?" Amy says.

"Such an ugly little girl." Mary-Margaret shakes her head and fingers her soft blue curls, not realizing she has spoken aloud.

Christmas

6

Ellen and James sleep in the front bedroom, a small room carpeted in gold, with gold curtains that hang in the windows as stiffly as paintings. The bed sprawls almost to the door, with a thin brown dresser wedged against the wall. Above the bed hangs a crucifix draped with braided palm fronds saved from many years of Palm Sundays. The eyes of Christ appear half open. His spindly hands are clenched into fists. He stares across their bodies, His gaze falling on the coffee table at the foot of the bed, where a blue plaster statue of Mary opens her arms to embrace the air.

James punches his pillow into the shape of a mushroom and lets his head fall into it, a sudden release, like letting a suitcase drop. When Ellen touches his shoulder, he jumps. "Cold hands," he says. "Don't." He rolls over on his side, facing her, the sheets clutched up under his chin. "If you think they'll let you pay for a real tree when they have a perfectly good *free* one in the basement," he says, "you don't know them at all."

"Would you eat an artificial turkey at Thanksgiving?" she asks, trying to tease him.

"That's silly," he says seriously. "People don't eat plastic. But there are advantages to an artificial tree. Pa's right — it won't wilt. It won't drop needles or drip sap. It's not a fire hazard."

"It's not a Christmas tree, either."

"I remember when they bought it — must have been twenty years ago. It was before anybody had heard of an artificial tree. Everyone came over to see it and they pinched it and asked how much it cost. Artificial trees look real, Ellie. You can't tell the difference."

"They don't smell real."

"We can get some spray, some room fresher, whatever you call it." He relaxes a little, the sheet pulling away, his bare chest smooth and hairless as a child's. "Everybody came to see it," he says. "Mother had me and Mitch serve them store cookies. The next year, they all got artificial trees, but we had the first one."

He strokes Ellen's foot absentmindedly with his, and she knows he is thinking of that plastic tree, the one his neighbors and relatives admired so long ago. He wants to be a teen-aged boy again, trailing behind his mother with a plate of cookies: not common, home-made cookies, but cookies bought at a store. *Offer them a cookie, Jimmy.* The old people in town still talk about what a sweet boy he was, so unlike his brother, so unlike his father. *Mama's boy.*

"But how long has that tree been down there?" Ellen asks.

"It's an *artificial* tree, Ellen. It's not like it's going to rot or anything. A live Christmas tree that's just going to die anyway costs ten bucks. We don't have the money, that we can buy every kind of thing we want." His foot against hers is frenzied; abruptly, he pulls it away.

"This isn't about money," she says, but she knows from the angry flutter of his eyelids that this is the end of the discussion. She turns out the light and stares up at the dark ceiling; it gradually becomes visible, the white speckling pale and irregular as the surface of the moon. Tomorrow is Christmas Eve. Tonight, Fritz finally agreed to let them put up the tree, provided there would be no hassle, no commotion. *I seen enough of this nonsense to last me a lifetime,* he'd told James. *Just cause you still got the appetite for it don't mean I should suffer, too.* And James seemed to grow smaller, his shoulders lifting with each careful breath like someone who has been crying for a long time.

Don't worry, Pa, he said, *we won't bother you.*

Thinking of this, Ellen moves closer to James, pressing her forehead against the cool, damp skin of his upper arm. He doesn't pull away, but he doesn't respond; it's as if she's falling asleep in a room of her own, something she's never done. She slept with her mother from the time her father died until she left home for school at seventeen. Even now, when she wakes up in the night, she sometimes thinks she's back in Mom's room with the dog lying between them and the cats braided together at the foot of the bed. In winter, frost angels played on the window-panes; in summer, Mom left the window open wide so the scent from the mock orange tree seeped into the sheets. During the night, neither awake nor asleep, Ellen would reach out with her foot to touch Mom's leg, which was always there, solid and serene, and Mom, without waking, would turn toward Ellen and pat her face with her warm, rough hand. Mornings after Mom got up, there were always sisters' beds to climb into, damp and warm and slightly sweet from the soap they used in their hair. "Aw, Ellie, it's so early," they'd moan, folding her into their arms. She'd doze for an extra minute or two until Mom's voice rang up the stairwell: *Girls! You got breakfast and chores, now, don't make me come up there after you.*

But whenever Ellen reaches out for James, he's ready with some excuse. He's ticklish; her hands are too cold; he's tired; he wants to be left alone. She tries to remind herself that, for James, being touched was often an act of anger, a slap, a shove, a beating. The artificial tree was a bright moment in all that. *Perhaps,* Ellen thinks, *I'm the one who's acting selfishly. I have so many good memories of my childhood, who am I to deny him this? It might even draw all of us together in a way no live tree could. James and his parents can remember better times, and the children and I will become part of that memory.*

"It's okay about the tree," Ellen says before she realizes he is sleeping. He begins to snore, a light, musical sound that seems to come from somewhere far away.

The next day, the children sit at the kitchen table stringing popcorn and cranberries for the artificial tree. Ellen is busy stuffing the goose, one from her sister Miriam's flock, that they're having for Christmas dinner. Amy cuts a star out of cardboard, paints it gold, sprinkles it with glitter. She has braided her hair clumsily with red and green ribbons; Bert, not to be outdone, knots a piece of ribbon into his own short hair. The decorations are laid out on the counter: clothespin soldiers, yarn dolls, candy wrapped in tinfoil. Drying on a cookie sheet are stars made of salt-and-flour dough. The color of the dough is light gray, almost blue. Later, they'll paint the stars red and gold, purple and green, even though Mary-Margaret says there are no such things as purple and green stars.

She sits in a chair by the kitchen window, a red flannel scarf wrapped around her neck, sucking on horehound candies. A granny-square afghan covers her knees. Periodically, she sighs. Mary-Margaret is always catching a cold, but Ellen has never known her to have one. She doesn't want to help Ellen fix Christmas dinner. She doesn't want to make Christmas decorations. She doesn't want to watch the game with Fritz and James in the living room. Now and then, she'll turn to comment on whatever it is Ellen is doing. *Mama always beat her eggs up two handed,* she says, or *Mama checked her cakes with a knife, not a fork.* Mary-Margaret's mother, Ann, has been dead for many years; still, they are having Christmas dinner tonight, on Christmas Eve, because that's the way Ann did it.

Mary-Margaret gets up to part the curtains and peer out at the yard. "Snow," she says, the way someone else might say *death* or *grief.* Perhaps she is remembering Christmas with

90

her mother and father and brothers and sister, all of whom are dead, except Salome. Salome is spending Christmas Eve at the rectory with the Ladies of the Altar Society. The Society sews the church linens, launders them, grows flowers for the altar, makes quilts for the missions, organizes bake sales, vacuums and dusts the church once a month. For a slice of ham and a dollop of instant potatoes, Father Bork will buy another year of hard labor, Ellen thinks. But then she is ashamed: it is Christmas Eve. She apologizes silently as she ties the drumsticks of the goose together with thread, rubs the skin with margarine.

"It's too early to put in that goose," Mary-Margaret says, sniffling.

"Do you think so?" Ellen says, keeping her voice level as she sticks it in the oven. She's known how to cook a goose since she was ten and her mother slipped in the barn, breaking both her wrists. It was the day before Thanksgiving, and the next day Ellen and Julia and Heidi cooked the meal as Mom directed them from her chair, her wrists held in place by heavy splints.

"Mama made goose so it would fall off the bone."

"How many geese did you keep?" Ellen asks to distract her.

"Oh, two, three dozen. Nasty things. Mean. Ate up the lawn. In spring, you'd step off the porch into muck."

She sits back down and rocks, lost in thought. Remembering the geese? Her chin nods to her chest, her hands clutch the afghan. Sometimes Ellen wants to make Mary-Margaret understand that in so many ways they are the same, that their lives were decided for them by forces they did not recognize in time. But when Mary-Margaret looks at Ellen, she sees her son's failure to marry well. When she sees Ellen's first child, she sees a girl who can give her nothing. She doesn't look up again until James comes into the kitchen, his cheeks flushed from watching the Packers.

"Who's winning?" Ellen says, even though she really doesn't care.

"Not us," he says. "This looks very nice," he tells the kids. Bert nods shyly; Amy shrugs. Ellen can feel how they are nervous, wondering what he wants, this strange man who is their father. But today he is trying; Ellen can see how hard he's trying in the way he stands, shifting foot to foot.

"Jimmy, that bird'll be all dried out if she puts it in now," Mary-Margaret says.

"Smells good," James says, not looking at his mother.

Ellen asks quickly, "When are you bringing up the tree?"

"Oh, soon," he says. "When you're done with this, I guess," and he gestures vaguely at the ornaments, the twisted red and white ropes of cranberries and popcorn.

"We're almost done," Ellen says. "I want to leave time for a nap after supper so we're all wide awake for Midnight Mass."

"What kind of tree is it?" Amy suddenly asks James.

"What?"

"You know, like is it a fir, or a Scotch pine?"

James considers this. "I guess you'll have to tell me when you see it," he says. "Maybe it's just a Christmas tree."

"Mama made goose so it fell off the bone," Mary-Margaret says. "This goose will be dried right up."

"I think it will be fine," James says softly. He kisses Ellen's cheek, surprising her, then heads back into the living room. Mary-Margaret sulks, wrapping the red flannel scarf more tightly around her neck, but she doesn't say anything else. After James is gone, Amy rolls her eyes and says, "There's no such thing as a *Christmas* tree."

"Use your imagination," Ellen says.

But Amy rolls her eyes a second time. Lately,

she's been studying James, looking for signs of weakness, for chances to prove him wrong. She's at an age where she is figuring out that her parents are not perfect; she resents it, resents them, but it is James whom she blames. It frightens Ellen sometimes to think of Amy as a ten-year-old girl, almost a teenager, certainly beginning to emerge as an individual person. She watches Amy work with the scissors, searching for clues that will tell her what Amy will be like when she's grown, eight Christmases from now. She wonders what all of them will be like, as she scours the countertop with bleach, thinking of James's unexpected kiss.

During halftime, James goes into the basement. He's down there for a long time before they hear him curse. His voice travels up the heating vent and echoes in the living room as if he were right there. "*Got*-dammit!" he says. The kids giggle and run downstairs. Mary-Margaret giggles too, sneaks looks at Ellen; her boy is being naughty. She sits in her parlor chair by the window in her pink chenille robe, her hair freshly curled, rinsed the color of the faintest blue sky. Beside her, Fritz sprawls in his La-Z-Boy. When Ellen moves the end table from between their chairs to make room for the tree, his sock feet stick straight up like exclamations.

"Where the hell am I going to set my coffee?" he says. "How the hell can I see to read without the lamp?"

"The Christmas tree will give off light," she says. "Or I can set the lamp up somewhere else, if you want."

Balloons fill the TV screen; the crowd cheers. It is time for the halftime show. Amy and Herbert race back up from the basement, and Ellen hears the sound of metal being dragged across concrete, then the *thump*-rest-*thump*-rest as James jerks the tree up the stairs.

"*Got*-dammit!"

"How's it look?" she asks the kids.

Herbert says, "Big."

Amy says, "Green."

"Where the hell am I going to set my paper?" Fritz says, just as James and the tree burst out of the stairwell in an explosion of painted bark and plastic needles. The tree is a vivid, neon green, strangled in wide ropes of gold and silver tinsel. Red glass balls glisten like wounds. The angel at the top is missing a wing, and one of her eyes is askew.

"It's already decorated," Ellen says.

"Less work this way," James pants. "You just bring it up, no hassles."

"Oh," she says, and he jams it between Fritz and Mary-Margaret's chairs, in the

95

space where the end table used to be. It is so tall that the angel is pushed flat against the ceiling. The smell of the basement fills the room: moist concrete, mildew.

"Some of the ornaments are broken," Amy says.

"Look, there's a spider," Herbert says. "Yuk."

"There's another one," Amy says.

"No problem," James says. "We'll just pick off the broken ornaments, and as for the spiders . . ."

He disappears into the bathroom and comes back with the Lysol. PINE SCENTED, it says in bold letters across the side. "That's expensive," Mary-Margaret says, but James opens fire on the tree. Spiders drop from the branches and scuttle across the moss-colored carpet. Amy and Herbert stomp most of them.

"There," James says. His eyes water through the Lysol, and the angel's skewed eye seems to be watering, too.

"I don't *like* this Christmas tree," Herbert says.

"Come on, now," James says, sounding playful, but showing too many teeth. "Isn't this the best Christmas tree we've ever had?"

It is the ugliest Christmas tree Ellen has ever seen. The tree forms a perfect triangle, and the metal trunk is painted a smooth, artificial brown, the color of tree trunks in children's books. Real trees are lopsided, too fat in the middle, skinny on top. Real trees have bald spots, ragged trunks, rough edges.

"How am I going to read my goddamn paper without the lamp, that's what I want to know," Fritz says.

"For heaven's sake, I'll set up your lamp on the other side," Ellen says.

"You forgot the cotton," Mary-Margaret says.

"The mice got into it," James says. "Pa, I'll set some traps down there if you want."

"There's no mice in that basement," Fritz says. "There's no goddamn mice any place in this house."

"What's the cotton for?" Ellen asks.

James gives her a funny look. "Snow," he says. "You know, you put the cotton under the tree so it looks like snow, and then you set the presents on it. Pa, it's crawling with mice down there. Why don't you let me set some traps?"

Fritz stands up, hoists his pants; James's face goes gray.

"C'mon, Pa," James says softly. "I don't mean nothing by it."

"We don't need to have snow," Ellen says, trying to smooth things over.

But Fritz is suddenly angry. "What," he says, and he snaps off the TV, "it ain't good enough for you, Jimmy? It ain't good enough for you here?"

"Pa, I didn't mean that."

"You think you can do better you are welcome to leave right now and take the rest of 'em with you and all their goddamn commotion. Bringing up this nonsense," he says, and he's yelling now, waving his arm at the tree. "All this bullcrap. Let me tell you something. This ain't no goddamn slum. There's no goddamn mice in the goddamn basement, do you understand?"

He grabs James by the collar and punches him in the face. Blood spurts from James's nose. He backs away, his head bent to his chest, making no move to defend himself. Fritz hits him again. The blow glances off James's shoulder; Fritz kicks him in the shins before he turns away, breathing heavily. It has happened so quickly that it doesn't seem real, but then James licks blood from the top of his lip, and Ellen hurts for him, she is burning with a clean, hot rage. She approaches Fritz from behind, not knowing what she will do, but James looks up and sees her. Then she feels how she is shaking all over.

"Get the kids' coats," he tells her thickly.

"No, Jimmy," Mary-Margaret says, but

James is pushing the kids through the room and into the entryway. Ellen follows with their coats, still trembling, hearing the crash and tinkle of the tree being thrown to the ground, Fritz grunting with the effort. James shoves them all roughly out the front door; the sudden cold air hurts Ellen's head.

"What about your mother?" she says to James.

"Pa won't bother her," James snaps. He wipes his mouth and chin with a tissue, fumbles the keys from the pocket of his coat. "All those years, it was always me and Mitch who took the brunt of it."

The kids stare straight ahead. Snow is still falling, and the smell of the lake is in the air: fish, sewage, cold green water. James unlocks his door, gets in, leans over to unlock Ellen's. She reaches around to unlock the back door. The sound of the locks is sharp as breaking ice. She wonders where they will go. To her mother? Maybe Julia? But even as she worries, she is exhilarated. They can't go on living with Fritz and Mary-Margaret after this. She realizes she's been holding her breath, and she exhales slowly, cautiously.

"Get in and buckle up," she tells the kids, and then she gets in too. She looks at James, his swelling nose, blood crusted around his mouth. "Oh, Honey," she whispers. "Do you want me to drive?"

He starts the car, squeals them out of the driveway. "Don't talk to me," he says fiercely. "Don't you say one goddamn word."

They drive for miles and miles, up to Cedarton, over to Schulesville, following Highway KW along the lake. By now it is dark; the windows of the houses they pass are lit with holiday candles; lights twinkle in the trees. Even with the heater on it's cold, and Ellen wishes the kids had their boots. Odd thoughts flicker through her mind: the road construction that was here in fall, a green print dress she once tried to make for Amy, the position of her feet, crossed neatly at the ankles. She thinks about the chewing gum she has in her purse, longing for a piece, but not wanting to disturb the uneasy quiet.

Snow spins in the glow of the headlights, and she remembers the blizzard of '59 that decided her life so quickly. James was driving her home when a storm set in, terrible and white. They pulled over, not sure if they were still on the road. All night they talked as they huddled beneath an old wool blanket, running the engine every half hour for heat, and in the morning, when the sky blew abruptly, brilliantly clear, and they heard the plow in the distance, they knew they would have to be married. For who would believe that a man and a woman could spend a night together in a car without making love? If they didn't marry, they both knew what the consequences would be, regardless of whether or not a baby came nine months later. To choose to marry was far better than to have your parents choose for you, to be taken to the church by your tight-lipped families, to listen to people say for the rest of your lives, *Them two, they had to tie the knot.*

"I have to go to the bathroom," Amy says and, wordlessly, James veers back toward town. They pull over at a family restaurant just south of Holly's Field. The broad front windows are like a stage, and Ellen stares greedily into other people's lives . . . the teenage couple sharing fries and pop . . . the group of women piling their coats cozily over a chair, arranging their purses and shopping bags around themselves in a way that makes her think of robins building nests . . . the old man stirring his coffee, licking a finger, a flick of gray tongue . . .

She fights a sudden, horrible urge to run.

"You coming in?" she says to James, but he doesn't answer. His face is swollen and homely, and she knows that, once again, anything she says will be wrong. "We'll just be a minute," she says, and then she takes the kids inside. The smell of frying burgers hits her stomach like a fist.

"I'm hungry," Herbert says.

She leads him and Amy through the restaurant to the back where the rest rooms are. She thinks about the goose she has cooking in the oven, ready to come out in half an hour, the dressing, the twice-baked potatoes waiting in the fridge, the *Kuchen.* "I don't have any money," she says. "Besides, you'll spoil your dinner."

"Daddy has money."

"Daddy feels really bad right now. It's probably best not to bother him or ask him for anything because that will make him feel worse. The way we can make him feel better is to just stay very quiet."

Bert's hair is still knotted with ribbon. She twists it free, then puts him in a stall to pee. Amy takes the stall farthest away from them. The rest room smells of toilet cleaner and strong musk perfume.

"He's going to leave us here," Amy says. Ellen can see her small feet swinging.

"What?"

"He won't be there when we go back out." She speaks slowly and clearly, as if she were speaking to a very small child.

"Of course he will!" Ellen says. She takes Herbert to the sink, washes her hands, helps him reach the faucet. She hadn't thought of that: James leaving them here, traveling on, anywhere, far away. What she had wanted to do a moment earlier. But didn't. Herbert lets his hands drift dreamily under the water. "Hurry," she tells him. "Let's not keep Daddy waiting."

"He won't be there," Amy says again, smugly. She comes out of her stall and sticks her hands defiantly in her pockets.

"Stop it!" Ellen says, hating her. "You're being silly. Now wash your hands."

Amy moves her hands through the water slowly, extra slowly, as Ellen's stomach falls and falls inside her. When they get back outside, the car is where they left it, idling hard, exhaust curling through the air.

It is dark when they turn back onto Vinegar Hill. Herbert is sleeping; Amy shakes him awake as they pull into the driveway. The snow is heavier now, wet, crunching an inch deep beneath the wheels. The house is dark. Ellen starts to get out of the car, but James doesn't move. The engine idles uncertainly.

"Aren't you coming in?" she says.

"I'm going out for a bit."

"I don't want to go in there alone."

James stares straight ahead. Amy opens her door and gets out. Herbert gets out too.

Finally, Ellen gets out.

"So you'll be back for Mass?" she says through the open door.

"Yes, dammit," he says. "Yes, I'll be back."

"Where are you going?" she says, but he pulls away, tires squalling on the ice. "Wait," she shouts, "I don't have the key!" and she chases him out into the street. He tosses it past her without looking, drives away. She picks it up; it's hooked to a key chain in the shape of a smiling face. The kids are watching. She's horribly embarrassed. Then she is numb.

"C'mon," she says briskly. "Let's get inside before we freeze."

"He's not coming back again ever," Amy says. Ellen pretends not to hear.

When she snaps on the living room light, Mary-Margaret blinks at them, owl-like, from her rose-embroidered chair. The Christmas tree is gone, the table back in place. "Where's Jimmy?" she says.

"Out," Ellen says, hanging up her coat, helping the kids with theirs. She can smell the goose. And Lysol. "He'll be back for Midnight Mass."

"Fritz went for dinner at Senior Citizens'," Mary-Margaret says. "They're having ham and scalloped potatoes, I saw it announced in the paper. But I wanted to wait for Jimmy."

"Did you take the goose out?" Ellen says.

Mary-Margaret shakes her head; her lip curls faintly. Pleased.

The kids follow Ellen into the kitchen, hugging the walls. The popcorn, the walnuts, the strings of cranberries: everything is gone. The counter is a wide white gleaming space. They look at each other and their faces close up. Ellen sees they are going to pretend this hasn't happened, that nothing is wrong, and she is relieved to pretend that too. She puts them to work setting the table, as Mary-Margaret leans against the wall, watching. "When is Jimmy coming back?" she says. She rubs her hand through her tight blue curls.

"He's never coming back," Amy says. "He said so."

"Amy!"

"What?" Mary-Margaret says.

"He's coming back," Ellen says. "He just went out for a bit. He's at the Gander with Hummer and Bill," and as soon as she says it she knows it's the only place he would go: back to his high school friends, to the booth where they always sat, squashed between the jukebox and the rest rooms. "He said he'll be home on time to go to Midnight Mass."

"He said he never wants to see any of us again."

"No, he didn't," Herbert says.

Mary-Margaret looks back and forth among all of them. Amy's eyes are bright.

"Believe who you like," Ellen says. "Food's ready."

They sit down to Christmas dinner. The goose is dry as bread. Mary-Margaret shakes her head at the first bite, makes a clicking sound with her tongue.

"Mama made goose so it fell off the bone," she says.

Ellen puts the kids to bed early, sets their alarm for eleven. There, on Amy's bed, is the star she made out of cardboard and glitter. So it was Fritz who threw their decorations away; Mary-Margaret would have saved nothing unless it belonged to Herbert.

"It's a good star," Herbert says. *Like me,* Ellen thinks, *trying to fix things, trying to make it all better.* And Amy, like James, who will be comforted by no one, crumples it into a ball that unfolds, bit by bit, after she throws it into the trash. It rustles there like a living thing as she turns away to get into her nightgown. Herbert dresses standing beside Ellen, his body gray hollows in the lamp light.

Mary-Margaret stops outside the doorway. "Come watch me take my pills," she says.

"In a minute," Ellen says. "We're saying prayers." She waits until she hears Mary-

106

Margaret move down the hall and the bathroom door click shut behind her. The children get into their beds and stare at the ceiling.

"*Angel of God,*" Ellen prompts them, and they continue with her:

> *My guardian dear*
> *To whom God's love commits me here.*
> *Ever this night be at my side*
> *To light and guard, to rule and guide.*
> *Amen.*

Their voices, chanting together, are like music in the half-dark, and when they finish they are quiet for a moment. The prayer itself means little to Ellen. It's the sound of the words, the feeling of so many people before her who spoke them with the same sadness, the same need. She said this prayer every night as a child, tucked into her mother's bed. When the light clicked off, bleeding into darkness, she was comforted by the thought of God watching over her. Prayers were a charm against loneliness. Prayers were an incantation warding off the razor-toothed fears that slept just out of sight, a constant humming presence. In the morning, there would be prayers before getting out of bed, prayers before and after meals, prayers for special intentions. On Sunday mornings, Mom drove them all to Mass; on Saturday evenings, they said the Rosary, kneeling shoulder to shoulder on the living room rug. Even now, Ellen can hear their individual voices, Heidi's light soprano, Gert's reedy whisper.

"Daddy is coming back," she says to Amy. "You know that, don't you?"

"I don't want him to come back."

The spell of the prayer is broken. "Get some rest," Ellen says. "You don't want to fall asleep during Mass."

"I don't want him to come back either," Herbert says, but he is sleeping, his mouth closing around Amy's words, repeating them like a lullaby. Ellen kisses them good night, then goes to find Mary-Margaret in the bathroom. She is dressed for bed in her pink gown with the billowy sleeves. Her breath smells of goose.

"Aren't you going to Midnight Mass?" Ellen says.

"Three . . . four . . ." She is measuring out her pills. She swallows them with water, coughs briefly. Then she bends her head forward and Ellen squeezes Ben-Gay into her hands, rubs her neck, her smooth shoulders beneath the gown. Mary-Margaret's skin is the softness of peach skin, the softness of babies and satin and water, the softness of rot.

"What about Mass?"

"I don't want to go without Jimmy," Mary-Margaret says. She gets up, pulling Ellen's hands with her under the gown, shrugs them away, and goes down the hall into her room. Ellen washes her hands, scrubs them with a washcloth to take off the greasy residue. When she comes out of the bathroom, she turns on all the living room lights: the lamp, the overhead light, the light above the TV. She goes into the kitchen and turns on the oven light, the big light over the counter, and she switches on the glass chandelier in the dining room. She bumps the heat up from sixty to eighty-five.

Wasting electric. Wasting oil.

She eats fingerfuls of cold stuffing from the dish in the refrigerator; soon it is all gone, and so is the leftover pumpkin pie. Still, she is hungry, she is raging with hunger. She takes the plate of *Pfeffernüsse* into the living room and turns on the TV, a Christmas special about an elf who cannot make toys. The first TV she ever saw belonged to her mother's sister and her family. They watched "The Howdy Doody Show," and while the picture filled the tiny screen, she and her cousins and sisters were silent, frozen, not wanting to blink or swallow or cough and accidentally miss a moment of that magic. Afterward,

Aunt Amelia was impressed, not so much with the TV as with the quietness of the children. TV was a wonderful thing, she said, because TV made children behave. Even now, staring at the screen, Ellen feels her hunger melt into a dull ache she can easily ignore. What will happen to the elf? Why can't he learn to make toys?

At ten, the show is over, and she wraps the gifts. A portable radio for James, chocolate lemon cremes for Fritz and Mary-Margaret. She bought the kids mostly clothes this year: boots for Amy, a down vest for Herbert, socks and underwear and lined mittens. Then, on a whim, she bought each of them a large stuffed mouse, one orange, one blue. Now she realizes they will both want either the orange one or the blue one. They will fight, they will cry. Someone will be unhappy. She wraps the mice, leaving only their long tails sticking out. Since there is no Christmas tree, she arranges the gifts around the TV, spreading them out so they'll look like more. Then she sits on the couch and stares at the reflection of herself in the window. Her skin is the color of pale bread; her eyes and nostrils are hollows. Her short, permed hair is uneven, curly in patches, straight above her forehead. She looks like any woman she might see in the grocery store.

When she was about Amy's age, she invented her future self from pictures she'd cut from the Sears catalogue. Her future self wore aqua shoes and hose and an aqua dress. Her hair was blond, swept up in the back, full in front. Perfect hair. Perfect body. Perfect clothes. She had eight children, and each of them had beautiful names. *Veronica. Evelyn. Ruth.* Her husband was sophisticated, dignified, certainly not someone who sold farm equipment. He worked in an *office.* Her aqua body greeted him at the door after work each day. Her aqua arms hung up his coat, led him to a table filled with delicious things to eat. The children sat, each in their place, and she turned to smile at them, one by one.

This is what my future self looks like, Ellen tells her reflection. *This is what a real wife and mother looks like.*

But she sees her aqua self shimmering behind her own reflection in the glass. It is almost eleven o'clock, and James has not come home. Her aqua self smiles her satisfied, perfect smile, the smile Ellen had chosen after scanning page after page, clipping many figures of women who weren't quite right. But now the smile gives Ellen a chill: there is something behind it, something desperate, something terrifying.

She jumps up and goes into the children's

room, turns off their alarm clock. Then she puts on her boots and her own thin winter coat. If she walks fast, she can make it downtown in fifteen minutes, grab James from the Gander, swing back for the kids, and get to church early enough to listen to the choir. For a moment, standing in the entryway, she smells the aqua lady's sweet sweet perfume. *Stay home with the children. Wait for James. When he comes home, be gracious, tell him it's all right.*

She leaves at a run with James's key in her pocket. Behind her, all the lights blaze in the house like fire.

She finds the car parked outside the Gander with its headlights on. The doors are locked. She doesn't have a key. The light from the headlights is a watery yellow against the snow. Cars and trucks are parked randomly along the street, facing each other, facing away from each other. Hummer's rusted Mustang has one wheel lodged on the sidewalk as if it is pulling itself toward the warmth and lights and smells of the bar, which have filtered out into the cold air of the street.

Her lungs ache from running. She pushes her way into the bar through the men standing by the door. One of them grabs her sleeve.

When she shoves him away, there is laughter. Ellen has always hated bars — the smoke, the noise, the groups of half-drunk men who always laugh in the same sly way. Before she married James, she sometimes went to bars with her girlfriends, but she always sat with her back to the wall, unable to feel safe. Marriage, she thought, would be shelter from all that, from men who look at you and laugh that way because you belong to no one. Yet marriage brought its own brand of laughter; on her wedding day Hummer kissed her full on the lips. *Warming her up for you, Jimmy,* he'd said, and the other men whistled when she slapped his face.

She spots James in his usual booth with Bill and Hummer and a woman she doesn't know. The woman is Ellen's age, but only another woman would guess it; to men, she would look younger with her stylish hair and painted nails, her sneakers with jingle bells tied up in the laces. She wears a cute red Santa's cap, and Ellen hates her for it. As she watches, the woman leans over, puts her tongue in Hummer's ear. James is sitting beside Bill, his head propped up on one hand, his skinny legs crossed at the ankles. He turns, looks at Ellen, but does not notice she is there, and she thinks wildly that perhaps it isn't him, that she's made a mistake and he's home right now, wondering where she is. Somebody touches her arm and she jerks it away, spins around.

"Oh, I'm sorry," she says quickly; it's one of the fourth-grade teachers from school. Ellen promptly forgets her name. It's Beatrice, maybe. Or Carol.

"I always pegged you as the quiet type, but here you are on Christmas Eve. Looks can be deceiving." The woman grins; then she looks at Ellen closely. "Hey, it's me, Barb. You okay?"

"No," Ellen says.

Then Hummer sees her, waves his arm. "Ellie!" he shrieks. He has a high, wandering voice. Mocking. "Me-e-erry Christmas!" he says. "Come and have a drink."

"That your husband?" Barb says.

"The one to the left," Ellen says grimly. "The one with his head on the table."

"Wow," Barb says, staring at James. "He's going to have one hell of a stiff neck."

"He's going to have more than that," Ellen says, and Barb laughs, but kindly, and squeezes her arm before disappearing into the crowd. Ellen sidesteps a group of slow-dancing couples, sits down next to James. Five people in a booth is tight, but she doesn't want anyone to be comfortable. James lifts his head and drapes a heavy arm around her shoulders. A

114

half-empty pitcher is on the table, certainly not the first.

"Whoops," James says. "I was going to get back for Midnight Mass."

The beer has wiped his expression clean. There is no trace of Fritz, the children, Christmas. No trace of her. Only his nose looks different: puffy, with traces of blood at the corner of one nostril. A few stained tissues are crumpled on the table in front of him.

Hummer checks his watch. It is gold, large, too big for his wrist. "Aw, shit, me too," he says sarcastically. "You Catholic?" he asks the woman.

"Used to be," she says. She takes a large swallow of beer. "Fuck that shit."

"That's sacrilege," James whispers to Ellen, truly amazed. "Did you hear what she just said?"

"I ain't been to Mass in years," Bill says. "I always mean to go, but then . . ." He smiles, shrugs, drinks his beer. "Hey, Ellen, you going?"

"If the car starts," she says.

James looks at her strangely.

"You left the lights on," she says. "Give me the key, I'm going to try and start it."

"Okay, okay." James says. "Okay, okay, okay, okay, okay." His hands work through his pockets like hands moving underwater. When she grabs the keys, the woman snickers.

"Looks like Jimmy's in trou-ble," she says, and she shakes her jingle-bell feet.

"Have a merry Christmas," Ellen says, and she leaves them to their beer. As she's struggling past the men around the door, her heel finds a toe, grinds hard, and then she's back on the street. She unlocks the car, gets in, turns it over.

Nothing.

She doesn't bother to try again. She puts her head on the steering wheel, thinking about the long walk home, the kids waking up in the morning to the presents strewn around the TV. The thud of the music from inside the Gander is as muffled as a heartbeat; snow falls, peaceful as the snow in a movie or a song. *Silent night, holy night.* It's a beautiful Christmas Eve. In the morning, the fields around her mother's house will be like a single cloth spread across a wide table, the pine trees shuddering with chickadees and juncos, the smell of wood smoke in the air. She thinks about how she will have to pretend to her mother, to her sisters, *Yes, what a wonderful Christmas we had, how was yours?* and her voice will be the voice of the aqua lady, charming and sweet and unreal. A lady's voice. The voice she chose for herself when she was just a little girl.

Lullaby

7

Their hands remind him of skeleton hands; their eyes the round, blank eyes of ghosts. As a boy, he'd been afraid of Halloween: the neighborhood children carved tiny jack-o'-lanterns and carried them, leering and lit, from farm to farm. From the window of the bedroom he shared with his brother, he could see strings of jack-o'-lantern smiles gliding through the dark fields. Sometimes, one of the smiles broke from the others, arced wildly, twisting as it fell, burst into blackness. Later, much later, his brother would come home, smelling of crushed pumpkin rot. He'd climb into James's bed and sit on James's stomach and pinch his nipples hard, saying, *chicken, chicken, chicken.*

James swallows, licks his lips. What kind of man looks at his own children and thinks of Halloween?

They are waiting for him in their beds, pale fingers thin and reaching. Their pointed chins remind him of witches. They are waiting to press their cool witch lips to his neck. They are waiting to breathe candy kisses into his ears. They are waiting for him to tuck them in, because he said he would do it. James stands in the doorway, not wanting to come in, not wanting those skeleton fingers even accidentally touching his own. He has never tucked them in before. He wants to be closer to his children.

"Have you said your prayers?" he asks. If he stands just so, his feet wide apart, his back straight, both his shoulders brush the door frame. He feels he is standing the way a father should: upright, firm, filling in the extra space. A lamp glows on the nightstand between the beds, and the shade of the lamp is painted with angels, white-winged angels in long, pale gowns.

"Yes," Bert says.

"No," Amy says. She has a bruise on her cheek: the shape reminds James of a lemon and makes his mouth taste sour. Amy says importantly, "Do you know what you're supposed to do?"

He wonders how she got the bruise. Little girls, he knows, get bruises now just the way little boys used to.

"You pull up the covers and ask us do the pillows feel okay, and if we say no, you say, oops, must be a stone in here somewhere, and you take the pillow and scrunch it and shake it and give it back. Then you say prayers and you kiss us good night."

She is such a plain little girl. His mother, he knows, doesn't like her. It isn't fair to dislike a little girl just because she is plain.

"That's what Mom does," she says.

Sunken cheeks. She does not have her brother's looks. Bert is small and sweet as an elf, except for the pointed incisors, too big for his mouth, which peep from the edges of his lips like fangs. He looks shockingly like James did at that age: delicate, pretty, mistaken sometimes for a girl. His eyes glitter; he is staring at James, he is always staring at James. He wants James to — what?

James looks again at Amy's bruise. Swallows the sour taste.

Bert's arms are wrapped tight around a large blue mouse; an orange one like it squats at the foot of Amy's bed. To James, both mice are gray: he is color-blind. But Ellen told him the colors, which he memorized. Because he is making an effort. Because he wants to be close to the children.

"What a nice blue mouse," he says.

He remembers something his grandmother used to sing to make children fall asleep. Her name was Ann, and she had long hair which she wore in braids and a bump on her chin where sharp black whiskers grew. When she died, they laid her on the kitchen table to prepare her body to be put into the ground where God would take it away. Once, when no one else was in the house, he lay flat on the table to see what it felt like to be dead. It was summer; flies buzzed against the windows, and a faint breeze smoothed his hair. He waited until he heard the flutter of angels' wings and smelled the sweet vanilla odor of their breath.

"Braun' Kuh, schwarze Kuh, mach' die Augen zu," James sings to the children in a quavery woman's voice.

His mother caught him there, stretched across the cold, hard wood, and he was punished, he knows he was punished, but can't remember how. It was one of the few times his mother ever punished him. He was the delicate one, sickly just like she was. *Hasenfuss,* Mitch called him. *Mama's boy.* The children look at him with their blank ghost eyes.

"Braun' Kuh, schwarze Kuh —" How does it go? Those black whiskers poking his cheek. The smell of grease in her hair.

"Daddy, what does that mean?" Bert says. Round eyes. Glitter.

"It means," James says, "brown cow, black cow." He waits for the words to come. "Make your eyes shut."

They think about that. Their cool witch lips

122

form silent shapes. Singing. Her braids twisted together, pinned high on her head, a nest of hair, smelling of grease. She stabs metal forks into the apples, one by one, then swirls them in caramel, lines them up on a platter. *When they come to the door, you give them these,* she says, and he waits, shivering in the drafty entryway, the jack-o'-lanterns drifting toward him, as though he is the center, the core, the magnet, his brother's brightest smile in the lead.

During the night he gets up, restless, untangling his breathing from Ellen's moist, deep breaths, leaving the stale cloud of warmth beneath the blankets. It is after midnight; he has been dreaming about the children. They clung to him as the air swarmed with bees. It was the sound of the bees that woke him, the shrill scream of a thousand wings, blending into song.

Braun' Kuh, schwarze Kuh —

He cannot remember the rest. His brother would have known; Mitch was older, he remembered everything, anything, when he wanted to. *A mind like a steel trap,* his mother said. Mitch was the smart one, good in school, while James was held back because he couldn't learn his colors, because he stuttered when he spoke, head down, voice almost too soft to hear. Skinny James, always frail like his mother, always with a black eye or a bruised rib or an arm in a sling. Accident-prone. Careless.

But James is alive and Mitch is dead. Mitch died when the truck he was driving over-turned, rolled deep into a culvert, burst into flames. Now he is buried at Saint Michael's Cemetery, asleep in the ground like the twin brothers James can barely remember. They lived less than an hour, not long enough to seem real, and his mother and grandmother denied that they had ever been born. But Mitch showed James what their mother said were two dogs' graves on the gentle swell of land overlooking the house. James liked to stand on their flat granite stones, each the size of a man's footprint, his legs spread wide as they could go, swinging his arms for balance. Once, Mitch gave him a shove, and James pitched forward onto his knees, embarrassed in front of his little brothers, who he knew must be laughing, like Mitch, at his clumsi-ness, their baby mouths black with dirt. The thought of them churned in his stomach, and he wouldn't visit their graves after that.

Together down there. Whispering secrets.

Even now, small children make James ner-vous. Smooth faces; blank ghost eyes. Tiny fingers and toes. He never knows what they are thinking. Their faces are masks, their expressions wiped clean of words. The slightest thing can kill them: a cold, a bump, a bruise. Then they close their eyes and disappear into the ground.

He gropes his way down the dark hall, past the children's bedroom, past his parents' bedroom. In the living room, he turns on the TV and sits down on the couch. The light from the TV fills the air like mist. His head is still thick with the dream: Amy's chin hooked over his shoulder, Bert's legs wrapped like a belt around his waist, the strange costume of their bodies against his own. The show is an old sixties movie, and he folds himself eagerly into the plot.

A man and a woman have married. In a quiet room, they kiss, the woman's head thrown back to expose her throat, the man's face impassive. They are just starting out; they call each other *Honey* and *Dear*. When the man wants to go out for a paper, he does it. When the woman wants to take a nap, she lies down. They are not being watched by tiny masked faces. They do not think of bruises in the shape of lemons. They are not forced to recall lullabies that make them remember other, bitter things.

When a commercial interrupts, James watches that too. He loves TV more than anything he can think of. It is small and neat; it is easy to understand. Wives love their husbands. Children love their fathers.

Brothers love their brothers.

In real life, he is away from home for weeks at a time, traveling state to state, selling farm machinery. When he comes back, Ellen's clothing has spilled over into his dresser drawers. The children do their homework at his desk by the phone. He doesn't know where to sit at the table: beside his mother like he used to? Or next to Ellen, his wife? He doesn't know which hanger to use to hang his coat: one of the stuffed gardenia-scented ones? A wire one? Cedar?

And then the children, the smooth skin of their foreheads so delicate, so uncertain. *Kiss Daddy hello,* they must be told. He hates the wet bite of their lips. He hates setting down his luggage, crouching, swooping them into his arms.

And Ellen, wearing clothes he doesn't remember, using words he doesn't know. *Remember the time we — ?* she says. He does not. The distance between them grows like a shadow at the end of a long hard day. Before they were married, they spent the night together in his car. The weather had turned bad, the roads swallowed in ice. They pulled into a ditch to wait it out and were buried to-

gether in the snow, forever close, forever sharing secrets. It was April 1959, and they
married one month later, in May, the first
buds just starting to show, and everyone eye-
ing Ellen's flat stomach, and the whispers, *All
night they were together in his car* —

She looks at him now as if he were an appli-
ance she doesn't think can be fixed. She wants
to move away from Vinegar Hill and into a
house of their own, a house where everything
will be even more different, and he will feel
even more out of place.

The children are growing up, she says.
Soon you won't know them anymore. Soon
they won't know you.

That's right, he says, that's good.

But of course he doesn't really say it; it
would be a terrible thing to say. And it isn't always true. Sometimes he feels his mind swallow him whole, the way a snake swallows a
plain, white egg, and inside the belly of his
mind he is not afraid of his children. They
come to him, soft as deer. *Daddy, look!* they
say, showing him this, showing him that, and
he always knows what to say, without Ellen
there to coach him.

Talk to them, she says. Say something.

But what?

He finished his last trip ahead of schedule
and came home two nights early, just as Ellen

and the children were sitting down for supper. The table looked different to him, smaller, and he realized that the center leaf was missing. The children were in their pajamas; Ellen had flour in her hair.

"Where's Ma and Pa?" he said.

"At Senior Citizens'," Ellen told him too brightly. "Kids, squish over for Daddy." She got a plate from the kitchen and filled it with chicken and dumplings. The children slowly edged toward Ellen's chair, leaving a small space for James between the table and the wall.

"I don't like chicken and dumplings," he said.

"I know that," Ellen said. She did not look at him as she set the plate down hard. "We weren't expecting you."

"We *love* chicken and dumplings," Amy said. Herbert nodded, his cheeks bulging.

"I thought you didn't like them," James said.

"Just because you don't like something doesn't mean we have to feel the same way," Ellen said, and the children lifted their pointed chins, a gesture of Ellen's he vaguely recognized. After supper, she played with them in the living room, hauling them up by the feet into handstands, then letting go. Their spindly bodies collapsed, knitted together, jumped up for more. *Me next! Me next!* they squealed. Each time a child crashed to the floor, James imagined a splintered bone. Their faces turned red; their hair swung in their eyes. Their shirts fell down to expose soft, puckered bellies.

"Careful!" he shouted, as Amy tipped over backward. "No more of this roughhousing!"

Ellen crouched, put her head to the floor, and pushed her body upward, uncoiling into a perfect, pointy-toed handstand. Her hips tilted slightly, keeping balance. Her breasts and belly flattened into one sleek line. James stared at her, shocked, for he realized *she* was angry. That night, when he got into bed, she rolled as far away from him as she could. "I will not live with a stranger," she said so quietly he almost couldn't hear.

This time, when he came home, he told her, I'll put them to bed tonight. But he stood in the doorway. He did not know what to say. He did not kiss them good night. He did not want to touch them.

Hasenfuss. Mama's boy.

All set? she asked, when he came into the bedroom.

Yes.

How did it go?

I sang a lullaby.

Did you kiss them good night?

129

When he didn't answer, she got out of bed, pulling both quilts along with her. "Ellie?" he said, but she disappeared down the hall toward the children's room. For a while, he lay shivering beneath the sheet, wondering what he should do. Then he got up to find a spare blanket. He looked in the chest of drawers and in the closet. He even bent to look under the bed. Finally, he called to Ellen through the wall, softly, not wanting to wake the children or his parents, but she didn't answer. So he put on his robe and lay back down, remembering how they had huddled together for warmth, the old Chevy swallowed in white, and how nothing wrong happened between them, although after that, it was obvious, they had to get married. What else could they do?

The TV flickers in the misty darkness. James's head sinks to his chin.

You're their father, she said.

Why would he dream of bees?

They love you, she said.

He cannot remember the end of the song. Mitch would know, but Mitch is dead. He is buried in Saint Michael's Cemetery, asleep in the ground like the twin brothers that died. He had a mind like a steel trap, but James cannot remember anything. He swallows, licks his lips. Without their faces before him, he cannot even remember what the children look like. Eyes, fingers. Sunken cheeks. Jack-o'-lantern smiles.

What kind of man cannot remember his own children?

The commercial ends; the lovers reappear. The woman twirls before the man, an angel in a long pale gown.

In the morning, he pretends to sleep as Ellen moves around the room, dressing for work in the semi-darkness. She steps into one of her teacher dresses, brown or blue — he cannot tell — that buttons up the front. A wide plastic belt cinches her waist. Her lips are outlined in lipstick; her short hair is curled tight, sprayed close to her head. He can see everything without opening his eyes. When her lips touch his cheek, he has felt it coming and does not wince, does not react to her sigh.

He would stay in this bed all day if he could stand it, his head half buried in his stiff, musty pillow, the blankets pulled up to his neck, bunched under his chin. But if he lies awake for long, his mind will wander and he'll find himself stretched out on hard, cool pine, hearing the buzz of flies and the beating of wings. The smell of vanilla. His mother's fierce scream.

He opens his eyes. In the kitchen, Ellen says

something sharp to the children; one of them answers back, *Wait*. No one answered back in his grandmother's kitchen. Children were to be seen and not heard. He ate whatever was set before him. If he didn't clean his plate, it meant he must be ill, and his grandmother gave him tablespoons of cod-liver oil. He remembers the oily taste, its slow, thick descent into his belly. His grandmother always watched him for signs of illness because his lungs were weak. In winter, he caught colds that lingered on for months. Feverish, he'd lie in bed, staring at the blankets his mother hung over the windows because light was dangerous to sick people. He tried not to fall asleep because he believed that was when people died.

Plates clatter, jackets rattle, quick footsteps brush the floor. James struggles not to listen, but it's too late, he's awake now, and the day stretching out in front of him like a field of snow, the distant fence posts frail as shadows, unable to contain him.

The front door slams. James is relieved. Now he hears Fritz rumble, Mary-Margaret moan. There are footsteps in the hall, the sound of the shower kicking in; once, twice. Mary-Margaret scratches at the door and pokes her head into the room. He can smell the salve she rubs into her joints.

"Jimmy," she says. "Are you sick?"

"No, Mother. I'm resting."

"He wants us to play cards at Senior Citizens'."

She means Fritz.

"Good, Mother," James says. "Go."

"I could stay home, if you wanted. You can ask him."

"No, Mother," James says. "I just need to rest." He closes his eyes, waits until he hears the click of the door. The way she fusses over him makes him feel unmanly. It embarrasses him to think that he came from inside her body, his face pushing out through her woman's parts, his mouth clamped to her woman's nipple.

It is only after they leave for Senior Citizens' that James finally gets up, moving slowly down the hall to the bathroom as if he were floating there. He has one more day at home before he goes back on the road, this time a familiar route near Rochester, driving fast in the company car, stopping to eat at diners with names like Sal's and the Eggery and Dew Drop Inn. He no longer notices the flat land twisting into hills along the Mississippi, doesn't taste the bacon and hash and toast gleaming with oil. His mind swallows him whole, and he lives in its belly for days. It's the driving that does it, and the lull of the road and the steadiness of the engine like a heart-beat. He shakes men's hands, smiles briefly at waitresses in coffee shops, but he is cocooned, invisible, serene.

Returning home is being torn from all that. Returning home is waking up at four-thirty on a winter morning, his grandmother's hand in his hair, and breaking ice in the basin to wash his face and neck. They milked thirty-six cows between them: James, Mitch, and Fritz, while Ann got breakfast in the house and Mary-Margaret sat wrapped in a shawl by the stove, sickly like James, never much help.

He brushes his teeth, shaves, steps into the shower, feeling as though he is not actually doing any of these things, but is watching himself, or someone like himself, from a window that's too small for him to see the entire picture. He has had that feeling before; it is how he imagines a dead person feels. Once, when he was eight or nine, Mitch invented a game called *Dead*. He took James out to the barn, to one of the small rooms under the haymow where the bins of grain were stored. It was August. There had been no rain for weeks, but today the air felt different: moist, hot, waiting. Thunder rolled in the distance, but it was a hollow, meaningless sound. Mitch pulled a candle from his pocket, lit it, used the hot wax drippings to fix it to a board.

134

Take off your clothes, Mitch said. *When you're dead, your clothes are the first things to rot.*

Bits of hay stuck to James's arms and legs. He could smell Mitch's sweat — bitter, like onions. As he took off his clothes, it was as if he were watching another boy slip out of his shorts and T-shirt, fold them in half, place them gently on the floor. Mitch tied this other boy's wrists and ankles with rope. He blindfolded him with a sock that was still warm.

Dead people can't move, Mitch said. *Dead people can't speak or hear,* and he pushed the other sock into the boy's mouth and stuffed warm wax into his ears. He lifted the boy into one of the bins of grain, and covered his feet and legs, his crotch and belly, his chest and shoulders. James heard the beating of the boy's heart, the sound of his breath rushing through his wide nostrils. And then James, too, couldn't breathe, couldn't scream, couldn't pray.

The soap is shaped like a heart. Rose-scented. Stinging in his eyes. The water drums his skull, and he opens his eyes into the stream, trying to flush out the soap, the smell of roses too strong, too sharp, ever to be mistaken for real ones. There were real roses at Mitch's funeral, and they were no more fragrant than ice. Now James is alive to remember their odor and it is Mitch who remembers nothing, it is Mitch who is dead. His casket was kept closed, the wooden lid covered with roses; they said there wasn't enough of Mitch left to recognize him anyway.

Mitch, the handsome one. Muscles like stones in his upper arms. Thighs thick as James's waist.

Mitch would have found a way to open the coffin to see if that really was his brother in there. But James was afraid, and now he'll never know. He'll never be absolutely sure. Sometimes he feels Mitch's hand hard on his shoulder. Sometimes he sees Mitch staring at him out of a stranger's eyes.

Hands the size of platters. Mind like a steel trap.

When James gets out of the shower, the mirror is steamed the color of milk. He stares into it, sees nothing. Feels nothing. Fritz and Mary-Margaret are at Senior Citizens' playing pinochle, sheepshead, rummy. Mitch is dead and Ellen at work and the children safely in school. The day stretches out like a field of snow.

For lunch, James eats sausage on buttered bread, reading the newspaper in the living room. Last night, a Milwaukee man came home from work and shot his wife, their two children, the dog, and then himself. A portrait of the family stretches across the front page; beside it, there's a small, blurred snapshot of the dog. All of them look ordinary, although neighbors say that the man had a temper, that the woman had been seen standing in the front window wearing her panties and bra. James reads the weather forecast; snow, but not enough for a travel advisory. There's an article about a local high school coach whom James doesn't recognize. There's a letter to the editor about a boy just home from Vietnam.

After finishing the paper, James wanders around the house, opening drawers and poking in closets. It is January, but there are still signs of Christmas. A half-eaten candy cane on his desk, its end sucked to a sharp point. Used wrapping paper folded neatly on the counter, pressed flat under the Bible, to wrap next year's gifts. A dying poinsettia on the windowsill, a gift to Ellen from the children, a gift she had liked.

One week before Christmas, finishing up his last route of the year, James had stopped for coffee at a restaurant in a little town one hundred miles from home. He cupped the chipped white mug between his hands, half-listening to the conversations of the people at the tables around him. *Aunt Emma's so hard to buy for,* a woman said, and he realized he didn't have a Christmas gift for Ellen. He paid for his coffee, then walked across the street to a small, shabby house with a sign hanging from the gutter that said Naughty Maudie's Lingerie. A cardboard lady in a Santa Claus hat and a nightgown stood in the window. THINK OF HER AT X-MAS was painted in block letters on the glass.

The shop was in the front room, and it was cluttered with mannequin parts, hangers, balls of tissue paper, and piles of small cardboard boxes. Nightgowns hung in a row from the ceiling. James thought they looked nice. He reached up to pluck at a white, lacy hem, wondering which one Ellen would like best.

"That the one you want?" a woman said. She was sitting at a card table at the back of the room. Behind her, James could see down the hallway to the kitchen, where several other women sat around a table piled with dirty pots and pans. They stared at him, and he looked away. Here he was not invisible. He could feel himself unraveling, becoming hesitant, unsure.

"Yes," he said. "How much is this?"

"Twenty," the woman said. She got up, grabbed a box off a pile, and brought it over to James. "I got the identical thing in here," she said. When she handed it to him, she let her hip brush his. "Who's this for?"

"For my wife," James said. "For Christmas."

"You want I should model it for you?" the woman said. "Or maybe another girl?" She nodded to the women in the kitchen. James could smell her teeth. He shifted, not knowing what she wanted from him. She was laughing at him. Maybe he should turn around and go.

"Do you gift wrap?" he asked.

"Sorry," she said, and she stepped away. She took the box from James and stuffed it into a plastic bag. On Christmas Day, when Ellen opened the box, he realized he'd never checked the size. The nightgown was an extra large. Later, in their bedroom, Ellen took off her clothes and picked up his hands and pressed them against her ribs. She guided him so they stood in front of the dresser mirror. James wished desperately to turn out the light. Her body, pressed against his own, was twisted and pale.

"Don't you remember what I'm like?" she said. She moved his hands over her stomach and hips. "Does this feel like an extra large?" He kissed her, but as soon as she let go of his hands, he pulled them away. Her body wanted to swallow his body, her breath suck away his breath. Her warm weight would fill him like water, like blood, until he felt her pulse beating in his ears.

James plucks the dying leaves from the poinsettia and throws them into the trash. He peeks out the kitchen window, then goes into the living room and stares out at the street. He sits down and tries to open the drawer to the coffee table, but the coffee table has been turned around, so the little drawer opens toward the TV. He is certain it opened toward the couch the last time he was home. Inside the drawer, he finds expired coupons, rubber bands and pens, a crumpled school paper of Amy's entitled *A Rainy Day*. Her handwriting is large and careful; her apostrophes and periods are small hearts.

> *When it's rainy I like to catch worms. I keep them in jars of dirt. If you cut a worm in half, one end will be a new worm, but the other end dies.*

He wonders if the new worm remembers the part that died. He thinks again of Amy's bruised cheek, how the bruise stands out on her pale, thin face. The thought of her being hurt, *bruised,* makes him queasy. He loves Amy, loves Bert. He cannot bear the thought of anything happening to either of them. Sometimes, when he sees them watching TV, or sleeping, or playing quietly at some game, he imagines their frail skeletons beneath their skin and is seized by the sudden fear that they will die. One slight bump, one false step, the screech of a car or the thud of a falling tree branch — this is all it would take. If it happens, when it happens, he doesn't know what he will do.

Better to choose the time, the method, yourself. Better to come home, like the man from Milwaukee, and get it all behind you once and for all, instead of waiting, helpless, for it to happen, the car, the branch, the illness, the closed casket. Better to break into your house with a gun: a violent lullaby.

He goes into the children's room, paces between their beds. The mice watch, their eyes fixed and mean. He remembers the smell of the bedroom he shared with Mitch when they both were in their teens, a smell that was far more Mitch than James: Mitch's deodorant, Mitch's shirts which he kept packed in cedar, Mitch's cologne, and at night, Mitch's onion sweat. The smell of Mitch when he was angry. The smell of Mitch when he turned mean. The smell of the sock, the smell of the barn. The weight of the grain.

James lifts Bert's pillow to his face, sniffs the way one might sniff at food about to spoil. He sniffs Amy's pillow. A shirt left on the floor. The curtains. He sniffs the mice. Relief floods his mouth with wet. Nothing smells familiar.

That night, he cannot eat. He sits at the table, passes the roast, the margarine and bread, the wrinkled peas. Across from him, at the head of the table, Fritz eats without looking up. Mary-Margaret, already dressed for bed, takes sips and little bites, each time shaking her head, for Ellen has spread a white cloth across the table and lit the candles that stand by the fruit bowl in the center. *Putting on airs.* James can feel the way this thought travels back and forth between Fritz and Mary-Margaret. The flames blink at him like hard, watching eyes; Ellen's eyes, flickering too close.

He knows she is waiting for him to speak. She has gone through all this trouble for him, because it's his last meal home for two weeks; the nice dinner, the candles, the white tablecloth which she's told him is hard to clean. He should say something, to her, to the children.

But what?

He watches the children, their small mouths opening and closing over their pointed teeth. It is seven o'clock; at eight, there's a good movie, plenty of action, something set in the Old West. He forces himself to take a mouthful of peas; the frail skins pop against his tongue as he chews. He fights to swallow. He should say something. He checks his watch; 7:02.

"So, what did you do today?" Ellen asks him, and for a moment the children freeze, forks in the air, eyes on James's face. *What did Daddy do?* they are thinking, he knows they are thinking that. They are thinking he is dull, peculiar, unlike themselves and their mother. Fritz snorts, bites savagely into his bread.

The movie starts at eight, a western, a good one.

"I don't know," James says.

"You don't know," Ellen says. "You must have done something."

"Don't bother a man while he's eating," Mary-Margaret says.

Ellen ignores her, keeps her smile fixed on James.

"I read the paper," James says.

"Then you saw about that man, the one from Milwaukee? Barb told me about it at lunch."

"What man?" Amy says.

"A very sick man," Ellen says, and her voice shakes, just slightly, but enough for him to think for the first time that, perhaps, she too looks at the children and is frightened by all the things that might happen, the cars and branches and caskets; that, perhaps, she too is afraid. He sees in her eyes a flicker, a flame, something he can almost recognize.

"A very sick man!" he says eagerly, but it comes out too loud, too strong, and she looks away. Mary-Margaret wipes her lips.

"This ain't proper table conversation," she says.

"That's right," Ellen says quickly, "you should be eating, you should eat more," and she abruptly stands up and heaps his plate with peas and bread, roast, a pat of margarine, a piece of fruit from the fruit bowl. The children watch with round, ghost eyes as she pushes him the salt and pepper. She gives him another piece of fruit. She fills his glass with milk. James fingers his knife and fork. There is something she wants from him, something he must do.

You should eat more, she had said.

He drops his head, and begins to eat. The roast, now the bread and margarine. The peas. The fruit.

"Wonderful," he says.

"I'm sorry," Ellen says quietly. She does not sit down. She is standing between the children. "I've given you too much."

"Delicious!" James says fiercely. He chokes down another bite of roast. He smiles at Ellen, smiles at his parents, who are staring, silent, at his plate. He will eat everything. It will be his gift to them all.

Knowing

8

Amy crouches outside her parents' bedroom with her ear pressed against the door. Inside, James sleeps fitfully; she can hear his breathing, rough as a cat scratching wood. The smell of his illness drifts through the house, clinging to the curtains, slithering along the walls. *Pneumonia. Bronchitis.* Beautiful words like the names of dolls. *Natalia. Clarissa. Pleurisy.* But Amy is almost eleven, too old for dolls. On New Year's Day, she gave her own dolls funerals and buried them in cardboard boxes in her closet. Ashes to ashes, dust to dust. Now they are sleeping in the arms of God.

"Where are Eliza and Missy?" Ellen asked when she tucked Amy into bed that night. Usually the dolls slept between Amy and the wall, their perfect heads propped up on the pillow. They looked sweet in the matching nightgowns that Ellen had sewn for them, yellow, with lace stitched to the collars.

"They are dead," Amy said in the deep

voice she had copied from Father Bork at school. "Do not speak of them again."

Now Amy imagines James's lungs like two pink mittens, swelling with air, rising up out of his chest, towing his soul to heaven. Dead people turn into guardian angels. Amy imagines James whispering advice into another girl's ear. *Wash your hands. Cheer up. Children should be seen and not heard.*

Perhaps he would like being a guardian angel. Guardian angels get to travel all the time, and whenever James comes home, he is eager to get back on the road. When he leaves, Amy forgets about him quickly. When he's home, she thinks about him all the time, and this is the second week he's been home sick, lying in bed, struggling for air.

Wash your hands. Don't chew with your mouth full. Turn out the goddamn lights.

Amy is certain Eliza and Missy have become her own guardian angels. Unlike James, they are practical angels, with practical things to say. *Your grandmother hates you. Your dad's really weird. If you imagine something hard enough, you can make it come true.* Because of Eliza and Missy, Amy knows things other girls her age do not. Eliza and Missy give Amy special powers, magical powers, that warn her of the many secret and terrible things that are hidden in this world.

Before Eliza and Missy, there was no one to look out for Amy, no one to protect her from those secret, terrible things. Last summer, she was walking in Autumn Lake because she had not yet learned to swim. The water was cool and tasted of iron. Ellen swam alongside her, graceful as a seal. "If you kick your feet, you'll float," she said, but Amy walked, step by cautious step —

Up to her hips —

Up to her waist —

Up to her chest and then her foot came down on something soft. There were sharp knobs buried within it. Amy grabbed one of those knobs with her bare toes and pulled the thing to the surface.

It was a drowned dog. The knobs were bones. The flesh was rotting, and it dissolved in oily pools on the surface of the water. "Drop it!" Ellen shouted, and Amy kicked at it and screamed, because she had never thought of a dog that way, as a thing made of bones and juices and skin. As Ellen guided her back to shore, Amy could *see* what the dog had been in life, a little terrier, white and brown, barking and circling and barking, just like Lassie always did when something was wrong.

What is it, girl? What is it?

The sound of James's breathing has

stopped. Is he dead? Should she call her mother? Amy puts her hand on the doorknob, and imagines James's long, narrow body sinking into muck, knobs for bones, dissolving. When the doorknob twists beneath her hand, she jumps back, slamming herself hard against the wall. A man is standing in the doorway, clutching his bathrobe to his throat, his hair a rumpled halo. Is he dead? Is he real?

"What do you want?" the man says sharply. "How come you're pestering me again?"

Amy runs down the hall to the room she shares with Bert. She slams the door, gets in the closet, and hides behind her dresses. It was here that Ellen found the cardboard boxes that held the bodies of Eliza and Missy. On the cover of each box, a cross was drawn in heavy black magic marker RIP 1967–1972. The eyes of the dolls were taped closed.

"They are deceased," Amy had said in Father Bork's deep voice. "Do not disturb their rest."

Ellen sat down on the floor of the closet with the shoes. Her shoulders moved up and down. "You're just a little girl," she said, and she stroked the matching nightgowns the dolls wore, smoothing the rumpled lace. "What is happening to you?"

That day at Autumn Lake, Amy had been furious with Ellen, a wild, helpless fury that left her shaking and cold. "Why didn't you tell me it was there?" she said, as the other children and their families stared. "Why did you let me step on it?"

"I didn't know," Ellen said.

"Yes you did, yes you did," said Amy.

But now she is older, and she knows better. When her mother explains, she nods and waits.

"You didn't know," she agrees.

At supper time, Amy comes out of the bedroom to help Ellen fix the meal. The kitchen is dimly lit, close, smelling of grease. Tiny yellow flowers watch from the curtains. Yellow eyes, patient, like the waiting eyes of dogs.

"Hey, Mom," Amy says. "What are we having?"

"Meatballs and rice," Ellen says. "Set the table and fix up some Jell-O for dessert."

Amy chooses lime Jell-O, careful with the boiling water, and then sets six places: Fritz at one end of the table, James at the other; Mary-Margaret to James's right, Ellen to James's left; Bert between Fritz and Mary-Margaret, and her own place beside her mother. Napkins. Salt and pepper. A serving spoon for the meatballs. In the living room, Mary-Margaret is playing the piano, and Fritz is watching TV. Fritz turns up the TV volume. Mary-Margaret begins to sing.

"So much for your father getting any rest," Ellen says. "I don't know why he's getting better between their noise and you pestering him all the time."

"He pesters me," Amy says.

"That's not what I am told."

"It's weird, having him here."

"Wouldn't it be nice if he could be here all the time? If he could find a job close to home?"

Amy knows Ellen wants her to say how it would be nice.

"It would be weird," Amy says.

"Maybe we could move into a place of our own. Like in Illinois. You remember Illinois?"

"That would be okay," Amy says, although what she remembers best about her father in Illinois is him sending her from the table whenever she picked up her fork incorrectly. *You don't want to grow up like a hick,* he said. Or *There's a right way to do everything.*

"Wasn't it nice then, spending time with Daddy when he came home from his trips?"

He liked Amy and Bert to sit side by side on the couch, doing nothing, saying nothing. Then he'd stare past them as if they weren't even there. Once, he pulled an envelope out of his desk, and showed them how much it had cost for each of them to be born.

"It was okay," Amy says.

You didn't know. You didn't know.

At school, beautiful Sister Justina tells them to start a journal. When Sister Justina talks, her hands shape the air into pictures for everyone to see. Her voice is something Amy can taste, something so good she can never have enough. All the girls in Amy's class want to enter convents when they grow up and wear the lovely deep blue Sister Justina wears and speak in Sister Justina's delicious voice.

"What should we write in it?" somebody asks.

"Thoughts, wishes, hopes, dreams," Sister Justina says. Her hands sweep together, collecting and polishing the words. "Things that have happened. Things that you want to happen. Anything you like. Take fifteen minutes now to begin."

Amy writes JOURNAL on the cover of her notebook, then opens it and stares at the first blank page.

I have nothing to say, she writes. *My dad is home sick, but he is better. Soon he can go back to work. I want to have a cat, but he says no because of fleas. I have a brother, he is six.*

When Sister Justina bends over Amy's shoulder, her dark blue habit sweeps Amy's cheek. "Was your father very sick?" she asks. Amy nods, blissful, too shy to speak.

At recess, the girls cluster by the fire hydrant, pretending to smoke cigarettes, exhaling puffs of warm air into the cold March wind. Kimmy Geib has a Magic Eight Ball, a round black globe with a clear window in which brief messages appear. *Yes . . . Maybe . . . Most Definitely.* The girls stand close together, making their backs into a wall that shield the Magic Eight Ball from the jealous gaze of Saint Michael's Church across the street. Occasionally, somebody twists her head to watch the boys, who are playing kickball in the dirt field next to the school.

"Isn't this a sin?" Jennifer Robbie says.

"Not if you don't really believe in it," Kimmy says. "Who wants to ask it something?" but everybody knows she'll pick Amy, because Kimmy wants Amy to be her best friend. Amy takes the Magic Eight Ball, closes her eyes.

"You have to tell us your question," Kimmy bosses, "and it has to be a question that can be answered yes or no."

Amy cannot think of a question. She waits, rubbing the cool, smooth surface of the Magic Eight Ball. She listens to the shouts of the boys, the *thunk* of the red rubber kickball. On Valentine's Day, the boys had tricked a first-grader into licking the metal hydrant.

The first-grader hung there helplessly, making low, grunting noises, like a pig or a cow. His tongue had been the exact same color as the kickball. At home, when Amy told them about it, Fritz had laughed. *Stupid one, just like Jimmy,* he said, and she'd understood that, once, her father had been that boy. The questions Amy has cannot be answered yes or no. Secret and terrible things are hidden everywhere in this world.

"Give it to me if you're just going to stand there," Lynne Peters says, and she grabs the ball away. "Magic Eight Ball, does Clayton Gordell like me?"

"The answer is no," Amy says, but Lynne shakes the Magic Eight Ball and peers eagerly into the window. Then she blinks and her mouth folds in on itself; she shrugs, pretending it doesn't matter.

"I told you," Amy says. "Clayton likes Jennifer Robbie."

Jennifer Robbie blushes; the other girls stare at Amy curiously. The bells ring, and Kimmy hides the Magic Eight Ball beneath her coat. "How come you didn't ask it a question?" she says, matching her step to Amy's, allowing the other girls to pass by so the two of them can walk alone.

"I already know everything," Amy says.

Kimmy shakes her head. "Saying that is an

even bigger sin than this Magic Eight Ball," she says, and she reaches out to touch Amy's coat eagerly, reverently. It's an ugly coat with worn rabbit fur around the hood, a hand-me-down from one of Amy's older cousins. "Trade coats with you next recess?" she says, as Amy knew she would.

Amy walks home from school dragging Bert by the hand, her ears pricked to catch the slightest whisper Eliza and Missy might send from the air. Bert hangs back, sucking his chapped thumb. His nose is running from the cold.

"Don't walk so fast," he says thickly, but Amy jerks him along, a fish on a line, and he follows her because he loves her and because he is the sort of little boy who always does what people tell him to do. When they get home, Mary-Margaret lets them in and wipes his nose with a handkerchief. The handkerchief is scented with gardenia and makes Bert sneeze.

"You didn't dress him properly," Mary-Margaret says. *"Schrecklich."* She is still wearing her bathrobe, and the ruffled belt pinches her thin body almost into two, like the body of a large, pale insect. The house smells of gardenia and Vicks. Peering down the hall, Amy can see the gray outline of her father, sleeping upright in front of the TV.

"I dressed him fine," Amy says.

"He's catching cold, just look at him."

"No, he's not," Amy says. She hangs up their coats, stretching high on tiptoe to reach the wooden bar. "Ask me any question you can answer yes or no, and I bet I'll get it right."

"Smart-pants," Mary-Margaret says. "You wouldn't give me sass if you was my gal."

"Ask me a question," Amy says to Bert.

"Let's watch cartoons," Bert says, and he goes into the living room and switches the channels, quietly, so James won't wake up.

"Smart-pants," Mary-Margaret says smugly to Amy. She sits down at the table, where she has a game of solitaire laid out, and carefully arranges the hem of the robe to cover her feet. "You don't know anything."

"You're going to lose," Amy says. "I'm sure of it."

But Mary-Margaret peeks beneath the turned-over cards, then shuffles through the extras until she finds the one she wants.

"That's cheating! You're cheating!" Amy says.

Mary-Margaret laughs. She peeks under another card. "You'll wake up your father, yelling like that, and then you'll catch it good."

"Cheater," Amy hisses.

Abruptly, just inches above Mary-Margaret's head, Eliza and Missy appear. They thrash the air with their wings. Their tiny pink mouths are open; their sharp white teeth are fierce. They tell Amy, *She will pay.*

"What are you staring at?" Mary-Margaret says.

That night after supper, Amy goes to her room and writes about angels in her journal. Without a guardian angel to protect you, there is no hope for you in this world, for only a guardian angel can see the secret things, the terrible things, that hide within every second. Say that you are walking down the street, and suddenly you feel you have to cross to the other side, you *must* cross to the other side, and so you do. Because that's your guardian angel looking out for you, and if you don't listen, a car could run up on the sidewalk where you were standing and squash you flat. Or say that someone is telling you a lie, and nothing about their face shows they are saying anything but the truth, but you *know* they are lying anyway, and you smile at them because you don't know what else to do. You don't need a Magic Eight Ball if you have a guardian angel. You already can *feel* all the answers to questions that can be answered yes or no.

She looks up to see Ellen watching her from the doorway.

"Homework?" Ellen says.

"We have to keep a journal."

"Sounds interesting."

"Not really."

"Then would you mind giving Bertie a bath? I'd like to go for a walk."

"Where to?"

"Nowhere in particular. You don't mind putting yourself and your brother to bed?"

Amy constructs a careful face. "I don't mind," she says. She doesn't ask if she may go along, because Ellen will come up with an excuse why she can't.

"Thank you," Ellen says formally, and Amy realizes her mother's face is as carefully constructed as her own. When she goes into the living room to fetch Bert, Ellen is already wearing James's big overcoat, her mouth and nose hidden by a scarf. She says, "See, Amy's here to give you a bath. I'll be back soon, Honey, I'll come and kiss you good night."

"No," Bert says. "Stay."

He is curled up on the couch, small and neat as a cork. Beside him, James is wrapped in a quilt. "Don't you start now," he says to Bert, who is sniffling behind his thumb.

"Little sissy boy," Mary-Margaret says.

"Don't go," Bert says, and he begins to cry.

159

"Bertie, I'll be right back. I'm just going for a short walk."

"*Hasenfuss,*" Mary-Margaret teases. "Mama's boy."

Fritz turns to James. "Jimmy, do we got to listen to this every goddamn night?"

"Herbert, that's enough!" James says harshly.

"Bertie, I'll be right back, okay?"

"It's you who's making him cry like that," James says to Ellen.

"I'm not making him do anything."

"It's you who's his mother," James says. "How come you want to leave him like this?"

"Because it's the only way I can get any time for myself around here!" Ellen says. "You're his father, even if you don't act like it. For once, you take some responsibility."

"I'm sick," James says. "I don't know what you expect me to do."

"I expect . . . *help,*" Ellen says. She gestures at Amy's grandparents. "I married you, not them," she shouts. "I didn't sign up to be anybody's servant! — Bert, *please,*" she says.

Herbert howls.

"Christ, Jimmy!" Fritz says. "She don't like it here, she is free to find somewhere else."

Amy steps forward and grabs Bert's hands. "C'mon, I'll get your water ready," she says and she tows him, still crying, into the bathroom. She closes the door and turns on the water, so the voices from the living room sound only like the echoes of voices. As soon as he hears the sound of the water, Bert stops crying and pulls down his pants to pee.

"She's going to be okay," Amy says.

"No, she's not," Bert says. He finishes, and steps out of his pants, dripping. "She's going to get bit by a dog with rabies. She's going to die and never come back."

"Arms up," Amy says, and Bert lifts his arms so she can pull off his shirt. She breathes in the boy-smell that comes off his body. If only he believed in angels . . . but she has tried many times to make him understand, to show him Eliza and Missy, to prove to him that her own guardian angels are powerful enough to protect them all. *But I don't see any angels,* Bert says. *You're not supposed to see them,* Amy explains, *you just have to know.*

"Ask me a question," Amy says. "Ask me any question that can be answered yes or no."

Bert gets into the bathtub, squats, bobs his bottom in and out of the water, getting used to the temperature. "Is Mom coming back?"

"Very definitely," Amy says. She gets a washcloth and rubs warm circles over his back, scratching around his shoulder blades until he straightens up and makes them stick out. *Wings,* Ellen calls them.

161

"Wings," Amy says.

"You don't know," Bert says sadly. "You think you know, but you don't. Only God knows if something's yes or no."

There's a scratch at the door, and James comes in, the quilt hanging from his waist like a colorful skirt. "What's going on?" he says.

"Shut the door," Amy says, "there's a draft," but James just stands there, staring at Bert's small body, at his penis which is curled and pink as a shrimp.

"Dunk your head," Amy says to Bert.

"Aren't you getting too old to let your sister see you naked?" James says.

"Shut the door," Amy says again, and this time James obeys.

"A big boy like you," James says.

Amy rubs shampoo into Bert's baby-fine hair. His head falls back against her hands, his eyes close. His neck moves loosely, and he makes a soft, contented sound.

"A big boy your age," James says.

They ignore him. He paces the two steps between the frosted window and the door, dragging the quilt through small puddles of water. He coughs, wipes his eyes.

"It's awful to be sick like this," he says, and he peers at himself in the mirror. Amy cups warm water over Bert's hair; he giggles when it runs into his ears. *Go away, you will go away*

162

now, Amy thinks as hard as she can, but it is several more minutes before James wanders out, leaving the door open behind him. Amy closes her eyes and sees her mother walking through the darkness, arms pumping, moving faster and faster until she lifts off the sidewalk and into the wide night sky, far away from Amy.

Amy tucks Bert into bed just like her mother would, saying the same bedtime prayer, kissing him on the same place beneath his chin. Then she gets into her own bed, leaving the lamp on the nightstand glowing, and writes in her journal. Perhaps there is no God or perhaps all of us together make up God, but with a guardian angel you don't need anyone but yourself, and soon, if you pay attention, you don't even need your guardian angel anymore. The angel kisses you good-bye and moves on to someone else, perhaps another girl or an old man or even a cat or a dog, because angels can't tell the difference. Angels can fall in love with anyone. Angels are the most beautiful things in the world.

She stops writing, and reaches out to touch the lampshade, which is decorated with angels in long white gowns. For a brief moment she is lonely for Eliza and Missy, who used to sleep beside her every night.

"Burning the midnight oil?" James says, and Amy whips her journal beneath the covers, because she did not see him, standing in the doorway, not exactly in or out of the room.

"Yes," Amy whispers, not wanting to wake Herbert. "Is Mom home yet?"

"No," James says. "*I'm* home."

"He doesn't want *you*," Amy says.

James takes one step through the doorway. His shadow stretches high on the walls. "Let me tell you something," he says. "It's hell having kids. Can you remember that?"

Amy does not say anything.

"Say it."

Herbert moans in his sleep.

"It's hell having kids," Amy repeats.

"Good," James says. He runs his hands through his hair. His eyes are wet; he blots them with a tattered tissue. Amy doesn't need Eliza and Missy to tell her how much he doesn't want to be here, how much he wants to be wherever it is he goes when Amy forgets to think of him.

They turn in their journals just before noon recess. When they come back inside thirty minutes later, cheeks bright with cold, Sister Justina greets them with an angry look which sweeps around the room until it descends upon Amy.

164

"Amy Grier," Sister Justina says, and her beautiful voice is filled with stones. "You will bring your journal to Father Bork. He is expecting you."

Amy takes the journal from Sister Justina, gets her coat from her hook in the hall, and walks across the street to Father Bork's office. The office is in the living room of the priests' house, which huddles against the side of the church. The housekeeper, Mrs. Hochmann, lets Amy in and ushers her with small, arthritic steps to the couch. Mrs. Hochmann is in her seventies and has been the parish housekeeper for over thirty years. The look on her face says she has seen all sorts come and go, but that undoubtedly Amy is something worse. She tries to take Amy's coat, but Amy clings to it firmly because she is terrified of Father Bork, just as all the girls are terrified of Father Bork. There are stories that he pulls girls' dresses up to spank them, and although Ellen says that's all garbage, Amy waits on the couch with her coat buttoned up to her chin.

When Father Bork comes in, he sits on the couch beside Amy without looking at her. He crosses his legs, folds his hands, and leans back into the cushions, as if he is planning to sit there for a long time. He fixes his lap with a gaze that is not angry, but very sad.

"Do you know what this is about?" he murmurs to Amy after several minutes have passed. His deep voice sounds as if it has been broken beyond repair.

Amy places the journal gingerly between them. "This, I guess."

"You guess," he says. He makes no move to touch it. "Do you know why what you have written here is wrong?"

"I thought I could write about whatever I wanted."

"It sounds here as though you think you are God. It sounds here as if you think you know things other people older — grown-up people — do not. And it admits that you have a Magic Eight Ball."

"It isn't mine."

"Whose is it?"

Amy does not say anything.

"I'm not angry," Father Bork says, and he fingers the journal, stroking it lightly. "But I am concerned. Think of how you are hurting God. Think of how much He loves you, yet look at the pain you are causing Him."

Father Bork puts the journal on the coffee table and drapes his arm around Amy. *He's going to spank me,* Amy thinks. *He's going to lift my dress.* She calls out to Eliza and Missy, *Emergency! Emergency!* but they do not appear.

"What I'd like to do is offer you the sacrament of confession. Just tell me you are sorry, and God will forgive you everything."

Amy imagines Eliza and Missy, their yellow gowns, their white, sharp teeth. *If you imagine something hard enough, you can make it happen.* But nothing happens, nothing at all. She is alone with Father Bork, sitting beside him on a couch that smells of cigarettes, his arm like a boa constrictor, squeezing her to his flickering tongue.

"Can you say, 'I am sorry, Lord, for my grievous sins'?"

Amy bursts into tears.

"Well, that's good enough," Father Bork says. "For your penance say four Hail Marys and contemplate humility. Then take what you have written and throw it into the trash. I absolve thee in the name of the Father, and of the Son, and of the Holy Ghost. Can you say Amen?"

"Amen," Amy whispers, hating everything.

After Father Bork lets her go, Amy does not return to her class as she has been told to do. She starts to walk home, but then she remembers Bert: how will he get home without her? It's an hour and a half before school lets out, and it's too cold to stay outside for that long. If she goes back into the school to wait, a hall monitor will find her and take her to Sister Justina. Amy has no choice but to enter the shelter of Saint Michael's Church, to dip her fingers in the holy water, to genuflect out of habit. She sits in the very last pew, hands tucked into her pockets as if they are hiding there.

9

For the past few months, Ellen has been waking at night, rigid with terror, afraid of her own death. The first time it happened she thought the feeling was something that would pass, like a bad cramp or a headache. She curled herself against James's silent body, nose pressed into the hollow between his shoulder blades. *Angel's wings,* she called those bones when she was a little girl. Her sister Julia could make them stick out at will, and with her wispy blond hair and wide eyes, she looked just like the paintings of angels at the front of Mom's old Bible. Ellen inhaled James's musty smell, and suddenly the thought of those angels horrified her. Dead people, dressed in white, floating through the air like dust. Toothless. Graceful. Bony fingers reaching for her throat.

The next time she woke in the night, she had dreamed of the angel of death. The angel looked like Julia with her feeble pink wings, but when she opened her mouth to speak,

Ellen saw two eyes shining from within the depths of her throat and knew she had come to drag her from her life. She sat up in bed, turned on the light, and those eyes dissolved into the air. That night, she was glad James was away, afraid her skin might crumble at the slightest touch, and instead of blood and guts and bone what would ooze from her would be dust.

Tonight she wakes up because she dreamed that she has died. As she lies beside James, breathing hard, she can still feel her bones being drained of calcium, the cells in her organs sloughing away, her very self dissolving. Just before he died, her father made a dollhouse for Ellen and her sisters, and after he finished it he carved a doll to look like each of them. He began with Miriam, the oldest; he had just finished Julia when he died, so Ellen was the only one who didn't have a doll. Still, she loved to look through the windows of that dollhouse and into the perfectly ordered rooms, where each doll was frozen before her single task, washing the dishes, ironing the clothes, making the beds, her feet held in place by tiny silver nails. In her dream, Ellen peered through the dollhouse windows and saw a figure carved to look like her. Delighted, she tried to reach for it, but her arms would not move, and she realized she was the doll, lifeless, an empty husk.

She gets up, puts on her robe, and goes down the hall to the kitchen. By now she has learned the secret sounds that the house makes after midnight — the hum of the refrigerator, the settling of the floorboards in front of the sink, the scratch of the crab apple tree against the window when the wind blows — and she senses she isn't alone even before she turns on the light. Amy is sitting at the kitchen table with her head buried in the crook of her arm. Her hair is unbraided, tangled against the back of her neck. She lifts her head, blinks sleepily.

"Honey," Ellen says, the nightmare fading. "What are you doing?"

"It's good for your back to sleep sitting up. I read it in a book."

"Does your back hurt?" Ellen says, and she rubs Amy's bony shoulders.

"No," Amy says.

"Would you like some warm milk?" Ellen says. "Milk has vitamins. That's good for a strong back too."

"I guess."

Ellen takes two cups from the cupboard and heats a pan of milk, grateful to have something to do with her hands. She knows she hasn't been spending time with either of the children the way she used to — inventing

weekend projects, poring over their assign-
ments from school. She just doesn't seem to
have the energy anymore; she is tired, short-
tempered, her mind always wandering. Six
months ago, she would have simply taken
Amy into her arms, asked her what was
wrong, and Amy would have told her. Now
she often feels awkward with Amy; Amy has
pulled away from her, keeping secrets, telling
occasional lies.

At work, she has been tired too, and the
students are starting to notice. She finds herself blowing up in the classroom over little
things that, once, she would have laughed at.
Mrs. Grier is a crab, she heard a little boy say
on the playground, and the circle of children
standing around him nodded their heads like
a small, fierce jury. "They're vultures," Barb
said affectionately, when Ellen told her about
it over lunch one day. "They start to circle the
minute they sense that something's wrong."

Ellen stirs the milk, and the skin sticks to
the rough wooden spoon. She has always
been a skillful teacher, a good mother. She
doesn't understand why that has changed,
why lately she isn't interested in anything anymore.

"I got in trouble today at school," Amy finally says.

"What kind of trouble?"

"They didn't like my journal. Sister sent me to Father Bork, and he made me take confession."

"He *made* you take confession?" Ellen brings the cups of milk to the table, sets them down, and sits in the rocking chair by the window. "Confession is supposed to be voluntary. What didn't they like about your journal?"

Amy gets the journal from her book bag by the door and gives it to Ellen, shivering in her bare feet and thin nightgown. "Here, come sit with me," Ellen says quickly, and Amy crawls up onto her lap, even though she is way too big and her legs spill over to the floor. It feels good to hold her this way. When Amy was a very little girl, she sat on Ellen's lap every night, and Ellen read aloud to her, book after book, until one day they discovered Amy had learned how to read. Now Ellen reads silently, turning page after page.

She remembers her own magical games she played at ten, at twelve, bringing the cows back up the lane for milking, never letting Number Seven take the lead because her bright white face meant bad luck. Her sisters, too, had their rituals. The toes of Gert's shoes met beneath her bed at night so Gert would never be lonely. Ketty wore her hair twisted into a bun on test days. Even Mom had her own beliefs: on holidays, an extra place at the table was set just in case someone (a guest? a spirit?) stopped by.

She finishes reading and rocks to and fro, wondering what to do. She knows what her mother would say to Amy about her journal. She would explain that, though she loves Amy very much, the Church and her teachings must always come first, and things Amy has written here contradict those teachings. *Who do you love more, me or God?* Ellen had asked Mom when she was ten or eleven. *God comes first,* Mom said, *before anyone, even your sisters and you.* Even now, she remembers the hurt, the sting, as if her mother had slapped her.

"So you made the confession," Ellen finally says.

The rocking chair goes *creak, creak.*

"No," Amy says. "Father Bork made it for me. I didn't say anything."

"That's good," Ellen says. "Father Bork is wrong. You don't have anything to be sorry for. Sometimes, I want to tell you —"

But she doesn't finish.

The rocking chair goes *creak, creak.*

After Mary-Margaret learned Ellen and James were getting married, she sent them to Father Bork for premarital counseling sessions. The first time they met, he made them

174

memorize *the surefire key to a successful marriage.* "Sacrifice is never easy," he told them solemnly. "Only love can make it easy. Perfect love," he paused, leaning toward them, "can make it a joy."

He waited.

They waited.

"Sacrifice is never easy," he prompted them, and, trying to keep straight faces, they chanted it after him until he was convinced that they'd remember it. They were sitting together on a couch that smelled of cigarettes, nervously holding hands, while Father Bork scrutinized them from behind his desk and sipped coffee from a beautiful cup painted with doves and olive branches. The housekeeper, Mrs. Hochmann, was a friend of Mary-Margaret's, and she kept coming into the room, first to empty the ashtrays, then to bring Father Bork more coffee. It was apparent that she was eavesdropping; afterward, James and Ellen tried to laugh about it, but they knew their marriage and its circumstances were the topic of many conversations.

They had to attend three counseling sessions, and at each one, Ellen promised more of herself to James. She must always obey him, because man is the head of woman as God is the head of the Church. She must bear James as many children as God saw fit. She must raise those children to be Catholic and, as their mother, she was responsible for their souls, and James's as well. *You are the hearth and home,* Father Bork said. *If the fire in the hearth burns out, the family dies.*

"Don't listen to what they say," Ellen says to Amy. "Just don't listen." Her voice is sharper than she meant it.

The rocking chair goes *creak, creak.*

Don't listen, don't listen.

The house is quiet except for the hum of the refrigerator, the scratch of the crab apple tree, the faint, distant barking of a dog.

Navigation

10

Ellen grew up with the man who is their waiter. His name is Roy and, though it doesn't show, she knows he has a rooster tattooed high on his forearm. In high school, he used to flaunt it, pushing up his sleeve, flexing his elbow to make the rooster stretch its neck as though it were about to crow. Kids crowded around him to see, and for a while all the boys talked about getting tattoos, what design was their favorite, what their parents would do. Now, like Ellen, Roy is past thirty, and a rooster tattoo is the sort of thing that makes people smile little, wise smiles and shake their heads. A rooster tattoo no longer fits into his life, which is quiet, perhaps even dreary, Ellen thinks, noticing the way he smiles at Barb as he guides the menu onto her plate. He winks before he turns away.

"It's my time of the month," Barb announces long before he is out of earshot. She shakes her head and her yellow sunflower ear-

rings clatter. "I could eat every last thing under *Dessert.*"

Barb's fourth-grade class has been moved
to the room across the hall from Ellen's fifth
grade. Sometimes Ellen is distracted by Barb's
high clear voice (*I should've been a mezzo,*
Barb likes to say) and she thinks of their growing friendship with a mixture of pleasure and
disbelief. They share their lunches in the
teachers' lounge; Barb is a vegetarian, and
over the past few weeks, Ellen has tasted interesting foods like bean sprouts and herb
cheese. Barb teaches in hip-hugger jeans and
brightly colored turtleneck sweaters, the clatter of her bracelets ringing like tiny bells. She
is the first person Ellen knows personally who
thinks there's nothing wrong with Women's
Lib. Once a week, they work recess duty together, walking between the swings and the
slide, taking turns patrolling the far edge of
the playground by the parking lot. Ellen wonders, with the same self-consciousness she remembers from childhood friendships, what
Barb sees in her. Whenever she thinks of herself, she sees a pencil sketch, wobbly and frail,
with arrows pointing to each part: *leg, arm,
hair.* There are ways, she knows, to imply
mother, wife, teacher, but there is no part of
herself which she can imagine labeling *friend.*

"What are you getting?" Barb asks, chipping fingernail polish from a tapering nail.

Moments ago, Ellen was grimly determined to stick to her diet and order just coffee, black. But the day calls for an ice cream sundae: this morning, walking to school with the children, she saw geese fly over Vinegar Hill, and she marveled at how they navigated through neighborhoods where all the houses looked the same, lined up in tidy rows without a river, a mountain, a lightning-split tree for a landmark. Flight is something Ellen can imagine, even wish for; navigation has always been a mystery. It is hard enough to travel through well-known streets and rooms and hallways, but how does one navigate wisely through tomorrow, the next day, the next week? Ellen sighs and closes her menu. There are only two more weeks of teaching until Easter vacation begins; still, she doesn't know how she can wait that long. At school, the children are restless, throwing mud balls at recess, doodling on their work sheets during math. At home, Amy and Herbert have divided their bedroom into sides, mine and yours, and they argue the borders with all the vigilance of two small hostile countries.

"A sundae, I guess," she says, just as Roy reappears.

"Excellent choice," he says, scribbling on his pad. "How's Jimmy doing?"

Ellen stares at his high, pink forehead, remembering how his hair used to grow curly and thick. "Um, he's okay."

"Is he home right now?"

"Until Saturday."

"Where's he off to then?"

"Somewhere west, I think," Ellen says vaguely. She doesn't like to talk about James in front of Barb, who is divorced and petitioning for an annulment. She tries to minimize the differences between herself and Barb whenever she can. Sometimes she pretends she is single too and can come and go as she pleases: eat whatever she likes, sleep in a bed with lavender sheets that smells only of herself, wear red and orange and purple turtlenecks that a husband would say are *too young*. James's name hangs between them like a foreign word, pretentious, something that doesn't belong.

"And what can I get for you, Hon?" Roy finally turns to Barb, his eyes suggesting endless possibilities. "A little shortcake, maybe? We got fresh strawberries."

"How fresh?" Barb says, loading the word.

"*Fresh,*" Roy says.

"Sounds good," Barb says, and Roy picks up the menus, sweeping the side of his hand across her arm. Barb watches the tight curve of his jeans as he walks back to the kitchen, and Ellen struggles with a vague sense of jealousy.

"He's married, you know," she says, somewhat sharply. "Four kids. And he has a tattoo."

"Tattoos can be interesting if they're in the right place," Barb says diplomatically.

"I wouldn't know."

"No tattoos on old Jimbo?"

Ellen laughs. *James with a tattoo!*

"Didn't you ever date a guy with a tattoo before you got married?"

"I never dated anyone but James," Ellen says, and as soon as she's said it, she feels she has stepped over an invisible line and become too intimate, too revealing. She imagines Barb is embarrassed for her, and she suddenly pictures Barb's adolescence: formals and dances, proms and homecomings, Friday night movies with boys who tilted their heads to hear the bright music of her bracelets, which must have been so risqué. Her own Friday nights she spent doing chores. To boys, she was never anything more than *a good sport, a cute kid.* "I was sort of a grind," she says quickly. "Always with my nose in a book."

"How did you meet James?"

Ellen searches for a lie, but can't find one. "He was one of my sister Julia's boyfriends, and she wanted to get rid of him. I was home for Easter vacation, and every time he called, she made me say she was sick. So one day he asked me out instead."

"Oh," Barb says. "Well."

They look away from each other and gaze awkwardly around the diner. It is small: six tables, two red vinyl booths, and a row of stools along the counter. Buoys hang from the ceiling, and one wall is covered by plastic sand dollars and lobsters and crabs pinned to a fishing net. The nautical theme is for the summer tourists, who will be too charmed by the quaintness of Holly's Field to remember that lobsters aren't found in Lake Michigan. Tourist season, though, is still months away and the diner is almost empty. A man dressed in coveralls perches on a stool, picking clay from between the cleats of his boots with a pencil tip. An older couple shares a piece of raisin pie, alternating bites. Ellen stretches her neck to peer out the window at Barb's red Camaro, which is parked in front of the fire hydrant. *My divorce car,* Barb calls it. Father Bork has summoned her to his office on several occasions, quoting letters from parents concerned about the moral integrity of a Catholic school that employs divorced teachers who drive flashy cars, smoke cigarettes in public, date men before their annulments are official. What effect might Barb have on young minds? these parents ask. What would Barb have Father Bork reply? She still takes Communion at Sunday Mass, staring him down until he releases the wafer.

"I've decided to get married again," Barb says abruptly.

"What? To who?"

"Oh, I haven't picked him out yet," Barb says. "Let's face it, the options are limited."

"I don't know why you'd want to get married again," Ellen says.

"I don't know either," Barb says. "Why do you suppose that is?" The day before he left for good, Barb's ex-husband locked her in the garage. The mail carrier found her on his rounds, then went on to spread the story throughout Holly's Field. Barb showed up for work the next day to face a classroom filled with nine-year-olds who knew all the details; "I guess it's because I'm turning thirty soon and I feel like that's too old not to be settled."

"Do you have to be married to be settled?"

Barb laughs. "Well, I think it helps. I mean, look at you. You're settled, you've got James and the kids — you know, someone to go home to."

Ellen shrugs, rearranges her silverware. She has no right to complain to Barb about her marriage. Barb would think her problems with James are silly after all she's gone through.

"So how will you find a husband?" she asks. "I mean, just *choose* someone?"

Barb laughs. "Of course," she says, but then Roy comes with their orders and she turns her smile to him. Ellen has known women like Barb all her life; her sister Heidi, for instance. Heidi can be talking to Mom or Ellen or her best girlfriend in the world, but when a man appears, other women become invisible. *It's natural,* Ellen reminds herself. *I don't mind. It doesn't make me angry.* She takes up her spoon and pushes it into her sundae, through the soft whipped cream, into the frozen center.

If I could have chosen, she wonders, *would I have chosen James?* She remembers the vinyl interior of his car, an old Chevy he'd bought from Fritz with two summers of work. Bits of hay clung to the foam that poked out of the cracks in the seat. A small blue statue of the Virgin was glued to the dash, and a Saint Christopher medal hung by a chain from the rearview mirror. The night of the blizzard, when they no longer could see the road, James slipped the Saint Christopher around his neck. *Don't worry,* he said, *This car never stuck me anywhere,* but soon, like a sleepy animal looking for rest, it nosed its hood into a drift. The windshield wipers grew heavy with snow, heavier still, until they froze to the

186

glass. *We can't spend the night here,* Ellen said; in a sudden panic, she tried to open her door and realized it was sealed with ice. *I'm so sorry,* James said again and again; he took her hand and for the rest of the night they talked, huddled under the stiff wool blanket, and in the morning when he said, *Well, we ought to get married, what do you think?* she looked into his kind, frightened face and told him, *Yes.*

She was twenty years old, home from college for Easter vacation, and she had known James most of her life, the way people know each other in towns like Holly's Field. Even now she can remember him as an altar boy at eight, stumbling over his robe and sending the gold serving platter flying like a discus into the pews. She remembers when he was held back at the end of sixth grade. She remembers him dropping out his first year of high school to help his dad with the farm the way kids often did back then. She tries to remember other boys, but she can't think of anyone in particular. There is only James, tall and thin, awkward in the old black suit of Fritz's he wore when he picked her up for their first date. Two months later, just after her graduation, they were married.

Her wedding dress was the one that Ketty, Heidi, and Julia had worn. Mom said it would bring her luck. It was yellowed under the arms and along the hem. The day of the wedding, Julia pinned the top of the sleeves to the bodice so Ellen would not forget and raise her arms; Gert stitched white flowers over the stains. As her sisters moved around her, Ellen watched them with her eyes half-closed, drifting, letting them take control. They were in the downstairs bathroom at her mother's home — after today, it would no longer be her own — and the air was close and warm as water. She doesn't remember fainting, but when she came to Mom was standing over her with a rag dipped in ammonia.

"She's just like Ketty was," Julia said.

"You're nervous," Mom said, though Ellen could see that she was afraid it was something else, and for one awful moment she hated her mother for what she was thinking. "It's like this for everyone."

"Not for me," Miriam said, suspicious too. "I wasn't nervous at all."

"Get her up," Mom said. "She's wrinkling the dress."

They smoothed out Ellen's dress, patted her face with a wet washcloth, and took her out to the truck. The fresh air stung her cheeks. It was a clear June morning, and the smell of the henhouse was in the air. *Ellen Grier,* she thought to herself, trying to make the name sound right, but in her heart she

188

knew she was still Ellen Schumaker, would always be Ellen Schumaker, and she was ashamed, going into her marriage with a selfish attitude like that.

She feels Barb's finger on the back of her hand. Barb is studying her with the same expression she uses when she suspects a fourthgrader of telling a lie. "You know," she says, "what I'd really like to do is move away from here, start fresh, maybe live someplace where nobody knows me. Honolulu or Mexico or something. I was just pretending about wanting to get married again."

Ellen licks her spoon, trying to act unconcerned even though she senses a trap. "Why?"

"I wanted to see what you'd say," Barb says. "I wanted to see if you'd try and change my mind."

Every diet Ellen has tried over the last few years has failed. Dressing for work in the morning, she avoids looking down at herself as she yanks her control-top pantyhose into place. Beside James and Fritz, who are bony as mules, or in the slender shadow of Mary-Margaret, or running after Amy and Herbert's quicksilver bodies, she feels bovine and slow, squat, hideous. And it's her own fault. All she needs to take charge of her life is a little self-discipline, a little self-control. But what she feels is out of control, out of focus, out of sync. Lately, she finds herself scrutinizing things so closely that they become unfamiliar. It reminds her of the way, when she was a child, she used to say her name over and over until the word stopped making sense and she became disoriented and afraid.

Last night, as she got into bed, she noticed her rosary on the nightstand. She picked it up and held the crucifix tightly in her hand, letting its sharp bones dig into her skin. James was already in bed, and, when she closed her eyes, still squeezing the crucifix, she did not think about how it would look to him, because she knew he would not notice. For years, she had looked at rosaries without thinking, but tonight, when she opened her eyes and looked into her palm, she saw not the crucifix but a man, *a dead man,* his face stretched in agony. A sudden feeling of nausea shook her; the rosary slithered away, falling to the floor with a clatter that made James turn his head. She saw herself as a young girl, lined up in church with Heidi and Julia, Mom and Gert, uncomfortable in her stiff black shoes and woolen stockings. It was Good Friday, and they were waiting to kiss the feet of the huge crucifix Father Bork cradled as gently as an infant. The line moved jerkily, step by step. As people touched their lips to

Christ's feet, the altar boy rubbed a white cloth dipped in alcohol over the painted pink flesh to kill the germs, although Mom had assured them that that wasn't even necessary: no germs could survive on blessed items. When Ellen's turn came, she froze, her lips already pursed, at the sight of those thick pink toes. She stared at the nail driven into His feet; blood oozed from the hole, and although Julia stood behind her whispering, "Kiss it! Kiss it!" Ellen could not. It was Father Bork who lifted those awful toes to her lips; Ellen herself never moved.

"What's wrong?" James said. His breath smelled of onions. She remembered how after they were first married he kept a tube of toothpaste beside the bed so his breath would be clean and sweet. At night, after he put out the light, Ellen waited eagerly for his hand to find her breast beneath the sheets. When he first realized how much she liked their sex, he'd laughed and shaken his head. Stunned, hurt, she grabbed her pillow and moved out to the couch; it was several weeks before she slept in his bed again. And after that, she always held back, unable to trust him fully, resenting how her new shyness seemed to excite him more. Now the thought of sex with him filled her with revulsion. She pointed at the crucifix that hung above the bed.

"Do you know what that is?" she said, and before he could answer, because she knew he would answer wrong, she said, "That's a dead man, James, a *corpse*."

Kiss it! Kiss it! Julia had said. Those thick pink toes.

James shrugged, rolled away.

"You think too much," he said.

Saturday morning, Ellen gets up before dawn to help James pack. He is going to Minnesota this time, to a sellers' convention that will last three days. He sits on the bed in his boxer shorts; she can feel him watching her as she moves around the dark room, filling the battered brown suitcase with his good pants, his casual pants, four crisp white shirts, socks, and underwear. He doesn't move to turn on a light and neither does she. She imagines that her back feels warm where he's been staring at it. A faint glow from the children's night-light in the hallway tinges the air like a scent.

"You better dress," she finally says, wishing he were already gone. She no longer suggests that he look for a job with regular hours. He was home sick for four weeks in March, and his presence surrounded the house like a shroud. He sided with Mary-Margaret whenever she complained about Ellen's poor cooking, Ellen's wastefulness, the inadequate way Ellen ran the house. He fussed at the children. He brooded in front of the TV. Now that he's traveling again, Mary-Margaret is subdued. She eats Ellen's cooking with a sigh but nothing more. Afternoons she sleeps on the daybed while Fritz plays cards at Senior Citizens', and when she wakes up she takes too many of the small yellow pills she keeps in a mother-of-pearl pillbox.

Ellen has her own supply of pills, though she is careful to conceal them. After several months of insomnia, she went to Dr. Heich for a checkup. "You're fine," he said in a way that let her know he wasn't really listening. Afterward, when she went to pay her bill, the receptionist handed her a prescription.

"Isn't this addictive?" Ellen asked.

"Doctor knows what he's doing," the receptionist said sternly. "It's something to help you sleep."

Now Ellen takes one every night, an hour before she goes to bed. Sometimes she takes an extra one because it doesn't seem like the first one is working, and she frequently takes one in the afternoon to smooth away what she feels when she thinks about going home, fixing dinner, cleaning up whatever mess Fritz and Mary-Margaret have made during the day. Dr. Heich has extended her prescription;

she may take up to four pills per day, as needed, and the new bottle allows three re-fills. She looks forward to each pill, the vague dizzy warmth that follows. She tries not to imagine saving them up, filling each new pre-scription until she has enough so she can swallow them all and completely disappear.

This morning, it is hard to keep her eyes open as she fingers James's clothes. She hears him stand up and begin to dress. When she turns to face him, he has put on his shirt; his arms and chest, which were invisible, glow white. It startles her briefly; he looks like a ghost. He says, "Do you believe that the Pope is never wrong?"

Ellen's thoughts have already drifted to the weather, because if today turns out nice, Barb will take her and the kids for a ride in the Camaro. Perhaps they'll drive up to Herring Bone Beach; the kids will amuse themselves finding gull feathers and driftwood while she sits with Barb on a flat, cold stone, bundled together in a blanket. James's question does not belong at the beach with the sound of the water, the weak gold sun, the throaty calls of the gulls.

"I don't know," she says after a moment. The question doesn't seem real.

"I want to know what you think."

"I'm not sure any of that stuff is true," she

hears herself say. She kneels on the suitcase, snaps the locks. James gets up and pulls on his trousers, and the sound of the zipper sends a chill up the back of her neck, it is so filled with rage. He says, "You shouldn't have said that."

The darkness breathes between them.

He says, "The Pope knows what's best for the Church just like I know what's best for this family. Living with my parents makes the most sense, even if you don't like it." He steps past her, picks up the suitcase, and carries it down the hall in his sock feet. Always, Ellen has fixed him a hot bowl of oatmeal, followed him to the door, kissed him good-bye, and then lingered in the cold air to wave. In Illinois, she had eaten with him, watching carefully as he traced his route in red marker on the map. *By noon, I'll be to Watertown. By six, I'll be at the Holiday Inn in Westdale.* His face would be flushed, still sleepy, and she'd kiss beneath his chin to feel the roughness there, despite his fresh shave, and he'd tilt back his head because he liked that, liked her special way of kissing him. Now she can feel that he is waiting at the end of the hallway, thinking to himself, *In a minute she'll come.* Perhaps he is remembering those mornings, too, when he would lean his chin on her shoulder as she washed the breakfast dishes; she felt his breathing, sad and slow, and she'd pause with her hands in the soapy water, matching her breaths to his own. Although he never spoke of it, she knew how nervous he got before he traveled. She knew that as he stood there, his chin digging into her shoulder, he was telling himself who he was — the husband, the father, the man — and because his fear did not fit those roles it evaporated into the morning air.

But she had said, *I'm not sure any of that stuff is true.* Surely he can sense what this might mean. Like Heaven, he is part of the natural order of things, something not to be questioned. And like Heaven, he has become more distant, more unknowable; like God, James has been slipping away.

Ellen has tried to be more religious, to recapture what she used to feel when she prayed. Some days, even now, she gets up early and goes to Mass before work. The wooden pews hold her erect, at attention; the Host rises up above the altar and magic surrounds her like a damp cloud. Then she eats God, swallows Him into her, waits for him to fill her up like those nights after work when she buys candy bars in the teachers' lounge and eats them, all of them, one by one, that bright forbidden sweetness. She tries to feel the smugness of faith, to know she is important and that her life has great, if hidden, meaning. But the more she has tried to claim God, the more He has rejected her. She wants to be lost in Him, but He vomits her out again and again, and each time He asks even more from her before He'll permit her return. She is proud, she is defiant, she is selfish, she is sinful. There is too much of Ellen in Ellen for God; she sticks in His throat like a bone. And perhaps James, too, finds her unpalatable, sour. *You should not have said that. You should not feel that. You should not be as you are.*

Across the hall, Fritz coughs in his sleep and begins to snore. It is growing light; James is no longer waiting. The front door opens, closes with a click. Even if she wanted to catch him, she could not, and reminding herself of that brings relief. She gets back into bed, settling into the still-warm sheets, and sleeps suddenly, soundly, completely, the way she did when she was a child. When she wakes up it is almost eight. The sun is a yellow slice beneath the curtains, and Herbert is tucked under her arm.

"You were *sleeping,*" he says in his funny way when he sees her eyes are open. His breath smells like peanuts. He sticks his thumb back into his mouth and sighs contentedly.

At breakfast, Mary-Margaret knocks the orange-juice pitcher to the floor. A piece of flying glass cuts Amy across the top of her bare foot, but no one notices this, not even Amy, until Ellen, on her hands and knees wiping up the mess, sees blood.

"Somebody needs a Band-Aid," she announces cheerfully; although a vein of blood trails across the floor, she is hoping it's not as bad as it seems. The kids look down, checking themselves out. Mary-Margaret glances at Amy's foot and faints, clattering forward into her plate. It happens so suddenly that, for a moment, nobody moves.

"*Ach,*" Fritz says, "she always faints at blood. How 'bout you, missy? You gonna faint on us, too?"

Amy looks at him disdainfully. "It doesn't even hurt," she says.

Ellen gets up and lifts Mary-Margaret by the shoulders, leaving damp marks on her pale pink bathrobe. Bits of stewed prune are smeared in Mary-Margaret's hair, and a bruise is forming on the bridge of her nose. A blue vein stiffens between her nose and upper lip.

"Is she dead?" Amy says, voicing Ellen's thought, but then Mary-Margaret opens her eyes.

"*Blut,*" she says, and as Fritz laughs, she

begins to cry, horrible choking sobs. Between breaths, she speaks in German, slapping Ellen's hands away. Then she gets up and goes down the hallway toward the bathroom, patting the wall ahead of her as if she has forgotten the way.

"Never could stand the sight of blood." Fritz chuckles, wipes his mouth with the back of his hand. "Good thing Jimmy ain't here or he'd keel right over with her."

"I *like* blood," Amy says firmly. Ellen washes her foot with witch hazel. The cut is deep but clean. She lets Amy bandage it herself while Herbert looks on, properly impressed.

"How come I never felt it?" Amy says.

"Stepped on a nail once, drove it into my foot," Fritz says, "through my shoe right up between the bones. Now all day I thought to myself, *I got something in my shoe,* but you know, I was so durn busy, I couldn't be bothered to take a look. Come nightfall, I couldn't get my shoe off. I'd nailed my goddamn foot to my shoe." He laughs, showing all six of his teeth, which are stained a cheerful gold.

"What happened?" Amy says cautiously.

"My foot turned black and dropped right off. That's why I got this here false one."

"You have a false foot?" Herbert says while Amy rolls her eyes.

"No he doesn't," she says.

"You don't?" Herbert says, and he looks from one to the other.

Fritz laughs and laughs. From the bathroom come the soft soft sounds of Mary-Margaret crying.

Barb stops by for Ellen and the kids in the afternoon. Ellen hears the horn in the driveway and scrambles the kids into their coats. Barb, like Ellen's mother, like Ellen's sisters, does not come inside.

On the way to Herring Bone Beach, Barb fiddles with the radio until she finds a Beatles song; she turns the volume way up. "I'm gonna clean out the gas line," she shouts, accelerating past eighty. Ellen marvels at the way Barb can talk about car things like a man. Logically, she knows that most human beings can pick up a manual and learn about transmissions and carburetors, but to Ellen they sound like the names of foreign countries in which she would be terribly, hopelessly lost. As Holly's Field fades behind them, the blue shine of the lake stretches far and flat to their right. There are no islands, only water that lifts to meet the horizon, the precise seam concealed by mist. She stares out across the rich lake farms, the edges of the fields still trimmed with snow. Ring-billed gulls litter the darkest soil for warmth, heads pointed north toward the farm where James grew up. The barn burned mysteriously five years ago, and the old stone house stands alone beside the deep, blackened hole, without even a shade tree for comfort. As they pass by, a red-tailed hawk lifts away from a weathered fence post, its shadow floating over the highway.

"How beautiful," Ellen says, but Barb hasn't seen it. Ellen glances back at the kids; they are both lost in the music booming from the speakers behind their ears, something with a steady, driving beat. James's departure seems like a dream, and she relaxes deeper into her seat, enjoying the way Barb controls the car, speeding up at just the right moments as they fly through the curves by the old grain mill.

"So did James take off again today?" Barb says.

"Yes."

Barb turns down the music. "Well?"

"Well what?"

"Doesn't it stink, him leaving you stuck with his parents like that?"

"I guess I've gotten used to it," Ellen says, surprised.

"No you haven't," Barb says. "No one gets used to anything, they just get numb. That's what's happened to you. You let him get away with anything he wants, him and his parents, too."

Ellen sees a white flash of rage. "What?"

"Now, look," Barb says, "we're friends, right? So I'm trying to help you stick up for yourself. Just because you married James doesn't give him the freedom to run your whole life."

"Not in front of my children," Ellen says, hating Barb fiercely.

"Oh, c'mon," Barb says. "Kids know these things before the rest of us do."

"No we don't," says Amy.

"*I* take my marriage vows seriously, even if *some* people don't," Ellen says; it slips out before she can stop herself.

Barb pulls over to the side of the road. Ellen wishes helplessly for another car to pass by, a deer to stray into the field, a dog to trot over from a nearby farm — anything to distract Barb, who wears the same look of fierce concentration she gets whenever she zeros in on a child's problem at school. Her teeth are sunk into her lower lip; her eyes are glittering, snake eyes. In another moment she will unhinge her jaws, swallow Ellen whole, crush her shell against her ribs, and digest whatever secrets spill out.

"This isn't the Dark Ages," Barb says. "Women have choices. I don't care what a priest will tell you, you shouldn't have to stay with a man who's hurting you."

"This is none of your business," Ellen says. "Maybe you better just take me home."

"I look at you and I see myself. You think it's going to get better somehow, but it won't. Baby, it just won't."

"Stop it!"

"Sometimes marriages don't work out."

"Take me home," Ellen says.

"Sure," Barb says. "Fine. Hide your head in the ground." She pulls the keys out of the ignition, tosses them into Ellen's lap. "But you're going to drive."

"I can't drive a car like this."

"What do you mean, *a car like this?*"

"With gears."

"You mean, you can't drive *stick.*"

Ellen glares at her.

Barb says, "Well, you're going to learn. When was the last time you did anything new, for Christ's sake?" She gets out of the car, walks around to Ellen's side. When Ellen doesn't move, she opens the door, pulls her out by the arm. The keys fall into the road and Ellen starts to hiccup. "Hold your breath," Barb suggests, but Ellen can't stop. The hiccups are shrill, painful. She bends over, hands on her hips, trying to catch her breath. "I'll crash," she says, her shoulders jerking. "I'll end up killing us all."

"You wanted to kill me a second ago, didn't you?"

"I still do."

"Drive," Barb says, and she picks up the keys, presses them into Ellen's hand.

They stall out twice before Ellen gets the Camaro into gear. "Push forward to find first," Barb says, but the gearshift sneaks to the left and Ellen, still hiccuping, throws them into reverse. The Camaro scoots backward into the ditch, stalls again.

"I can't do this," Ellen says.

The kids are holding each other's hands. "Don't flood it," Barb says. "Go easy now," and Ellen starts it up again, kicks up dust, then lurches onto the road.

"Use your clutch. Shift. *Shift*," Barb says, and they almost stall but then they don't. Ellen peeks at the speedometer; they're steady at thirty miles an hour. She keeps both hands on the wheel. She hiccups, checking the rearview mirror, but there are no other cars in sight.

"I thought you wanted to go home," Barb says after a while.

"I do."

"You're going the wrong way."

"I *know* that! I don't want to have to turn around."

"You could turn around in a driveway somewhere."

"No! There's not enough room."

Barb turns up the radio again, settles back. "What are you going to do, then?"

"I'm going to turn around in the parking lot at the beach where I won't hit anything. Turn that noise off so I can think."

"Do you think I'd let you drive my car if I thought you were going to wreck it? *You* turn down the music," Barb says, but Ellen doesn't want to take her hands from the wheel. She hiccups three times in rapid succession. She has read in the *Guinness Book of World Records* about a man who hiccuped for seventeen years straight before he died, and she wonders if this is how something like that starts. Barb turns to the kids and says, "Your old ma's a pretty good driver, hm?"

Ellen checks the mirror again and sees the children look at each other as if they think both she and Barb are crazy.

Five miles and fifteen minutes later, Ellen coasts into the beach parking lot and the Camaro stalls again. Before she can start it up, Barb has the keys. She says, "Say, kiddos, why don't you play on the beach while your mom and me have a chat?"

They leave the car like sparks darting away from a fire. Amy yanks up Bert's hood before they walk down to the ice along the edge of the water. There they stand, shoulders touching, two small dark figures on a wide gray surface. "I'm sorry about what I said before," Ellen says to Barb. "Hey, my hiccups stopped," and she starts to cry. Barb passes her a tissue, another tissue, another. She strokes her hair. She finds a linty roll of Life Savers in the bottom of her purse and tries to get Ellen to take one. She offers Ellen blush, rouge, cherry-flavored Chap Stick. Green eye shadow. The blunt cap of an acorn. A pen. Ellen cries and cries.

"I just wanted you to talk to me," Barb keeps saying. "I just wanted you to know that you're not all alone."

That night, Amy takes Ellen by the hand and pulls her into the bedroom. Herbert is already in bed, his thumb wedged into his mouth. Ellen expects to be bombarded with questions: *Why did Barb say those things about Daddy? Why were you crying in the car?* But Amy closes the door behind them and puts her finger to her lips. "Shh," she says. "Look what she gave me."

She lifts her pillow and there is Mary-Margaret's piano-shaped bottle that used to stand beside the empty ballerina on the top bathroom shelf, the bottle Amy has always loved.

"She gave you this?" Ellen says.

"Can I hold it again?" Herbert says.

Amy picks it up and turns it over and over in her hands before handing it carefully to Herbert. Ellen listens to the musical flow of the perfume inside it.

"She said she didn't mean to hurt me," Amy says. "She said I could have bled to death and then it would be her fault. She said I could have *died*," Amy says, and her eyes are huge.

"No one dies from a little cut, honey. Your grandma was just upset."

"I know that," Amy says. "It was really, really weird." Herbert returns it and she tucks it back under her pillow. "You know," she says, "I don't even want it now. I'm too old for it. I don't know what to do with it. And besides, she doesn't even like me." She doesn't look at Ellen; Ellen feels her tense, as though she expects to be contradicted.

"But you're going to keep it," Ellen says.

"Yes," Amy says seriously. "I have decided to keep it."

The Way of
the Cross

11

At night, when her hunger becomes tangible, thick and cold as iron in her gut, Salome dreams of a small house filled with many small doors. It is a cozy house strewn with handbraided rugs. A fire burns in the fireplace; family pictures line the walls, and the solemn faces look familiar, although Salome can't place where she's seen them before. On the floor, two children, twin boys, play naked with their toes. Salome picks them up and walks from room to room, a baby clutched beneath each arm, calling out, *Is there anyone here?* She doesn't quite hear the sound of something pattering behind her. When she turns to look, it's too late: a wolf, yellow-eyed and icy-toothed, leaps out at her with the silence of a cloud, and in that silence Salome begins to run, scattering rugs and crashing into furniture, the babies banging her hips. She dashes through door after door, until she reaches the last one, which is locked. Then she falls on the babies and devours them herself —

The wolf disappears —

Salome swallows, blinks her yellow eyes —

She awakens with the taste of blood in her mouth; she has bitten her lip again, the chapped flesh split pink. As she sits up, the odor of her body wafts from beneath the quilts. On New Year's Day she caught a bad cold and for months it has lingered in her chest and throat, the long ache of fever nesting in her limbs. Now, after walking to Mass in the morning, it is too much of an effort to bathe, to shop, to go to the Laundromat, to clean the gritty plates piled up in the sink. She turns on the light, and shadows scatter across the walls of her tiny apartment, slip away into the darkness through the single window overlooking the water treatment plant. There is no place lonelier than the night, even with the Lord keeping watch, even with His gift of dreams and the promise of His reward. She watches a mouse dart along the windowsill, dark eyes bulging velvet; she sings to it softly, an old lullaby of Mama's.

Braun' Kuh, schwarze Kuh, mach' die Augen zu —

When Salome was twelve, she awoke in the night and knew something was very wrong. She lay perfectly still in the cold, dark room,

212

feeling the warmth of Mary-Margaret's small body beside her own, listening to the ragged snores of her brothers in the room across the hall. Slowly, she moved her hand across her neck and shoulders, over her chest, and down toward the hot aching core of her belly. She rolled on her side and her thighs stuck together; the sheets were moist, and she recognized the smell of slaughter and sickness, of birth and death. She sat up, shivering as the air licked the tops of her arms, and she lit the candles on the nightstand. Shadows opened their eyes on the walls and stretched their long dark limbs. The shadow of the rocker by the window was a man; the shadow from the lip of the water pitcher was the sickle that he carried, and Salome believed Death had come for her.

When she pulled the Rosary from beneath her pillow, she saw the white sleeve of her nightgown was stained with blood. The blood was the color of pine pitch and it was everywhere, streaked on her thighs and hips, the sheets, her gown. Mary-Margaret stirred sleepily and opened her eyes. When she saw Salome, she sat up too. Her shadow on the wall wavered beside the man, who stopped and let his sickle fall to his side.

"Get Ma," Salome whispered, afraid to move.

Mary-Margaret looked at Salome's bloody lap and leaped out of the bed with a shriek. Her breath left a white twist hanging in the air. When she saw blood on her own gown, she screamed again, louder, dancing up and down on her small bare feet. The motion of her shadow consumed the ghost upon the wall, abandoning Salome and her shame to the world of living people, of fathers and mothers, brothers and sisters, where no one ever forgets.

It was the boys who came into the bedroom first; they clogged the doorway with their tousled heads and wide-awake staring eyes. Mary-Margaret was sobbing, wiping at her gown with the washstand towel. "We should tell Ma," one of the boys said, but Mama was already there, pushing them aside. Salome bent her head, waiting for Mama's sharp slap, for she knew by this time where the blood was coming from. But instead of hitting her, Mama poked her fingers into Salome's back and belly.

"Hurts here?" she said briskly. Her nightgown was sprinkled with small yellow flowers, each like an eye, harsh and accusing. Salome nodded.

"Anywhere else?"

When Salome shook her head, Mama leaped at the boys. "Out!" she told them. The boys slunk into the hallway, averting their eyes, for the voice Mama used was a familiar one. It was the voice that answered the indecent questions of the younger ones and scolded the impure thoughts that were written on the faces of the oldest. It was the voice that said, *You don't look at your sister that way,* and *You come away from that wash line,* and *You throw them drawings in the trash barrel.* The boys crept away to their beds without speaking and soon Salome stood numbly clean, lost in a fresh white gown that belonged to Mama. Between her legs, thrusting forward like a pouch beneath her belly, was the cloth bundle Mama had given her. The bleeding would come back every month, God's curse upon all women since the time of sinful Eve. Mary-Margaret sat quietly in the rocking chair, still flushed from crying, dressed in a gown of cherry-colored wool that had belonged to Salome when she was just an innocent girl, not a grown woman like she was now.

"Wash your cloths in cold water," Mama said as she finished making up the bed with fresh linens. "Let them soak in the covered bucket behind the backhouse."

"Yes, Ma."

"Don't talk about this to nobody. When you get like this, stay away from the boys."

"Yes, Ma."

"Mary-May, I hope you're listening. This'll happen to you someday, though I hope you'll be older than your sister here."

"It will *never* happen to me," Mary-Margaret said fiercely. "Do I still have to sleep next to her?"

"Silly little cricket," Mama said, and she kissed Mary-Margaret affectionately. "Go to sleep quick and the angels will bring you good dreams." She scooped Mary-Margaret up and plunked her into the bed, drawing the quilts up over her nose. "You too," she said to Salome, and Salome lay down awkwardly, feeling the cloth bundle shift between her legs. She hesitated, then felt with her hand to make sure it was still in place. She did not know if it was wrong to touch herself that way or not. Mama pinched her cheek and blew out the candles. "Try not to think about it," she said. As soon as she was gone, Mary-Margaret rolled as far away from Salome as she could get.

Sometimes at night, as they were falling asleep, Mary-Margaret played a game of make-believe, waving her small, ringed finger in the air as if it were a magic wand and everything she said would come true. "Someday I'm going to live in my own house on the lake with a porch made out of stone. Guess how many horses I'll have?"

216

Then Salome had to guess, and she always guessed wrong, because Mary-Margaret changed her mind each time they played.

"Every day I will choose a different horse to ride, and some will be yellow and some will be green and some will be purple and some will be blue. In the afternoon I will practice on my own piano so big that I'll keep it in a special room. I'll travel all over the world and give concerts until I'm famous and rich. Guess how many dresses I'll have?"

And she would describe each of the dresses, one by one, using the beautiful words Mama taught her, *magenta, alabaster, incarnadine,* weaving them with her voice until Salome could see them hanging on hangers made of ivory, the smallness of Mary-Margaret's hands and waist, the lace twisted through Mary-Margaret's hair, and Salome would forget it was a sin to think that way, to be filled with pride and vanity, and she'd secretly imagine such dresses for herself, though she never said so aloud because she knew she was too plump and plain to wear such beautiful things.

But this night, Mary-Margaret said nothing. Salome thought she had fallen asleep when suddenly Mary-Margaret said, "When I'm grown up, I'm not going to bleed and stink up the bed with my smell."

Salome closed her eyes, feeling the weight

of the darkness on her eyelids.

"Nothing like this is ever going to happen to me," Mary-Margaret said. "I'm going to be famous and rich. I'm going to travel all over the world. Say it," Mary-Margaret said.

Salome said nothing.

"I will *never* be anything like you! Say it! Say it!"

Your sister isn't strong, Mama always warned Salome, and *You mustn't upset your sister.* Salome helped Mary-Margaret with her simple house chores; she bathed her and dressed her and on Saturday mornings she wrapped her hair in rags so she would have curls for Sunday Mass. Mama had lost both girls born before Mary-Margaret, and Mary-Margaret herself had almost died several times. *Mary-May is a gift from God,* Mama liked to tell people. *God has spared her so many times I am convinced He has saved her for a special purpose in this world.*

"You will bleed between your legs just like me," Salome said. "You will have babies and they'll hurt you, there, when they come out from inside you."

Mary-Margaret reached across the space between their bodies. She pinched Salome's thigh as hard as she could, twisting the skin between her fingers. "Take it back!" she hissed, pinching and twisting. "Take it back!"

218

but Salome would not. In the morning, Salome had a bruise that stretched down her thigh like a beautiful tapestry, swirls of magenta, alabaster, incarnadine. Her leg felt wooden when she walked. By the time the last trace of color had faded, it was late summer, August, the season of tornadoes. Mary-Margaret never touched Salome after that. Even today she is careful when she hands Salome a curler, a bobby pin, so that their fingers do not accidentally meet. Salome takes special care of Mary-Margaret's hair; she curls it, trims it, tints it the faintest shade of blue. Her fingers move by rote over the familiar landscape of her sister's scalp, wrapping each thin lock of hair into its own sweet nest. Her touch is brisk, certain, the touch of someone from whom there are no secrets. The touch of a confessor, or even a lover. A mother's touch.

Mama said Salome's dreams were the Devil's mark, but Salome knew they came from God because her dreams always spoke the truth, and truth comes from Heaven alone. She had just turned thirteen when the dreams first came; on a sticky August night she dreamed God's fingers reached down from the sky and walked across the land. Winds blew and trees fell. A hollow roar swelled from within the earth, like the groan of an old and angry woman. Her brother Quinnie shook her awake.

"Tornado," he shouted. "Get down cellar with the others. Don't you have a lick of sense?"

Mary-Margaret's side of the bed was empty, still faintly warm, musty sweet. *She could've woke me,* Salome thought. *But she left me here to die.* She lay motionless, feeling the weight of the hurt that swelled in her chest and stomach. She saw God's fingers whirling like dancers, picking her up lightly, carrying her away.

"Come on!" Quinnie screamed. "Wake up!" He shook Salome until she struggled out of the arms of the dream and followed him down into the cellar. The other boys were perched in a clump with Pa; Mary-Margaret sat holding her little gray cat in Mama's lap, wrapped in a blanket, her beautiful hair like yellow paint in the light of the lantern. The cellar was square and small, with a packed-dirt floor and crates stacked high for shelves. Three dead hens were strung from the low ceiling; another had fallen but no one moved to pick it up. Salome stepped over it carefully and crouched between the watermelons and the rough woven basket of eggs.

"You could've woke me," she said to Mary-

Margaret, but Mary-Margaret didn't open her eyes.

"She's just a little girl," Mama said. "She was frightened, she didn't know better."

"I could've got killed," Salome whispered.

"Hush . . ."

"You better put out that light," Pa said, and Mama snuffed their faces into darkness. Then there was only the sound of the thunder and wind, the smell of damp earth and the sauerkraut barrel. In the brilliant eye of her mind Salome saw the window beside her bed burst into diamonds and knew that she would have died horribly had the Lord not chosen to spare her. She saw the dogs, huddled under the porch; the sheep matted together into one wide card of wool; the whites of the horses' eyes. She saw the trees Pa had planted for a windbreak bend over neatly, a row of tottering children touching their toes.

"We'll be lucky to keep the roof," Mama said after a while.

"Our place will be fine," Salome said without thinking. "But all that's left of Ubbinks's is the cellar hole."

"The girl thinks she's a prophet," Mama said, but in the morning they found the Ubbinks's had been blown clean away. The only thing ever recovered was the butter churn, which had landed in the schoolyard;

when the children opened it, a small bird flew out and disappeared into the trees. One of the cows gave birth to dead triplet calves, each of them white with blood-pink eyes. A flock of starlings descended on the currants: too gut-swelled to fly, drunk on the fermenting juice, they skittered around the barnyard, frightening the horses, drowning in the water troughs. A distant cousin died; then a not-so-distant cousin. There were rumors of tuberculosis and Mama thumped their chests and hung garlic wrapped in burlap around their necks.

On the day the goats climbed the fence to get into the cabbage plot, Mama fixed her calculating gaze on Salome. "What have you done that the Devil finds you so interesting? You with your unholy dreams. All I need is my oldest gal running after some craziness in her head."

"There's nothing in my head, Ma," Salome said.

"I do believe that's true," Mama said grimly.

But Salome knew it was *she* who had been spared by the Lord for a purpose known only to Him. One Sunday during Mass, she saw each Station of the Cross spring to life. She watched, horrified, as Christ was scourged, mounted upon a rough cross, thrust into the cradle of the sky. Tears came to her eyes, but as she looked around, she saw the rest of the congregation was unable to hear the lash of the whip, unable to smell the sour breath of Christ as he gasped for air. Children were playing with the hat clips, trying to snare flies with long pieces of hair. Fathers drooped in their seats, resting sharp chins on their chests. The faces of the mothers wore distant looks, and Salome felt with her mind how they were planning dinners, tallying crops, wondering where they had mislaid a thimble, a piece of calico, a letter.

She burst into strangled sobs, hands clamped over her mouth. People exchanged knowing glances; Mama had had a sister who died young, convinced she could fly from the milkhouse roof, coaxed by angels no one else could see. *Es ist im Blut,* they said, *it's in the blood,* and they shook their heads as Mama led Salome from the church, weak and trembling, barely able to walk. In the wagon, Mama slapped Salome across the mouth.

"You need to get some sense, young miss," she said. "You think you're some kind of saint, is that it? Tell me why God would send a vision to some dirty-minded gal! Sounds like it's the Devil you got whispering in your ear."

"It weren't me the Devil wanted all them years," Salome says to Mama now. But there is no one to hear; she peers stiffly beneath her bed, she glances into the gaping black mouth of the closet, she looks out the bedroom door down the hallway into the kitchen. The apartment is empty; Salome is relieved. She snaps on the radio and listens to a strange man's voice speak of places she will never go, people she will never see, and she is comforted despite the smell of her flesh, the knot of hunger pulsing inside her like a child.

At dawn she wakes up abruptly clearheaded; she fills the bathtub with water and scrubs the dried skin around her elbows and ankles and knees. She works Ivory into her hair, rinses it clean, untangles the worst of the mat of curls at her neck with a stainless steel comb. Now she wants to fill her mouth with cheese and bread, soft ripe bananas, coffee rich with cream. But the brief spurt of energy has been washed away, and she bends over coughing, coughing, a sound as hollow as a dog's angry bark. A tiredness enters her body, and she can't bring herself to put on her coat and step into the first sweet day of sunshine Holly's Field has had in weeks to walk downtown to buy food.

In the kitchen, she eats Spanish olives from the jar, squirts the last of the ketchup onto a spoon. She searches the cupboards for something she might have missed, knowing she ate the last preserves for supper, yellow beans, swallowing them cold from the jar. She re-arranges the shortening can, the dark bottle of vanilla, the baking soda and blackstrap molasses. Sunlight plays on the brittle geraniums lining the windowsill, and their leaves are patterned with maroon crescents which warn of their longing for sunlight, nutrients, warmth. At the bottom of the cookie jar, Salome finds the remainder of one of Ellen's gifts: the crumbling heels of a loaf of homemade bread, still soft inside a piece of plastic wrap. She toasts one, spreads it with shortening, keeping the other for later. Even her jaw feels heavy; she concentrates hard on chewing, pausing for breath between swallows.

Several times a week, all through the month of January, Ellen came in the night to knock on Salome's door, startling her as she listened to the radio. *Go,* Salome hissed through the chain, *this is no time for you to be out.* But always Ellen coaxed her way inside, a *Kuchen* or a jar of apple butter in her hands. She sat down on the couch as if she'd been invited, and talked about uninteresting things. She gave Salome vitamin tablets for her cold, fresh soft fruit, a pair of warm wool stockings — she seemed a nice enough girl, if lonely, but one night she began to pry. *What was your sister like when she was young? What do you remember most about your mother?* It was then that Salome realized she came not for company, but for information.

"You'll learn nothing from me," Salome said, and she showed the girl and her cherry crisp to the door and locked it. She felt Ellen standing on the other side, craftily waiting for Salome to check if she was gone so she could slip back inside. In the morning, Salome found that cherry crisp beside the door, frozen solid in the pan. She left it there for one day, for two. Several nights later, Ellen's knock came at the door, but Salome got into bed and pulled the quilts up over her eyes. The next day, the cherry crisp was gone, and Ellen did not return with her questions.

Now, Salome can almost taste that cherry crisp, the tart bite of fruit smothered in sweet sweet crust. Mama made cherry crisp each summer. Once, when Salome was a little girl and Mary-Margaret just a baby, Pa stole a crisp off the porch where it was cooling. He gave a bite to each of the dogs, just enough to stain their muzzles guilty pink. Then he beckoned Salome and the boys into the barn, where they divided it, hot and sticky, with their fingers, the barn cats stamping impatiently, sipping the air with their noses.

When Salome opens her eyes it is late afternoon; her cheek is flat against the cool Formica table. She has dreamed about two small children, toddling twin boys with lips and skin the pale blue of china. They babble silently and, though Salome searches their faces, she cannot understand what they are saying. One takes a bite from the other's cheek; the skin tears away easily. The cheekless one bites his brother's mouth, tugging his tongue out by the roots. Both children seem delighted as they consume each other's ears. *Stop!* Salome shrieks, but they bend to swallow each other's genitals, and Salome knows that there is no hope now, they are voracious, and after they are eaten up there will be nothing left.

It takes her a long time to hear the knock at the door, a series of *thumps* followed by laughter. The whorl of hunger in her stomach tightens. She pulls herself up and walks to the door through the bright dream of fever, marveling at the way the kitchen table and chairs, the countertop, the dying geraniums and rubber garbage pail all look so small. She is a giant, each foot falling to the floor from a great distance, and when she gets to the door it is a long reach down to find the knob.

The twins are at the door. Salome recognizes them immediately, even though they are so much older and their cheeks and ears are whole and pink. Horror swallows her greeting, and she waits, staring at them, wondering

227

what they want. They look at each other and giggle. Each carries a paper bag: one holds a box of cookies in his hand.

"Um," they say together. Then one says, "You wanna buy some cookies for the Middle School Marching Band? We got chocolate mints and Savannahs."

"And those cracker ones," the other boy says. "We got samples here if you want to try some, but it takes six weeks to get your order. We're trying to go to Canada, I mean, if we sell enough cookies by Easter. They're only a dollar twenty-five." He holds out a box of cookies and Salome can smell the sweetness through the garish cardboard wrapping.

Surely they have come from beyond the grave, knowing so well how to torment her. "Come in," she says gruffly. If she doesn't let them see she is afraid, perhaps they'll go back where they came from, to that terrible world between God's Kingdom and the sorrow of the Pit. Undoubtedly, they wish to entice her there; they are lonely, they long for a woman's touch to soothe the burn of unconsecrated soil against their skin. The boys step inside, wrinkling their noses, and Salome can see Mary-Margaret in their faces. The scornful high cheekbones, the slender beauty. Yellow hair the color of paint. She tries not to imagine the taste of mint, the thick melt of chocolate on her tongue.

"What do you want from me?" she begs them. "Honor thy father and mother, the Good Book says it. I had to do what Ma told me."

The boys look at each other. "It's just a dollar twenty-five," one of them says. The other is looking past the dirty dishes in the kitchen to the cluttered living room, breathing through his mouth.

"I never done nothing to either of you while you lived," Salome says. "I pray for your souls every day."

The boys are watching their feet now, moving toward the door, but suddenly Salome cannot bear to see them go. She had chosen their granite stones from the wall below the barn, chipping them free with the pickax, and as she lifted those stones to the wheelbarrow, she'd felt a searing pain deep in her womb. This is the pain that burns her now as she remembers how she hauled those stones to the rise overlooking the house where the earth was loose from rabbit burrows, where a shovel could puncture the cold clay crust and bury itself in soft peat. "I dug the graves," she cries out to them. "I freely admit that to you. But I did not help you die."

One of the boys giggles, a high nervous cackle, and in that sound Salome hears the hollow wail of an infant. She smells the birthing room; sees Mary-Margaret's flushed face; hears the clop of Fritz's heavy boots as he moved in and out of the doorway, smoking, letting the cold air in. "There ain't nothing wrong with you," he said. "Lots of gals drop babies without half the commotion you make." And Mama's face as she stared after him, hatred raw in the set of her lips. *Over my dead body,* she said, *will he lay claim to either of these sweet children.*

Salome starts to cry and reaches for the closest boy, but he wriggles out of her grip, dropping his bag of sample cookies. "I never done you no harm," she begs, but both boys duck past her and slip out the doorway, their sneakers squeaking on the icy steps. Salome stares after them, rubbing a pinch of her dress between her fingers. *Not my will, but thine,* she prays, imagining their long trip back to the netherworld. And just as suddenly as they have disappeared, she understands they are messengers, and that, once again, in His own way, the Lord who will not let a sparrow fall has provided for His own.

She lifts the bag from the floor. It is filled with boxes of cookies, some opened, some sealed. Her hands shake as she selects a chocolate mint. She chews once and swallows, the shards scraping her throat, and then she is filling her mouth with chocolate mint cookies, peanut butter cookies, shortbreads, sesame crackers, white flour, sugar, egg. The pleasures of the body flood her soul, and she feels the first rush of energy run through her veins like new, strong blood. That night, as she climbs into bed, she glances down the hallway into the kitchen to note the proud sleek shine of the countertops, the chairs neatly fencing the table, the swept floor. Tucked in the refrigerator, safe from mice, are three boxes of cookies for tomorrow, the day after, the day after that. By then her legs will be steady again. She'll walk to the bank, cash her Social Security, fill her cupboards with all the food she can carry. She falls asleep with her full stomach rising and falling under her hand as light spills across her face from the round, high moon that wavers above the water treatment plant.

12

Mary-Margaret feels the changes deep inside her body. At first, she does not understand. Mornings, she is dizzy and nauseated; she creeps to the kitchen, one hand trailing along the wall for balance, and sips at the tea Ellen makes for her, not speaking, afraid she might vomit or weep. Her ankles are swollen, grotesque, and though she tries to keep them hidden beneath the hem of her robe, that gal won't leave her alone. *You want me to fix you some Epsom salts?* she asks. *You think you should see a doctor?* But Mary-Margaret waves her away. She's short of breath. She cannot think. She sits at the piano for hours, hands draped loosely over the keys.

At night, she lies awake watching the pale green limbs of the clock beside the bed. There is something familiar about the way she feels, but the memory teases her, swimming the edge of her consciousness, just out of reach like a half-forgotten song. Then, one afternoon as she lies down for her nap, she feels tiny hands grip the ladder of her ribs. The babies have grown back inside her; they clamp their mouths tight against her lungs, nursing air, kneading at the tender tissue with their fists. Mary-Margaret pounds her chest and sides, her soft flat belly, but she cannot shake them loose.

She tries hot baths and enemas. She clips a novena from the weekly paper: *Thank you Saint Jude for favors granted. Pray to Saint Jude for all your needs for 9 consecutive days, say 3 Our Fathers, 3 Hail Marys, and 3 Glorias.* But as the days pass, the babies only grow bolder, kicking their feet when she speaks the Holy words, climbing up and up until they lick at her heart with half-formed tongues. She remembers how they were born so small, wrinkled as lambs, and squalling. She hadn't wanted any more children. She had had enough with the nausea, the swelling of her feet, the bite of the slimming corset she wore so the vulgar push of her belly wouldn't show. She had had enough with Fritz's rough hands. After James was born in '36, she spent six months in bed, sick with what the doctor called *milk poison,* but what she knew was a sickness of the soul. Soon after that she made up her mind to go against God and Nature.

You be grateful what you got, she told Fritz the day she got back to her feet, *you won't get anything more out of me. Go into town to fill your needs, go in the barn with the pigs for all I care.*

For the next year she was strong as Mama, strong as Salome, strong as the women she met in church who looked their husbands in the eye and never carried an arm in a sling or favored a fresh-crushed foot. She slept in the boys' room with the thick oak door bolted shut; during the day, she carried a knife. Each day, she worked hard, digging bushels of potatoes and onions from the garden, splitting her own kindling at dusk, and as the months passed, the residue Fritz's body had left on her washed away like soft lard soap. She slept deeply at night, her little sons draped warm as cats against her sides, with no rough hand to pinch her throat, no thick wedge of flesh rasping away inside her. Fritz eyed her at the supper table. *I got me forty acres, you know two sons ain't enough for all that.* Once, he brushed his hip against hers, but he stepped out of reach of the quick wink of steel, and then Mama stood behind him with a chunk of stove wood.

I told you not to interfere, he said to Mama. *Remember how I warned you.*

He surprised Mary-Margaret one cold, bright January day as she lifted her skirts in the backhouse. She did not have time to think. He hit her once in the forehead with a brick and pulled her out into the snow. Blood ran into her eyes as she ran blindly, her only thought to move, to keep moving, until the brick found the back of her head. Then she lay still as he emptied himself inside her, and when he finished, he pissed yellow circles around her body. The warmth of his urine melted the snow and stung against her face. She prayed for a miracle even as his seed took hold, but she had been the one to defy God's will, to refuse the marriage bed and the new souls it might bring. *Not my will but thine be done*, Christ cried out to God from the agony of the Cross, and Mary-Margaret understood that it had not been a prayer but a torn white flag. Whatever God wanted He would take as His due. If Christ could not resist, how could she?

When Mama found out what had happened, she made a special secret tea to shake the seed from Mary-Margaret's womb, but though she held the cup to Mary-Margaret's lips, Mary-Margaret refused to drink from it. She knew now that God would have His way, if not through this child, then another. But perhaps, if she became small enough, God might start to overlook her. Perhaps, if she kept His commandments, lived by His rules, He wouldn't take notice of her ever again. Surely the Heaven that followed this life would make up for whatever she'd suffered. And so she knocked the cup from Mama's hands and prepared for another birth.

Willow, Mama said, *you may bend but you won't break,* but Mary-Margaret knew that she was broken, her limbs clipped and bound for kindling, her trunk chopped off at the knees. This pregnancy was worse than the others. Mornings, she lay helplessly in bed, waiting for Mama's strong arms to lift her out of the sheets still damp with Fritz's smell, to hold the basin while she vomited, to slap her feet until she had enough feeling to lower them to the ground. Then she braced herself against the wall as Mama tightened the stays of the slimming corset that hid her shame from the eyes of the neighbors, the children, the parishioners, the priest. After that, it was all Mary-Margaret could do to walk downstairs and help get breakfast for the hungry little boys.

By the eighth month, Mama had to slit the corset so Mary-Margaret could breathe. One day, Mama even suggested she go downstairs indecent. *He never looks at you,* she said. *You be sitting at the table and he might not even notice.* But Fritz did notice, and in front of the boys he told her how she disgusted him. *You go on back upstairs,* he said, *and don't come down till you look like a Christian, not some hea-*

then gal with your business hanging out.

"To him, we're no more than the animals," Mama said, as she laced Mary-Margaret back into the corset. "But I'm going to fix it so he knows we are worse. He won't want nothing to do with you after that."

"He will never leave me alone," Mary-Margaret said.

When her time drew near, Fritz went to Milwaukee to fetch Salome, who moved through the house like a shadow, frightening the little boys with her strange and silent ways. Mary-Margaret sat in the kitchen, sipping shepherd's-purse tea to help bring on the labor, and hating her sister for her simple, silent body. Salome had never been sullied by a man's coarse touch. Salome's belly had never filled up with blood and guts that turned themselves into a child. Salome, like the Saints, was a Virgin, pure, and she would sing with the angels someday, her small, plain mouth opening wide to release a music that Mary-Margaret could only dream of hearing. *Mary-May is a gift from God,* Mama had said when Mary-Margaret was a little girl. But Mary-Margaret knew now she was no gift to anyone, slow and obese, breaking wind, chained to the earth by the cruel will of God while Salome rose before her eyes.

It was a cold fall day when she went into labor; the night before there had been a mild frost, but the ground still squished beneath her boots as she dragged herself to the house from the backhouse, warm water flooding her thighs. Inside, Fritz sat on the good parlor couch, rubbing tallow into his boots. The little boys sucked on their fingers as Mary-Margaret followed Mama up the stairs to the bedroom, and the eyes of the older boy went curious and wide.

Throughout the birth, she screamed with rage, but eventually her voice weakened, faded, then dried up altogether. She could do no more than hiss by the time Mama pulled the babies' bodies from her own, their wet skin steaming in the chill. Their cries brought Fritz, who stood in the doorway as Mama and Salome scrambled to cover Mary-Margaret properly.

"Don't wait up on me, Sweetheart," he leered. "I'm going out to celebrate my two new sons."

Mary-Margaret closed her eyes. Beyond all doubt she wanted to be dead, but she did not die, and in the morning, when she woke, the cradle beside the bed stood empty.

"Where are they?" she asked Salome, who was sitting at the foot of the bed. "I want to touch my babies before he does."

But Salome dropped her head into her

hands. "There are no babies," she said, and she was shaking. "You better talk to Ma about all that."

"Where are they?" Mary-Margaret said again, but Salome was yelling, "She's awake!"

When Mama came into the room, she held Mary-Margaret's face between her hands. "He had no right to those children," she said, "after all he done to you."

Still, Mary-Margaret did not understand.

"Look at how he is with Mitch and Jimmy," Mama said. "What I done, I done for these babies as well as for you," and she helped Mary-Margaret to her feet, neatly made up the bed, opened the windows to air out the room, and took the bloody linens to the barrel to be burned. When Fritz came home, bleary-eyed with beer, they were sitting in the kitchen as if it were any ordinary day: Mama, Mary-Margaret, and Salome, the boys wearing bibs and eating scrambled eggs. "What, you up already?" he said, but Mama just shook her head: what did he mean? They were eating breakfast. It did not take long for him to discover the two small graves on the hillside overlooking the house, but Mama laughed at him and said they were dogs' graves, God knew he'd killed enough of them over the years.

"What babies?" Mama said, and she

laughed at him for weeks. "So drunk you can't remember how many boys you got? Any more boys you think you got coming, they'll be in your imagination too. Crazy old man, the next thing you know we'll be calling up the neighbors to put you away."

For years, Mary-Margaret would catch him looking at her in the horrified way she had once looked at him, as if she were a piece of rotted meat, rancid and foul, and a deep satisfaction warmed her because she knew that he was afraid. *She-devil,* he'd said to her. *Just to hear your voice makes my skin crawl.* It made up for the nights she lay awake, trying to remember those newborn faces, weeping for those starfish hands. It almost made up for the anguish she felt after Mama died, when she dreamed of Mama writhing in eternal fire and heard her voice as clearly as if she were still living.

What I done, I done for you.

But the will of God is more powerful than women. On the ninth day of the novena, Mary-Margaret begins to weep, for once again her prayers have been ignored. She doesn't go with Fritz to Senior Citizens' anymore. She doesn't linger after Sunday Mass to shake Father Bork's smooth hand. She doesn't call Salome to come over and curl her hair. She is a tree, axed and bound for kindling, submitting her life to God's will the way Mama would not. Now she spends the days sitting quietly on the couch, watching "Let's Make a Deal," "The Dating Game," "Jeopardy." Outside her window, it is finally spring, but Mary-Margaret doesn't notice. In her mind, it is a cold, bright January day, the snow stinging her forehead and chin. She feels the great weight on her back, hears the sharp grunts in her ear. Over and over she prays the prayer she whispered as a new bride, *Lord, help me to accept what I cannot change,* until the beginning of it and the end of it run into each other, the way you cannot tell when one breath ends and the next begins.

Money

13

Swimming lessons begin in June; Ellen enrolls Amy and Herbert in spite of James's complaints about the cost. "*If* we're going to live near a lake," she tells him, "they have to know how to swim." James, she knows, is afraid of water, afraid of the sound it makes as it enters your ears, engulfing you, pinning you down until you work *with* the feeling of it rather than against it, when it buoys you up like a gentle hand. Amy is afraid of water too. Since she stepped on a dog skeleton in Autumn Lake, she will not place her feet where she cannot see them. *What were you thinking of*, James still says angrily, *letting the children into that dirty water?*

But Holly's Field Pool is chemical clean, dyed the appropriate shade of blue. Lifeguards prowl the edges; the temperature is kept at an even seventy-eight degrees. There are no dead leaves or fish, no sharp rocks that might cut a child's heel, no skeletons or sunken beer cans filled with mud. Even James agrees it's perfectly safe, but he says *money, money, we don't have that kind of money* until, on their wedding anniversary, Ellen takes the checkbook from his briefcase, goes downtown, and pays the nonrefundable registration fee.

For the past ten months, James has banked all of her paychecks, and usually some of his, too. But the more money they accumulate, the more James panics at the thought of spending any of it. Ellen studies him with an oddly clinical interest as he dresses in old shirts with yellow, frayed collars, drives three blocks out of his way so he won't have to put a quarter in a parking meter, pockets occasional loose change from the muddy church parking lot on Sundays. At night he talks about *the future*, dreams that money will buy for them all. Amy will be a pediatrician; Herbert will practice law. He paces the room in his boxer shorts and T-shirt, talking about the situation in Vietnam, the economy, the nation, the TV humming behind him like a chorus. Ellen lies in bed, not speaking — for it is not a response James wants — and waits for the warm wash of sleep, the aftertaste of the pills she swallowed still bitter against her tongue. With this new prescription, she has enough pills so she doesn't have to ration. She keeps most of them in the bathroom, hidden in the body of

Mary-Margaret's empty ballerina, safe from James and the kids. The rest, she carries in her purse. It's hard to think about cutting back, even though she knows she's been taking too many.

But she hasn't had insomnia like this since after her father died. Then sleep had brought nightmares of long tangled mazes. Men were coming for Daddy, and Ellen struggled to hide him in the pantry, in the root cellar, high up in the silver dome of the silo. Often he was so small he fit neatly into the palm of her hand; once she even hid him in her mouth, but the men always found him, always carried him away through a series of twisted paths which Ellen could not follow.

Now, each night she pokes her fingers into the ballerina's belly, and in the morning she wakes up in the position in which she fell asleep, sometimes with her hand numb beneath her pillow. She sleeps fiercely, dreading the buzz of the alarm, the flash of sunlight beneath the drapes. "Just five more minutes," she pleads with the children when they tap on the bedroom door. The aqua lady of her childhood would certainly not behave this way. The aqua lady would be up at dawn to make homemade muffins for her family. She'd wear sweet gingham aprons and aqua hose, high heels to show off her legs.

Mornings, Ellen pulls on the same shorts and T-shirt she wears each day, stares into the mirror at the plum-colored welts beneath her eyes, trying to find something in her face that is familiar.

"I can't believe you did that," James sputtered when she dropped the pool receipt into his lap, muttering *Happy Anniversary* under her breath. He and Fritz were playing cards, their faces the same in the half-light until James tipped his chin forward, embarrassed in front of his father. "You listen to me," he said firmly, grabbing her arm.

"Good night," Ellen said, twisting free, and she went down the hall to the bedroom without saying anything more. She was half undressed when James came in and shut the door behind him.

"What's *wrong* with you?" he said. "You just aren't yourself anymore." She unhooked her bra and he looked away uncomfortably. His gaze traced the fine cracks in the ceiling plaster, stroked the tops of the window frames. But she did not put on her nightgown. She did not cover her breasts with her hands. Goose bumps rose on her arms; she realized how thin she was, how much weight she had lost over the past few months, and she laughed a little because it was so ironic — she didn't even bother to diet anymore. Her body was angular, knobbed with bone. Her breasts sagged against her ribs.

"Are you laughing at me?" James said. "Why are you laughing at me? You're the one standing there naked. You're the one not making any sense." His voice was high, uncertain. When she didn't answer, he said, "Put some clothes on, you'll catch cold."

He still did not look at her.

"Do I embarrass you?" Ellen said, moving into his line of vision. "Does this embarrass you?" She touched her breasts, and his face grew sharp with disgust. She couldn't imagine ever loving him, wanting him, his damp, nervous body locked against her own. What she wanted now was to frighten him with her own flesh, with what he had rejected; to make him feel ashamed the way he made her feel ashamed.

James flinched. "You shouldn't talk that way," he said, "as if you're crazy."

"You're the one who's crazy. You're the one who won't even spend the money for our kids to learn how to swim."

"I just want what's best for everyone."

"You want what's best for you. How much money is enough, James? How much before it will make you safe?"

"You had no right to go behind my back."

"Let me tell you something: you will never

be safe. All the money in the world and you'll still be the same person you are now, still under your father's thumb."

"In my family, we learned how to save money," James said shrilly. "In my family, we didn't waste money on every little thing we wanted."

Ellen sat down on the bed. "Go away now," she said quietly, "because if you don't I'm going to break every last thing in this room. And when your father comes running to see what's wrong, I'll dance naked on what's left of the furniture."

She slipped the nightgown over her head so she wouldn't have to see the sickly look on James's face. By the time she pulled the nightgown down, he was gone. The door closed gently behind him. Covering her face with her hands, she tried to feel remorse, but she was distracted by the darkness of her palms and the way light filtered red between the edges of her fingers. She knew that to anyone watching she would appear stricken with grief. But Ellen didn't feel anything. After a while, she gave up trying. She spread her fingers, closed them, idly watching the dresser, the statue of the Virgin, the crucifix hanging on the wall as they appeared, disappeared, reappeared.

She drives the children downtown for their

first swimming lesson, partly to help them sign up for their lockers and keys, but mostly to make sure that Amy doesn't slip away and spend the hour in the library reading books from the Young Miss section, slim paperbacks with horses and dreamy-eyed girls on the covers. The poolhouse smells strongly of popcorn from the concession stand. Candy wrappers are scattered on the floor; the trash can by the rest rooms is overflowing. Older boys lean against the soda machines, wearing only their swimming trunks, their postures both arrogant and shy. They glance at Ellen, then look away, eyes narrow slits.

"What a dump," Amy says. Her towel and suit hang loosely around her shoulders. Bert's are rolled up neatly, tucked beneath one arm. He trots into the boys' locker room before Ellen can say good-bye; he's excited, he's meeting a friend from school who has told him swimming is fun.

"Do I have to do this?" Amy says.

"Yes."

"Can you at least give us a ride home?"

"I gave you a ride here. It's not far to walk."

Amy storms off toward the girls' locker room, her small square shoulders rigid. For a moment, Ellen wavers, almost calls her back. But she just can't play the mommy right now, patient and cheerful, ignoring her real self, which feels hollow, drained of everything except the desire for sleep, for quiet, peace. Lots of kids take swimming lessons — Amy will take them too. And Ellen has bought herself two sweet hours: James thinks she'll be watching the lesson from the bleachers with the other mothers; the children think she's gone home. She winces as Amy turns at the locker room door, fires one long last look of sheer hate.

"She doesn't hate you," Barb assured Ellen the week before, as they sat drinking coffee in the diner. That morning, Ellen had told James she had gone to early confession at Saint Michael's. *So confess,* Barb said, grinning. *I absolve thee.*

"I know she doesn't hate me," Ellen said. "But she doesn't *like* me either."

"If you left Holly's Field, it would be easier. Just you and Amy and Bert, minus the rest of the menagerie. There are openings at the public school in Schulesville. You could get by on what they pay, plus support."

Ellen had already called Schulesville for information on those jobs, but she did not tell Barb. Telling Barb would make leaving James seem like a real possibility.

"Ellie, you're better off than lots of women. At least you have some options."

"But if I did something like that," Ellen

said, "my family —" and she stopped, trying to think of a way to explain how they would look at her and see someone who had done a terrible, selfish thing, who had committed a mortal sin, who had lost her respect as a woman. "Maybe I should talk to one of my sisters," she said weakly. "Maybe it won't be so bad."

"It killed my mother when me and Rick split up," Barb said quietly. "It's never been the same between us. That's why I'm trying for the annulment, even though there's no chance of getting it." And they drank their coffee, not saying anything more. But the next day, Ellen visited Julia, because Julia was the youngest, the one most likely to keep an open mind. Julia was pregnant again, her belly so big that she had to turn sideways to open the door. She wore one of her husband's roomy old robes and a pair of tennis shoes; her two oldest sons danced around her waving Styrofoam airplanes, while the youngest shrieked from a playpen in the center of the living room. Over coffee, while the kids played jail between the table legs, Ellen grasped Julia's hand and held on to it tightly. "Please just listen, okay?" she said. "Don't tell Mom, but I'm thinking I might leave James for a while. Not a divorce or anything. Just, you know, a separation."

Julia's face drained of color, and she pulled her hand away. "Kids!" she snapped. "Upstairs to your room, pronto!" The boys scuttled out from under the table like silverfish. Ellen tried to reassure them with a look, but the ice in their mother's voice had frightened them. They filed up the stairs with their heads down, as if they expected to be punished.

"You can't do this," Julia said, as soon as they were gone. "It's wrong, you *know* it's wrong."

"Please listen."

"No."

"*Julia.*"

"You shouldn't even say something like that. You took sacred vows, you made a promise." She stood up angrily. "What are you going to tell me next? You're taking birth control pills? You're having an affair?"

Ellen got up too. "Look, forget it. Just don't tell Mom, okay?"

"Every couple goes through bad times. You should talk to Father Bork, find out what you can do to make things better. It's not like . . . James hasn't hit you, has he?"

Ellen shook her head. "It's not like that."

"Well, you shouldn't expect it to be easy." Julia sat back down again, ran her hands through her hair. "I forget how different things are for you, being younger. Young people want everything to be easy. But think about it — Christ didn't have an easy life."

Ellen said nothing.

"Maybe you should have another child."

"Oh, God," Ellen said. "You're not listening. Even divorce is better than having a child with somebody I don't love."

"But you love James," Julia insisted. "You love him, you just *do*. Have another baby, you'll see."

What Ellen saw was that Julia was going to tell their mother.

"Maybe you're right," she said, and quickly sat back down.

But of course, that was a lie. There will be no more babies, no more boiled rubber nipples, first words, first steps. She tries to recall what it felt like carrying Amy and Herbert inside her, but what she remembers most is the loneliness rather than the kicks or the backaches or the strange flush that lingered on her cheekbones. The more she wanted to talk about the changes in her body, the less James wanted to listen. "It'll all be over with soon," he told her, but she didn't want it to be over with. She wanted it to *last*, to be wonderfully significant. When he told her, "Don't worry, women have babies all the time," it made her feel like some kind of animal, a cow who calved every year in spring without anyone thinking anything about it.

She lets her hand fall to her stomach; it is flat now, and lifeless, unlike the plump, proud stomachs of the flocks of little girls in their swimming suits, digging through their small plastic purses at the concession stand. Over the past few months, she has lost muscle tone. Exercise, Barb tells her, is the key to feeling better, but sleep is what appeals to Ellen most, delicious sleep, dreamless sleep, the sort of sleep that nearly always eludes her, even when she takes an extra pill. She no longer goes for walks at night; Bert cries, James complains, Fritz and Mary-Margaret shake their heads at what they call *foolishness.* For a month or so, she visited Salome because Mary-Margaret certainly couldn't object to that. But Salome became strange, suspicious. *Why are you here?* she often said. *What do you want from me?* The last time Ellen visited, Salome would not let her in, and after that she couldn't think of where else she might go.

Perhaps it's best that she stays in at night. She hears stories about groups of teenage boys, about men who get drunk at the Sunburst by the waterfront and follow young women home. Just two weeks ago, a young girl hitchhiking south of town was raped. Who knows what might have happened to Ellen, had she been walking alone that night?

But right now it's broad daylight, almost noon, and she decides to take a walk down to the lake. She loops her purse strap over her shoulder and sets out at a brisk pace; after two blocks, though, she is dizzy, out of breath, and she looks for a place to sit down. The sun glares off her glasses, burns the tip of her nose. A group of boys flash past on skateboards, and their colorful T-shirts and sneakers look sinister. "Shit, lady, move it," one of them says. Across the street, the doors of the bank open toward her like welcoming arms, and she can feel how it will be inside even before she gets there, the coolness of the tiled floors, the sedate blue colors, the hushed adult voices.

She goes in and sits self-consciously in one of the chairs that line the wall, listening as the tellers talk softly with one another. The dizziness fades, leaving her forehead and temples slick with sweat. She looks in her purse for a tissue, and beneath it she finds the checkbook which she meant to return to James. The check she wrote was number 221, but there's no record of the check before it.

Well, she's at the bank, she might as well find out the amount of that check so she can figure the new balance. Won't he be surprised, smug James, when she returns the updated checkbook. She walks up to the tellers somewhat nervously. Banks, like churches, make her vaguely uncertain with the unspoken rules and private gestures she associates with solemn occasions.

"I'd like a balance on my account," she says, "and the amount of the last check to clear."

While the teller looks up the ledger, Ellen studies the paintings on the walls. Geometric shapes mostly: blue circles, yellow squares. Meaningless. Non-threatening. So different from working in a classroom decorated with anguished tempera paintings, twisted clay pots, clumsy poems labeled LOVE or HATE. Alone at her desk, Ellen studies these frail reconstructions of her students' lives — a lost pet, an angry parent, a distant older sibling. It's too easy to find pieces of her own portrait here in a mother's scold, a daughter's rigid stance. How wonderful it must be to handle money instead of people, to be responsible for balances and quotas rather than wishes and rages and dreams.

The teller scribbles on a slip of paper, passes it to Ellen, ten months' worth of savings. Six hundred dollars and seven cents.

Six hundred dollars?

"Excuse me," Ellen says. "There should be over six thousand dollars in this account."

"Let's see," the teller says. Ellen stares at

blue circles. Bright yellow squares. Breathes in the clean, cool air; traces a finger along the smooth countertop. "The balance is correct," the teller says. "Two weeks ago, *here*" — she points to the ledger — "a withdrawal was made for six thousand dollars. Check number two hundred twenty."

Ellen tucks the checkbook back into her purse and walks out of the bank into the bright sunshine. She feels dizzy, hollow, as though she's had the wind knocked out of her, and she sits down on the curb, watching the traffic straggle past. Their money, *her* money, gone. If she tells her mother, Mom will say, *It's not your place to worry about money* or *He probably had a good reason.* Her sisters will say, *Well, men know more about that kind of stuff anyway.* Father Bork will remind her that just as God is the head of the Church, the man is the head of the woman, and that Ellen should place her trust in James. *You are the hearth and the home,* he had said. *When the fire burns out in the hearth, the family dies.*

Ellen works her hand into her purse, grips the pill bottle tucked into the side pocket. It seems that something must be sacrificed soon: the head or the hearth, God or the soul, James or Ellen, and it is Ellen who does not fit, who is always unsatisfied, ungrateful, unhappy. *Dear God, please,* she begins, but she doesn't know what to ask for. She feels the way she did when she was a child waking up after one of her dreams, not knowing which of the twisted paths to take, the voices of the men fading in the distance.

Amy's swimming suit is an old one from last summer and it pinches her beneath the arms, rides up in the back to expose her hips. It is green with bright yellow flowers; a frill of material hangs from the waist. When she steps into the water, it floats up in a babyish way until Amy holds it down with her hands. She is older than all the other kids, and some of them are looking at her curiously. Herbert is talking with his friend from school; he pretends not to know Amy, and Amy pretends not to know him.

The teacher is a teenage boy. He says his name is John and they should just go ahead and call him that. All the kids look at one another — did he really think they would call him *mister?* But everyone watches when he executes a perfect backflip off the diving board. He pops back to the surface, plunges forward, porpoiselike, swims over to where they're waiting in the shallow end, and tells them that, if they work hard, they'll be able to do the same thing someday.

Right now, though, they have to put their

faces into the water and blow bubbles. Amy turns her back to John so he won't see she is keeping her face dry except for her chin. Herbert has his entire head beneath the water. When he comes up, John makes an example of him, asking can anyone else go all the way under too? Amy creeps behind John, staying carefully out of his line of vision. The other kids don't notice because they are underwater most of the time, practicing holding their breath. Some of the mothers in the bleachers notice, but they just point and laugh.

A girl jerks her head out of the water and coughs; Amy's stomach shrinks into a small, hard ball. The water smells bitter, and it sucks at her chest, pushes against her stomach and hips. She cannot imagine surrendering to it, arms beating like awkward wings, feet thrashing. Solid objects waver and dance; things in water are not the way they seem. Amy is careful to test the bottom of the pool with her toe before she steps all the way down. At any moment, the concrete could give way and send her plummeting to a pit filled with beasts. At any moment, the water might turn to a boiling bath of oil. In the basement Amy has found old books of her grandmother's about the lives of the saints, and on rainy days she re-reads her favorite parts: Saint Martina, who bled milk after the emperor stripped her naked and slashed her body with knives; Saint Fausta, who endured one thousand nails hammered into her skull; Saint Euphemia, whose limbs were ripped from her body, whose feet were severed the way Amy's feet look severed, distant, far off under the water.

"Okay!" John says. "I think you're ready to swim. What do you think about that?"

They all look at one another, dripping, uneasy.

"We'll start with the dead man's float," John says. "And our volunteer to go first will be the girl who still hasn't put her head in the water."

John looks at Amy. Amy looks at John. A few of the kids titter. The water tickles in Amy's armpits, swells against the hollow between her shoulder blades.

"Swimming doesn't interest me," Amy says with as much disdain as she can muster. She keeps her hands at her sides, holding the skirt of her swimming suit in place.

John smiles at the other kids and says, "How come do you think a big girl like her is afraid of water?"

"I'm not afraid of water. I'm just not *interested* in swimming."

He ignores her. "To do the dead man's float," he explains to the class, "you have to be perfectly relaxed. Take a deep breath and the water will hold you up, like this . . ." He glides into a float, his long thin body stretching. He stays that way until the kids start to whisper to each other. Maybe he is unconscious. Maybe he died right in front of them and they didn't even know it. They all jump when John finally pops up out of the water, slicking his hair back, grinning.

"Now you," he points to Amy. "What's your name?"

Amy doesn't answer.

"Amy Grier," one of the mothers calls.

"Amy is going to be my volunteer. She's going to relax and fall forward into the water, and I'm going to hold her up."

But Amy is weaving through the other kids toward the steps.

"Get back here," John says. "You and me have the whole summer to go yet."

The mothers in the bleachers are laughing, and so are the kids in the pool.

Amy stops. "What do I have to do to pass this class, so I don't have to come anymore?" she says. "I mean, what does everybody have to do at the end of it?"

"Dive," John says smugly.

Amy gets out of the pool. A few of the kids yell *fraidy cat* and *girl;* she feels as though she is watching herself from somewhere far away. All of this is her mother's fault, and if Amy dies that will be her mother's fault too. She walks to the deep end of the pool, climbs up the steps to the diving board. She imagines the funeral, her mother dressed in black, weeping over the coffin in which Amy lies, dead, astonishingly beautiful. Abruptly, Christ appears above her, his feet moving gingerly over the air, as all of Amy's relatives and friends and everyone she's ever known bow down in front of her body. Christ opens His shirt, exposing his Sacred Heart the way he did for Saint Margaret, only now, because of Amy, everyone can see it, everyone can see how much Christ grieves just for her. The mothers are calling to her, clattering down from the bleachers, but Amy pretends they are cries of anguish from the mourners.

"Hey! Stop!" John yells, climbing out of the water. The last thing Amy sees is his shadow gliding toward her along the concrete. She closes her eyes, fills her lungs with air, lifts her arms, and pitches forward.

The shock of it, the coldness, and the hollow, watery sound stiffen her body and she glides until her clenched fists scrape the bottom. She opens her eyes and sees the liquid yellow surface above. What if her mother doesn't come to her funeral? What if nobody cares that she is dead? Men will fish her body out of the pool with a hook. What should we do with her? they say, and when no one claims her, they bury her by the edge of the pool, in unconsecrated soil, where her mother will never come to visit and Christ will never find her. The sudden bullet shape of John hurtles through the water; Amy thrashes her legs and, miraculously, she lifts away from him. She moves her arms, keeping rhythm, until she feels cool air against the top of her head, and then she lifts her chin to breathe, scraping her forehead against the pool wall.

"What a stupid thing to do," John shouts from the middle of the pool. "Get back to the shallows and stay there."

She struggles up out of the pool, her legs and arms shaking wildly. She is not dead. She is not dead. A group of mothers comes down from the bleachers saying, *Sh, Sweetheart, you're okay.* One of them tries to wrap her in a sweet-smelling towel, but Amy walks away, kicking her legs out proudly until she reaches the locker room. The mother follows, sitting down beside her on the low wooden bench in front of the lockers and this time when she slips the towel over Amy's shoulders, Amy holds it against herself. "Did you see me swim?" she asks the mother, closing her eyes so it can be Ellen who is stroking her wet hair and calling her *sweetheart, baby, love.*

★ ★ ★

Ellen finds James asleep on the patio, stretched out in a lawn chair, a dish towel draped over his head so the top, where the hair is thin, won't burn. Next door, the Muellers are watering their lawn. Mr. Mueller wields the nozzle, calling directions to Mrs. Mueller, who trots behind him lugging coils of hose. The hose moves between them like a living thing until Mrs. Mueller drops it and stands, arms akimbo. Mr. Mueller whirls, brandishing the nozzle angrily, and then he sees Ellen watching. With his chin, he indicates the house to Mrs. Mueller. She goes inside, and he follows her, flinging the nozzle to the ground.

Now that the weather is warm, their fights trickle through the open windows, more a fragrance than a sound at first, subtle, then slowly building. It's the night fights that disturb Ellen the most. The voices remind her of a strange, atonal opera, the sort of thing she sometimes hears on public radio. She takes a sleeping pill and lies down in the middle of the empty bed, imagining James in some far-off motel room, and wonders if he's thinking of her even as she knows he's not. He will be sleeping soundly, the television buzzing at the foot of the bed, his knees curled to his chest so that his body takes up as little space as possible. Ellen spreads her legs, spreads her arms, invading the space that would belong to James if he were here. She tries to breathe deeply, tries to relax, until the angry music of the argument fades.

One morning in spring, Mrs. Mueller came to the door clutching a paper bag beneath her arm.

"Keep this for me, will you please?" she said to Ellen. She spoke as if she were afraid that somebody else might hear. "I'm leaving him, and these were my mother's things, her jewelry and some old pictures. I can't have them with me until I know where I'm going. I don't want to carry anything of value."

"Of course I'll keep them for you," Ellen said. "Let me know when you get settled and I'll send them on."

But Mrs. Mueller was gone only three days. She came by to retrieve her things early in the summer, and though she waves at Ellen from her yard, they have not spoken since. When Ellen told James about it, he simply shrugged. "She learned what it's like out in the real world," he said. "Makes things look pretty good where she's at."

His face was smug, certain, *right;* the expression he's wearing now. Ellen sits down on the patio floor, feeling the rough concrete bite the bare backs of her thighs. She says,

"James," but he doesn't move. She can tell he is awake. His eyes skitter beneath his lids, and his Adam's apple bobs once. In the harsh sunlight, she can see every pore of his skin.

"James, where is our money?"

He sits up abruptly. "What?"

"I went to the bank. We have almost nothing —"

"What were you doing at the bank?"

"It's my bank."

"Where are the kids?"

"Swimming. What did you do with it?"

"Well," he says, "I've been meaning to tell you. I invested it."

"Uninvest it."

"I can't. Not for eighteen months. But the interest —"

"You mean we're going to live here for another year and a half?"

James clears his throat. "We'll talk about this some more when you calm down." He closes his eyes.

The ground spins away from Ellen and she remembers her father's death, because the feeling then was oddly the same. He'd fallen from a wagon and landed wrong; still he walked back to the house unassisted and nobody thought it was serious. Ellen had crawled up beside him on the bed, and she remembers playing with his fingers as she drifted off to sleep. She woke up, confused, in Miriam and Ketty's bed, and ran downstairs just in time to see the coroner and another man she did not know lift her father's body onto a hard, flat stretcher. Daddy looked the same, but, in fact, he was different. He had changed as soon as she'd closed her eyes. She clung to her mother during the funeral, howling with what everyone thought was grief, but what she knows now was rage.

And now that same fury floods her body, fresh and sharp, only there is no one to run to, no place to hide. She stands up, breathing hard, trying not to look at the soft, pale stretch of James's throat as he lies in the warm sunshine waiting for her to give up and go away. Cool-headed James, patient James, serene beneath his flickering eyelids. Whatever the storm, he will wait it out; he knows he is right as simply as he knows that Ellen is wrong.

Ungrateful. All he does for you.
The hearth and the home.
Sacrifice.

Ellen's anger is like a fire, spreading in gusts, licking at larger and larger things. She walks over to the Muellers' and picks up the hose. It is long, cold, serpentine. She drags it until she stands only several feet away from James, pulls the trigger on the nozzle. James shrieks, topples out of his chair as the water slaps his face, knocks the towel from his head. He writhes beneath the stream, which she aims against his chest and tender belly, the notch between his legs. She is silent, deliberate, her mind closed to everything but the water and just beyond it where a faint rainbow wavers delicately above the grass.

James whips in through the back door, slams it. Ellen hears him shoot the lock, hollering from inside the house . . . Crazy! . . . Childish! . . . She aims the water at the door, at the windows, moving the stream over the brick walls, and it comes to her what she is doing, what she has been doing. She is writing her name in wet block letters six feet tall.

14

What James sees isn't land or water or sky, just the long, gentle tongue of the road swallowing him into the horizon. Sometimes, on the rural highways, he stops to urinate behind a clump of trees, inhaling the familiar, tangy odor of his piss with satisfaction as it darkens the bark. Walking back to the car, the sun hot against the sunburnt part in his hair, he lifts his arms to catch the breeze and remembers other warm Julys when he was working in the fields with his father and Mitch, not riding in shirtsleeves in a company car with the windows rolled all the way down. Back then, they wore coveralls and hats and long-sleeved shirts. *The more you sweat, the cooler you feel.* Once he fainted and came to upside down, carried over Mitch's shoulder, his face bouncing hard against the seat of Mitch's pants. When he kicked, Mitch's steely fingers tightened on his thighs, and James vomited helplessly onto his heels, leaving a wet trail through the pale new leaves of the corn.

In the car again, slipping easily onto the road, he remembers his first job, when he was ten, working for his father, walking milk to the row of summer cottages along the lake two miles away. The cottages were made of good fieldstone, the porches decorated with flowers planted in wooden barrels or hanging from the gutters in clay pots. James smelled white flour biscuits, smoked ham, apple pie, and his stomach felt small and hard inside him. "Milk today, ma'am?" he said shyly at each door; the children of the rich summer people put out their tongues while their mothers pressed the cool coins, one by one, into the palm of his hand.

Look out none of them Chicago ladies grab you, Fritz teased, poking at the fly of James's coveralls. *I hear them city gals are wildcats for a skinny little bastard like you.*

But James admired the women at the cottages. They spoke of the weather in low, soft voices as he ladled milk into the sleek mouths of the pitchers they placed beside him on the porch. When their children pinched their noses at the manure on James's boots, the women shooed them inside and apologized sweetly. At home, Mary-Margaret pressed him for details: What did the women say? What did they wear? Once, she put on her

Sunday dress and walked along with him, carrying her shoes in her hand so they wouldn't be dirty when they reached the first neat cottage. But though she peered eagerly past the screens into the high-ceilinged kitchens, none of the summer women suggested she come inside, and when they got home Fritz pinched the soft insides of her arms, bending her backward across the kitchen table into the leftover breakfast dishes, into the pork skillet shining with lard. *Putting on airs,* he'd spat. *What we got here's good enough for the likes of a she-devil like you.*

James still has the dollar Fritz gave him at the end of the summer. He keeps it in a jewelry box with two pairs of cuff links, a broken watch, and his birth certificate. Every now and then, he shows it to Amy and Herbert, wanting them to understand that the value of a dollar goes beyond what it can buy. The true value of a dollar lies in its *potential.* He calls them out of their bedroom, or up from the basement where they play behind the sump pump, and makes them sit, side by side, on the couch. Their pointed chins are like Ellen's pointed chin. Their spindly legs churn the air. They giggle and nudge their sharp elbows against each other; he is careful not to look into their faces, afraid of what he might find there.

"Even at your age, I knew the value of savings," he says, pacing the length of the living room, and then he tells them the story of Rockefeller picking up the pennies his son would have left on the floor. Five pennies make a nickel, ten pennies a dime; one hundred pennies make a dollar just like the one James has saved so carefully. There were many times when he could have spent it. There were many times when he almost gave in and told Mitch where it was hidden away. But each night, he lay awake thinking about that dollar and how it was just a beginning, how the following year he'd have another dollar, and the year after that, another.

"It's dollars that pay for college educations," he explains to the children. "It's dollars that pad you a nest egg for retirement, or pay up doctors' bills if something goes wrong."

But the children stare at him with blank ghost eyes. They are not interested in the value of a dollar. They are not interested in the safety that a dollar can buy, even though James believes this safety is the secret of the rich, the key to the smooth serenity he remembers in the faces of the summer women. The rich can buy whatever they need. The rich are never afraid the way James is afraid. "Listen to me," he says, "you're not listening," and he tells the children as much as he can remember about the summer people, their calm politeness, the clean, slender fingers of the women who shook his hand.

He is two hundred miles from home before he lets himself think about Ellen, who, like the children, does not understand about money the way Rockefeller did, the way James does now. He convinces himself that she is not really angry, that by the time he comes back home things will have worked themselves out. Surely she must know he only wants a better life for the children, the way his own father wanted better for himself and Mitch. But just wanting something isn't enough. Wanting something won't make it happen when there are so many other, terrible things that are waiting to happen too. The fever. The stranger with a fistful of candy. The mad dog, the loose bull. The overturned truck blossoming into flames.

The day after they moved back to Wisconsin, James took Ellen and the children to Saint Michael's Cemetery to visit Mitch's grave. From across the street, the tall steeple of Saint Michael's Church brushed a long-fingered shadow over the gravestones, stroking the plastic roses and daffodils, disappearing like a slender ghost behind the trees. Ellen took James's hand and they followed the shadow until they reached the Grier plot, a sunken square between two dying oaks. James used his foot to clear Mitch's granite slab of leaves and debris while the children played leapfrog over stones farther up the path. He remembered the funeral, the winter wind pinching his ears, the sour feeling in his belly that was not loss. *God took my good one instead of the weak,* Fritz told people bitterly. *Even God won't have Jimmy or his mother.*

"Look, Mommy!" Amy shrieked; she scuttled up the back of a towering angel and leaped from between its wings, Bert tumbling after her. James saw them lying cold and still, their quick lips sealed with wax. He saw their flesh unwrap from their bones and small, blind creatures make nests in the hollows of their skulls.

"This is a graveyard!" he yelled at them suddenly. "Show some respect for the dead."

They froze, their faces closed as doors. Ellen let go of his hand and stared high up into the branches of the oaks, which he knew were bright with autumn colors he would never see. He wondered about what color meant, if not being able to pronounce a thing *red* or *purple* or *blue* was significant enough to account for the differences between Ellen and himself. He understands her less and less; like color, she cannot be explained. She won't go with him to the cemetery anymore; she won't let him take the children. Sundays after Mass he walks over by himself while she chats with her sisters and her sisters' families. He cleans the face of the granite slab with his handkerchief, pulls dandelions and chicory from around the stone's edge. Mitch doesn't have a company car, white cotton shirtsleeves, money in the bank. Mitch has a shallow box, a hole in the earth, a dirt sky. Sometimes James still hears him in the ragged laughter of drinking men. He sees him in the bold, loose stride of teenage boys. Mitch the handsome one. Mind like a steel trap.

The one God chose to call home.

It is late afternoon when James reaches the Traveler's Rest, a motel south of De Kalb. He steps into the air-conditioned lobby, pauses to sip from the water cooler beside the door. As he waits for the receptionist to give him his key, he pockets two packs of complimentary matches, eats stale mints from the hospitality bowl, takes a coupon for ten percent off at the Ponderosa next door. It is money, he knows, which allows him to do this, along with his white cotton shirtsleeves, his briefcase, his ID card from Travis Manufacturer. The smile of the receptionist is bought by money too; he thinks of the sneers of the summer people's children, the skirting glances of the town girls whenever he spoke in school, the nuns' distasteful stares when he and Mitch opened their lunch tin and took out a bent spoon, four biscuits wrapped in a handkerchief, and a snuff tin of molasses. Tonight he will eat prime rib and charge it to the company account. When he leaves town in the morning, there will be no one to watch him go, no one to say, *That little Jimmy Grier, I remember his old man, I remember his brother.*

James worked the dollar up into the lining of his Sunday coat where Mitch wouldn't be able to find it. Every day, all through the fall, Mitch hunted for it patiently, methodically. He upended James's dresser drawers, leaving a scattered rainbow of clothing across the bedroom floor. He dug his hard hands deep into James's pockets whenever he caught him alone. He searched James's schoolbag, the root cellar, the rafters of the smokehouse. Once, he even walked out to the two small graves on the hillside, and dug with a penknife around the flat granite stones until Mary-Margaret chased him away.

Where is it? he whispered across the breakfast table, between the sharp blows of the ax as James chopped wood, in the darkness of the bedroom as James knelt to say his prayers. Over the summer, Mitch's body had started to change into the body of a man. Hair sprouted on his knuckles and chest, on his belly, beneath his chin. His privates swelled against the cool morning air as he stripped off his pajamas.

Where is it? Where?

It was Ann who walked into the milkhouse one bright September day and found Mitch pressing James's face into a bucket of milk. James's forehead was plastered with heavy cream; he breathed thickly through his mouth, coughing white bubbles that clung to his lips. Milk leaked from his nostrils and dribbled from the corners of his eyes. When Ann cleared her throat, Mitch took his hand from the back of James's neck. Barn cats scuttled in around Ann's skirts and lapped at the concrete floor.

"He's been playing in the milk," Mitch said. He towered over Ann, his wide shoulders swaying. "I told him Pa'd wear him out."

"He'll wear you both out if you don't get this mess cleaned away."

"It's Jimmy's mess. He'll clean it up." Mitch smiled and walked toward Ann, big boots clomping; after a moment she stepped aside to let him through. When he was gone, she went to James and gently slicked the hair out of his eyes. Milk was caked behind his ears, around the edges of his nose.

"Why do you let him find you alone?" she

said, and then she shook her head. "You get this cleaned up quick, maybe your pa won't even find out. And get these kitties out of here," she said. "I got to get supper started 'fore they miss me."

After she left, he lay down in the puddles of milk, his body knotted close on the concrete floor. His head hurt from holding his breath. The barn cats moved around him, pink tongues working, a flicker against the back of his neck, a warm rough rasp on his ear. He lay motionless as they cleaned him, trying not to weep at how good it felt to have their mouths moving over him as though he were one of their many babies, their cool noses kissing his skin.

That night, when Fritz's belt cut through the air like a scream, James's mind dwindled smaller and smaller until it was only a speck of dust that could easily drift away, past the house, past the backhouse, past the barn, over the fields until it reached the woods, and the lake beyond the woods, and sank into the silence of the water. Afterward, Ann came into the room. She sat on the bed and sang to him in a soft sweet voice, until he came up out of the silent water and through the woods and across the fields, until he lay on the sheets with his wrists tied to the bedposts. She untied him and pressed a white cotton towel to his back, blotting the design of the belt, and then for a long time she was silent. *This can't go on,* she said at last, and she wept, clutching a pillow over her face so she would not make a sound. The next day she died and they laid her out on the kitchen table to prepare her body to be put into the ground.

One hot day the following year, James crawled up onto the table and stretched out to see what it was like to be dead. He closed his eyes and waited. By the time Mary-Margaret found him there, he was deep underwater and refused to open his eyes. She screamed and beat on his chest with her fists and poured whiskey under his tongue. Opening his eyes was the hardest thing he has ever done.

For the next week he visits distributors, hawking a new line of pea harvesters, his Travis Manufacturer cap clutching at his head like a mother's firm hand. He drinks bitter coffee in tiny offices gray with cigar smoke; he walks the lots with the managers, noting comments about the performance of various machines. The managers sense the farm in him easily. They pump his hand and call him *young man* and ask him about his family. At each stop, James tugs his wallet from his hip pocket, and he shows them a picture of Ellen, who, he proudly explains, is a schoolteacher.

He shows them a picture of Amy at six, with Bert toddling beside her, holding onto her thumb. The managers show James their own pictures: *my Maisie, my Scottie, my first grandchild, Michael.*

Later, alone in his motel room, James studies Ellen's picture. She looks no different from the other men's wives; she is smiling, she is happy. He remembers Ellen as a little girl, three grades younger than himself, rolling up the worn sleeves of a dress he recognized as her sister Julia's. He can't remember ever speaking to her, though, and after he left school in the ninth grade, he never thought of her at all. It was Julia who lingered in his mind, the way her small mouth opened wide when she laughed, the way she never seemed to notice Mitch's gaze following the back of her skirt down the narrow halls. Ellen laughed with her mouth closed to hide her crooked teeth; now she doesn't laugh at all. Her eyes are red-rimmed, heavy-lidded; she frequently yawns behind the back of her hand. When he talks to her he feels she isn't really listening.

His last stop this trip is at a family farm called Riverland. The owner has big money to spend; the distributor, a man named Monty Fried, arranged for James to meet him at the place. It helps to have a Travis rep come right to the house: makes the distributor look good, impresses the farmer. Often, after they finish talking business in the kitchen, the wife will ask them to dinner, and they'll all sit down to ham and potatoes, fresh coleslaw, creamed corn, and rhubarb pie.

James is looking forward to this visit. He has worked with Monty before; Monty likes his whiskey, and an evening can get interesting. He parks in the courtyard behind Monty's truck and gets his briefcase from the backseat. His father's farm was laid out much the same as this one: the wide gravel courtyard with the house to the right and the barn to the left behind the low stone wall; the clothesline strung between the house and the corner of the chicken coop; the high clover fields behind the house; the cow pasture in the low land around the barn; the pea fields stretching beyond it. He turns to admire the placid herd of Holsteins, the broad slope of their backs, their slender swinging tails. Two big dogs sniff at his heels; he pats their handsome heads and inhales the almost-sweet odor of the clover. Chickens bathe along the rutted driveway, fluttering dust into their feathers. In the distance he can see sheep, their coats shorn short and clean. The cows begin migrating, two or three at a time, to stand before him, curious and calm, stretching their chins above the low barbed-wire fence and lowing.

He remembers his father's cows, their ragged teats pink and oozing, Fritz's foot in their bellies when they kicked at his rough hand. He remembers the sheep, savagely sheared, their staccato bleating. How one spring the smell of the blood drew dogs, and in the morning the sheep parts were scattered across the field, the dead smell rising from the ground. How he and Mitch hauled the sheep legs and sheep bellies and sheep heads, torn off at the throats, to be burned. How he found a half-formed unborn sheep in the grass, the birth bag still intact, the frail beating heart the size of a child's thumb. He remembers the kittens congealed into a cold wet lump at the bottom of a tin bucket. He remembers the dogs, one after the next, that got too old, too lazy, too stupid, too slow. He remembers the gunshots, two, three, four, the frantic pedaling limbs, the fixing eyes. *Always was a goddamn lousy shot*, Fritz said. *Can't hit the broad side of a barn. You try it, boy.*

But James refused.

And when he refused, there was always Mitch, who could do whatever it was James could not. Because Mitch was his father's son, while James was his mother's boy, sickly and frail, no use to anyone. *How come God took the strong one is what I want to know,* Fritz shouted into the winter wind, but even Fritz did not guess Mitch's strength. Only James knew that Mitch wasn't gone. Only James knew that Mitch would never leave him. *Look how your legs are like mine,* Mitch said as he stripped back the covers, one hand holding the candle, tracing James's body with the light of the flame. *Look how your hands are my hands.*

He jumps at the clap of Monty's hand on his shoulder. The dogs bark, sensing his fear, muzzles slung low to the ground.

"Jesus." Monty laughs, waving the dogs away. "Jimmy, you look like you've seen a ghost. This here is Mr. Wally Donovan."

"Fine place you got here," James says quickly, and he shakes hands with the owner, nods as the owner introduces his oldest son, Josh, his second-oldest, Bobby. But he feels Mitch's hand in the owner's firm grip. He sees Mitch's smile in the owner's strong teeth. Tonight it will be Mitch who drinks Monty's whiskey. It will be Mitch who heaps his plate with bread and country ham. Mitch will smile at Wally Donovan's wife, the way James remembers him smiling at Julia, red-lipped, white teeth flashing.

James wakes up in a room that smells of

mildew. His suitcase is unopened at the foot of the bed; a TV stands in the corner, bolted to the floor. Someone is tapping on the door, rattling the knob. James opens his mouth to speak, smells whiskey.

He does not remember where he is.

"Just a minute," he says.

"Check-out time is ten and I'm not waiting around for you."

"I'm sorry," James says. "I overslept."

"Fifteen minutes I'll be back," the woman says, "and you better be dressed and decent. I know all the tricks. Don't you dare try anything."

He hears the creak of the cleaning cart, and then he remembers pulling into the parking lot, paying the night clerk, falling into bed without undressing. He is in Illinois, at the Sweet Dreams Motel and Bar, three miles down the road from Riverland, still five hours from home. He gets up, splashes water on his face, and carries his unopened suitcase to the car. On his way through the lobby he takes a complimentary cup of coffee and two complimentary Danish.

Thunderheads bruise the horizon. James gets on the interstate, balancing the coffee between his knees. He twists the radio on for a forecast: tornado warnings across Illinois, Wisconsin, Indiana. He accelerates to sixty, to seventy-five, as gusts of wind rock the car. Hot air laps at his face and neck, and the back of his shirt clings to the seat. He watches the west, letting his gaze sweep across the flat gray landscape, lingering on the occasional crisp white outlines of a farmhouse, the hulking shadow of a barn. The crops — field corn, peas, wheat — bend to the east, as if turning their faces away. He passes a windbreak of hickory trees and hears the snap of the branches. He is remembering gathering those hard sweet nuts as a boy, when the light is sucked away.

Too late, he begins to roll up his windows. The radio voices are shattered by static; the drum of the hail against the roof fills his ears, and he cannot hear if there is anything behind it — the train roar of a twister, or more likely, three. When he was eleven or twelve, Fritz took him out onto the porch during twister weather. James had been sitting with his mother on a burlap sack of potatoes in the cellar, listening to her chant the Rosary in a hushed, dry voice. Twisters always frightened her; she believed they came from God. Suddenly, the cellar doors flew open, but it wasn't God, just Fritz coming down the stairs in a gust of rain.

"You come on up with your brother and me," he said, and Mary-Margaret released

James's hand. After Ann's death, she never argued with Fritz over anything.

"Mother," he said, but when she did not answer, Fritz pulled him up the stairs and across the barnyard to the house. Rain came in spurts, warm as bathwater, and it seemed to James as if there were tiny figures darting through the air: devils, ghosts, angels. He clung to the porch railings as one figure grew closer, larger, running up from the barn, and then he saw it was Mitch with his hair sleek against his head, his wet shirt billowing.

"There!" Mitch shouted, and he pointed at the two ribbons that descended from the clouds, skipping nimbly over the Hansens' field three miles away. James forgot to be afraid. The power of the twisters amazed him; they were truly afraid of nothing. They went where they wanted, did what they wanted, and people were helpless to stop them. James felt that if he could get close enough, he could learn what made those twisters what they were. Perhaps he could become like that, too. He let go of the porch railing and began to walk toward them until a hand grabbed him by the shoulder, held him tight.

"Ain't they something," Fritz said into his ear.

James nodded, unable to speak. For the first time in his life he felt close to his father, and it was Mitch, whooping and shrieking as lightning split the sky, who did not understand.

Afterward, when Mary-Margaret emerged from the cellar and picked her way across the muddy courtyard, wrinkled and squinting as a mole, James felt proud that he was a man like his father, like his brother, unlike his mother, who had huddled helplessly in the ground. From then on he looked at her differently, and when she put her soft hand on his arm, he quickly pulled it away. "I'm too big for that, Mother," he said, and when she tried to kiss him: "I'm too big for all of that."

Now he wishes he were underground, where he hopes Ellen has taken his parents and the children. He hopes she has remembered to leave the east windows open three inches. He hopes she has remembered to unplug the TV. He hopes she won't let Fritz bring the children upstairs to spot the funnel. He sees their small bodies lifted easily as twigs, spun high into the air, dashed to the ground like loose bales of hay. The thought of this seizes hard in his chest; he pounds the steering wheel, his rage as sudden as the hail, and lukewarm coffee pours down his legs. It's not right of Ellen to say he doesn't love his children. It's not right of her to say he is distant, to call him a stranger, to say he doesn't care. He is driving home as fast as he can, he will not stop until he gets there and sees that everyone is fine. He loves his daughter, he loves his son. Ellen just does not understand.

Grace

15

Amy stands in the driveway watching the cherry lights of the ambulance reflecting off her bare arms. How she wishes her skin could stay this color, flushed warm and pink, like the skin of a girl in a magazine. Two stout men lift the stretcher and slip it between the open double doors; Amy strains for a glimpse of her grandmother's face but it is covered by a plastic mask. Mary-Margaret's blue curls are frizzed around her head, and they are the last thing Amy sees before the men climb in and pull the heavy doors to themselves. Briefly, Amy wants to cry, but she does not; she is a magazine girl with magazine skin, cool and detached, slumped against the garage door in her pink tube top and pink short shorts as the ambulance warbles once, twice, glides out of the driveway.

All the way up and down Vinegar Hill, people are standing on their porches in the feeble afternoon sunshine, carrying babies to the edges of their driveways, peering out of their windows. A morning of tornado warnings kept them in their cellars, and now they move stiffly, hands cupped to shade their eyes. *Who is it?* someone calls to Ellen as she gets into Fritz and Mary-Margaret's car to follow the ambulance. *Who is it?* they call to Amy, their eyes inquisitive and bright. Chipmunk eyes. Their noses work, sniffing the air for secrets. James isn't due home until later this afternoon, but they will keep watch for him, eager to be the first to tell what they know, what they suspect.

Is it the grandmother? Is it the grandfather? Is it the little boy?

Without the red pulse of the ambulance, Amy's skin is ugly and gray. She tosses her hair like a magazine girl, but she feels stupid now, too many people watching, and that hurting feeling at the back of her throat as if — but she won't — she might cry. She is glad Bert is away, staying with Auntie Miriam and Uncle Darby for the weekend, helping Uncle Darby fence a new pasture. Bert would throw back his head and howl if he were here. Bert would allow the neighbor women to wrap him in their arms, push crumpled tissues against his nose, usher him back to their houses for lemonade and cake.

Is it the grandmother? Is it the grandfather? Is it the little boy?

But Amy will not be bought. When she sees Mrs. Mueller, long-legged as a doe, step over the ditch separating the yards, Amy ducks inside and closes the door behind her. She pulls the drapes and sits down on the couch, listening to the clear chime of the doorbell, the scuffle of footsteps on the braided twine mat where she and Herbert have to wipe their feet. She touches her newly pierced ears, fingering each pale green stone like it's a charm. The lobes are still tender; Kimmy did them with a blackened needle as Amy sat on the toilet seat in the Geibs' tiny bathroom, trying not to jump.

"What some people need is a good dose of buckshot," Fritz says, coming down the hall from the bedroom, and Amy does not breathe, imagining Mrs. Mueller galloping across the front lawn, wide-eyed, skirt flapping like a tail as Fritz squints down the barrel of the shotgun he keeps on a rack in the hall closet. But Fritz just sits on the couch beside Amy, and soon the doorbell stops ringing. By now Mrs. Mueller must be on her way back to her yard, speaking with the other neighbors, who are also eager for answers. By now the ambulance must be at Saint John's Hospital in Cedarton, the stretcher unloaded, Ellen trotting behind it, disappearing into a room marked QUIET or KEEP OUT or ADULTS ONLY, a room where Amy would not be allowed to go.

She is eleven now, old enough to shave her legs, to wear musk-scented deodorant, to step into the closet each morning and, hidden from her brother's curious eyes, slip her arms through the straps of a crisp cotton bra, elbows jangling the hangers. She is old enough to carry a purse, to smear Plum Passion or Very Cherry lip gloss on her lips and not lick it off. She is old enough to read friends' copies of *Seventeen* and *Mademoiselle*, magazines her mother throws into the trash if Amy forgets to hide them. And she is old enough to know all about boys. But still, her mother has left her behind. *Stay near the house and be good,* she said. Amy rubs her smooth smooth legs and imagines herself in a hospital waiting room, inhaling the mentholated smoke from a cigarette, ankles coolly crossed. Her hair is thick and wavy; her full breasts rest on the shelf of her arms. She wears a low-cut black satin dress. The nurses look in on her now and then, whispering to one another.

It's her grandmother, you know. They were very close. Look how strong she is. Look how well she's taking it.

"Well now, missy," Fritz says musingly. His thick glasses have slid down on his nose; sweat shines on his forehead and cheeks, and he gives off a sour cheese smell. Amy stares at his hands, which are folded on his knee like spiders embracing, or fighting to the death. Each hand squeezes the other in turn, ugly hands notched with warts and scars, the pinky finger missing from the right hand. A magazine girl wouldn't have a grandfather with hands like these. A magazine girl wouldn't be left alone with such hands, wondering what they will do. Lately she feels Fritz looking at her as if she is someone else, someone he doesn't quite recognize —

Yet.

"Maybe we should pray," Amy says, because that's what Mary-Margaret would suggest at a time like this. *Lord, help me to accept what I cannot change* is Mary-Margaret's favorite prayer; it is written on the prayer card that's taped to the bathroom mirror with crumbling yellow tape, and Amy sometimes picks at it with her fingernail while she's brushing her teeth. All week long, as twisters hopscotched across the state, Mary-Margaret said that prayer as she watched the sky, and *Oh Jimmy*, she sometimes said. Amy pictures her grandmother lying alone in a cold, white room, and wonders if she is praying now, or if she is already dead. Perhaps her ghost has freed itself and is rustling through the air like a leaf. Perhaps it will return to familiar places:

the rocking chair in the kitchen, the parlor chair embroidered with roses that stands just several feet from the couch where Amy is sitting now. The back of her neck feels strange, and she wishes her mother would come home. Outside on the street, a child laughs shrilly, and Amy jumps, thinking it's her grandmother's voice she has heard.

"Pray for what?" Fritz says.

This morning in the basement, waiting for the siren at the top of the water tower to sound the all clear, Mary-Margaret had been oddly silent. The house rattled with wind, the floorboards creaking overhead as if a strange, gigantic creature were pacing in the kitchen, waiting to devour them as soon as they came upstairs. Amy and Ellen played cards while Mary-Margaret watched and Fritz slept, his snores like a dog's warning growls.

"You go on and pray if you want to," Fritz says and his voice is a sneer. "Me, when something goes wrong, I don't wait on Jesus to fix it."

"Me neither," Amy says. She had noticed Mary-Margaret first, but she hadn't said anything. Mary-Margaret's lips and fingernails had turned the same dark purply blue as the sky; her eyes crossed so deeply that she seemed to be staring into her own self as she slid down in her chair. *War!* Amy shouted, slapping her cards on the table, and Mary-Margaret clattered to the floor, her rosary beads tangled in her fingers.

"I learned to do for myself," Fritz says. "Nobody ever did nothing for me. From the time I can first remember, I worked to earn my keep. But you're growing up soft, gal, soft as your grandma." He pokes his blunt finger into Amy's side, hard, harder, hurting her; when she gasps, he cuffs her cheek, almost affectionately. Amy tries not to inhale his sour cheese smell. She tries not to see Mary-Margaret thrashing her heels against the basement floor. The way Amy herself did nothing, shuffling the cards again and again while her mother ran upstairs to call the ambulance. The way she and Fritz looked at Mary-Margaret, and Mary-Margaret looked back at them, and no one said a word. She is frightened, she is shaking. She wants to be with her mother, tucked against her mother's side like a bird. She wants to be a magazine girl in a black satin dress who is not afraid of anything. Fritz's front teeth gleam yellow as the teeth of old horses: long teeth, mean. Amy starts to get up but it's as if her legs are concrete; she cannot move, cannot twist away. He touches her newly pierced earlobes, twisting the small green stones until tears form in her eyes. "What's all this foolishness?" he says, and he sweeps his hand down the almost-flatness of her chest. "Putting on airs! Just like your grandma. Pretty soon the young bucks will come sniffing around, and next thing we know you'll have a belly out to here."

He stands up and stuffs one of the square satin couch pillows up under his shirt. "There," he says, "now I'm a mama. Just like you're going to be one someday. Right? Ain't that so?"

Amy doesn't answer. Her earlobes burn. She wants to touch them, to see if they're bleeding, the way she checks between her legs whenever she feels wetness, but it never is blood down there, just sweat or a little pee, she isn't sure. Maybe blood is running down her neck and she doesn't know it, like the woman she and Kimmy saw downtown with the dirt-red stain on her white shorts. Maybe Fritz can see the blood and he is secretly laughing at Amy the way Amy and Kimmy secretly laughed at the woman. Fritz paces back and forth in front of her, one hand holding the pillow in place, lifting his feet high so they fall to the floor with each step, *boom, boom.* She sees that he wants her to laugh, so she tries. He rips the pillow from his shirt, hurls it at the lamp, topples it along with a potted philodendron. Its long trailing vines thrash the air as it falls, arms searching for a grip.

"That's what'll happen to you someday when a man puts a baby inside you."

He kicks her grandmother's embroidered chair; it slides into the wall, unresisting. Her grandmother's chair looks empty, braced against the wall, but her ghost might be sitting there, watching. Her ghost might pick up the fallen lamp and bring it down on Fritz's head, or slip into the telephone wires and cause the phone to ring. It will be the police on the line, telling Fritz he is under arrest. He will be put in the electric chair and Amy will pull the switch. None of this can be happening, but if it is, something else will happen to stop it. Amy is not helpless. Amy is not alone.

"Your grandma had four of my babies," Fritz says. "The last two was twins, and I went out to celebrate it. By the time I come home, there's no sign of them. *What babies?* your grandma says to me. She and her mama."

When he looks down at Amy, she knows he isn't seeing her, but somebody else, a woman resting her breasts on the shelf of her arms, a woman wearing a black satin dress, a woman whose body swells like bread because of what she and men do together. She scuttles backward, her spine pressed into the wall of the couch, feeling the soreness of her ribs where he poked her. She isn't a magazine girl. She isn't who he thinks he recognizes.

"Folks said that night I got so drunk I thought I had twice the sons I did. *What babies?* her mama tells me. *You never had any more babies but the two you already got.*

He kneels down beside her. His face is a mountain, the tufted eyebrows like trees, the eyes pond-water gray and speckled with floating leaves. He blinks, and water runs down the slope of his nose, a clear stream that veers off to trace the deep lines beside his mouth.

"You tell me," he says, his voice almost kind, "what kind of devil is a woman who kills two little babies?"

Amy doesn't know.

"You really are devils, all of you," he says. "You are born with it in you, like a bull is born to meanness. Devils to the last."

Amy sees herself with a forked tail and hooves, bald red skin, a pitchfork like a Halloween devil, even though she knows real devils can look like anything they want to: a pig or a fish. A girl. An old man. She swipes at her ears, feels wetness there. Her face burns with shame.

"You pray for your grandma, if that's what you want. *Me*" — Fritz punches his chest — "I hope she rots in Hell with her ma."

He gets up stiffly and goes down the hall to the bedroom, closes the door with a sound that is as soft as a kiss. Amy goes into the bathroom and turns on the overhead light. Her left ear is bleeding, the pierced hole ripped into a jagged oval. She works the earring free and washes the lobe with water and soap. Then she takes the other earring out and washes that lobe as well. She tosses the earrings into the trash beneath the sink and washes her hands and face and neck. New blood seeps from her torn ear and she blots it with toilet tissue, waits, then checks to see if it's still bleeding. For months she has hoped for her bleeding to start, for the stain on her white cotton panties that means she's a grown-up woman like Kimmy, like Kimmy's friend Jennifer. Now it has happened, she is finally bleeding, and even though it's different it means the same. She is a devil, just like Kimmy and Jennifer are devils, like her mother certainly must be. But she isn't going to tell them that. Nobody ever has to know.

She goes back into the living room and finds her sweatshirt where she left it on top of the TV. She pulls it on over her pink tube top and picks up the knocked-over lamp. She straightens her grandmother's chair. She takes out the vacuum cleaner and sucks up the dirt left by the philodendron, which she replants neatly, wrapping the long viny arms protectively around the pot. By the time she is finished, the room will look exactly as it did before. No one will be able to tell the difference.

Ellen doesn't stay in the gray little room where she has been told to wait. Shivering in her shorts and T-shirt, she hooks her purse over her shoulder and walks down the long hallway, avoiding the nurses' station, looking for a sunny window away from the air-conditioning. The hospital smells of coffee and disinfectant, and she wonders why every hospital she's been in has smelled the same. It's a smell that reminds her of having a cold, one that gets up into your head and stays there, making even your own skin smell strange.

As Mary-Margaret was being rushed from the ambulance into the hospital, she cried out for her mother, her voice muffled and thick behind the plastic mask. Now Ellen cannot shake the sound from her mind. She wonders if James has come home from his trip yet, if perhaps he has arrived at the hospital and is sitting in another cold gray waiting room that smells of coffee and disinfectant. She imagines him with his knees spread wide, his feet pointing away from each other, listening for the sound of Mary-Margaret's voice the way Ellen has been listening, as if those thin cries could filter like smoke through unseen cracks in the walls, *Mama, Mama.*

She turns the corner and almost walks into a man lying on a stretcher. His feet are uncovered, and his tapering yellow toenails are both beautiful and grotesque. She has heard that after people die their hair and toenails continue to grow, but she can't remember if this is really true or just something kids tell each other at school. This man is in his forties, big-bellied, his face grizzled with beard. He stares at the ceiling without seeing it, and Ellen wonders what he was doing when he first realized, however vaguely, that something intricate inside him had failed. Perhaps he was at work, soldering one meaningless piece of metal to another, or lecturing a new employee on protocol, rules he once believed in which mean very little now. He might have been with his family, sitting down to supper. He might have been playing with his dog, or thinking thoughts that made him stare at the ground and smile soft, secret smiles.

Mary-Margaret had been watching Ellen play cards with Amy, her hands clasped over her stomach, her rosary braided between her fingers. She had fallen from her chair without a word, her thin legs treading air as if there were somewhere important she had to go. Ellen imagines Mary-Margaret lying on a stretcher just like this one, her toenails just as yellow, just as thick, and growing. Farther down the hall, a woman in white bursts through a set of double doors. Ellen turns away, but the brisk *squeak squeak* of the woman's white shoes is close behind. She has the feeling that even if she broke into a run, the woman would follow at exactly the same distance, businesslike, efficient.

"Ma'am, I must insist you stay in the waiting room," the woman whispers loudly.

"I'm sorry," Ellen says, whispering too. "It's just that I'm so cold. Isn't there a warmer place to wait?"

"Try the chapel, second floor."

"Thanks," Ellen says, but the woman is already gone, sucked between another pair of double doors that seal themselves neatly after her.

She leaves a message for James at the nurses' station, then takes the elevator, trying not to look too closely at the couple riding with her because she's afraid that if she does she'll grab them by the collars or clutch at their sleeves. *My mother-in-law had a heart attack and all I could do was watch,* she'll say. *She fell on the floor. She couldn't breathe. I saw it happen.* But that won't be what she means, what she wants to say. She feels disconnected, as if she's looking at everything from behind a thick lens. In the basement, she had held Mary-Margaret's hands, talking to her softly while Amy stared and Fritz stood over her with the look of a farmer assessing a sick animal. "Here, you sit with her too," Ellen said, but Fritz turned away. Soon she heard him clumping up the stairs, and by the time the ambulance came he had locked himself in the bedroom.

"Keep an eye on Amy, at least," she shouted at him, drumming her fists on the door. "*If* that isn't too much to ask while I take your wife to the hospital."

Then she saw Amy looking up at her.

"I want to come along," Amy said. She had changed out of the sweatshirt she'd been wearing into a skimpy pink top; she held her purse in one hand. Ellen knew if she opened up that purse she would find lipsticks hidden inside the innocent tissue packs, a slim mascara worked into the lining. Amy put her hands on her hips, small and fierce, defiant and frightened, and Ellen could not look at her. She ran past her down the hall, calling over her shoulder, "Stay near the house and be good," as if this could somehow keep her from growing older and more fierce and more afraid until one day she too would be clutching her heart on the cold concrete floor of a basement, the lipsticks and skimpy pink tops long forgotten, blue-veined legs thrashing air.

The chapel is empty; a dozen narrow pews,

an altar the size of a picnic table. Ellen walks to the front and kneels before the metal trays filled with candles. Most have been lit, some recently, some burned down into a flat, shiny pool, the dark wick at each center like the pupil of an eye. Ellen digs through her purse for a quarter and slips it into the donation box. Then she lights one of the few remaining candles, holding the match against it until her fingers sting.

She and her sisters had gone with Mom to light a candle for their father every Sunday after Mass. They'd line up with the Feiderspiels, who had lost their oldest daughter; the Oosters who had lost their mother; the Klepners who had a sickly son. All of them knew each other's grief. Everyone waited patiently as the others took their turns at the kneeler, clattering coins into the donation box, praying for health, for rest, peace. *I can't think of what to say,* she told Mom the first time she was allowed to light the candle. *You don't have to say anything,* Mom said. *God knows what's in your heart.*

The candle burns steadily. The outer husk is sun yellow, surrounding the darker core.

Dear God, Ellen begins.

She does not want God to know what's in her heart. Last week, Barb took the kids for the morning so she could drive to Schulesville, an hour away, and interview for an opening at the public school there.

Dear God.

The next day, the principal called to offer her the job. She answered the phone in the kitchen as James and Fritz watched TV in the living room; afraid they might hear, she accepted in a whisper. Afterward, she sat down on the floor by the phone, waves of panic rippling over her.

Who called? James said later.

No one.

No one? he said. It seems peculiar you would want to talk to no one for so long.

Now Ellen feels as if what has happened to Mary-Margaret is her fault. But that's crazy. But that's how she feels. But she's done everything she could for Mary-Margaret, cleaning her house, fixing her meals, rubbing salve into her soft peach shoulders. But she cannot stop seeing those thin legs walking, walking nowhere, growing still.

God.

Schulesville Public pays much more than Saint Michael's. With child support, she and the kids can get by, and when she gets her share of the money back she'll be able to buy a car. But how can she even think about leaving at a time when James will need her so much? If there was ever a chance that her

309

mother and sisters would understand, that chance does not exist now. *You promised for better or worse,* they'll say. *How can you live with yourself?*

God.

The word is empty. She gets to her feet and sees that a man is standing in the doorway of the chapel. Light streams from behind him, making his body glow. For a moment, Ellen thinks of the saints and their visions of Christ, His body wrapped in light. Perhaps He has come to chide her for her selfishness, and in His presence, filled with Grace, she will finally be certain, *this is right; this is wrong.* But the man simply walks into the chapel, stops, shifts foot to foot. She sees he has been crying, and she has never seen him cry before. "James," she says, but his name in her mouth is as empty as God's; she doesn't have anything to say to him.

"I thought," he says, talking in gasps like children do when they've been crying very hard and for a long time. "When I came home. When I came home and they told me about the ambulance."

Then he comes to her and embraces her, his sharp nose chiseling her neck. Ellen feels nothing except sadness and, perhaps, an awkward disbelief.

"I know it's wrong, but I was so grateful."

He sobs into her shoulder. "When I found out it was Mother. Because I thought it might be one of the children. I thought it might be you."

Choice

16

Miriam arrives at the house late that night, Bert leaning sleepily against her side. She wears a windbreaker that belongs to one of her grown-up sons and carries a duffel bag that another grown-up son left behind when he moved out. "I keep my family with me," she jokes, kicking off her husband's big boots. She hugs Ellen and Amy, then moves toward James, arms outstretched. "Can't you give your sister-in-law a kiss?"

"It's good of you to come," James says formally. He tries to sidestep the hug, but Miriam is quick and she links him into her arms.

"I can stay as long as you need me," she says, following him into the living room. "Sarah can take care of Darby and the house. Sometimes I forget she's just fifteen, but they say the youngest is the most down-to-earth."

It's the first time one of Ellen's sisters has been invited inside. Ellen is suddenly aware of Bert's fingerprints on the walls, the dust on the TV set, the clutter of newspapers, cups, and shoes. Miriam walks around the living room, fingering Mary-Margaret's knickknacks and vases, straightening the shade on the lamp. James phoned her himself to ask if she would take care of the children for the next few days, so Ellen can stay at the hospital with Mary-Margaret. He's arranged this with the nurses. He is organized, rational, calm. There have been no more outbursts of weeping.

"So how is she?" Miriam says. She brushes a balled-up sock from the couch and sits, pulling Bert into her lap.

"The heart attack wasn't severe," Ellen says.

"Are you going back to the hospital tonight?"

"No," Ellen says, just as James says, "Yes."

Ellen can see James's mind at work, dividing her into shifts: take care of my mother, check on the kids, talk with the doctor. Already he has mentioned she might want to take a leave of absence in the fall. Ellen still hasn't told him that by then she will not be here; she cannot imagine saying *James, I am leaving you,* packing only the things she and the kids absolutely need, carrying the suitcases out into the driveway where Barb's red Camaro would be waiting to take her . . . where? "There's nothing we can do for her tonight," she says. "They'll call if there's any change."

"And your pa is already there with her, I imagine," Miriam says to James.

"He's in his room," Amy says. "He won't come out."

"Oh, my," Miriam says.

"He says he thinks Grandma is the Devil."

"What?" Ellen says. All she needs is for Amy to act up in front of Miriam. Miriam is already convinced that Amy is growing up *wild* because Ellen isn't home with her the way a mother should be. Suddenly, it is important to show Miriam that she *is* a good mother, that Amy is under control, that Ellen knows how to handle her children. "Don't tell lies," she snaps.

Amy's eyes are bright with hurt, but she does not contradict. Instead, she chews on her thumbnail, ripping the cuticle with her teeth. She does not look at Ellen, does not look at anyone, just tears the skin from her finger with a deliberateness that makes Ellen wince. "Why don't you and Bert go to bed now," Ellen tells her weakly. Amy takes Bert's hand, pulls him out of Miriam's lap, and leads him away without a word. Ellen gets the set of spare sheets from the linen closet in the hall; she presses her face into the clean, stacked towels, feeling absolutely terrible.

By the time she has fixed up the couch for Miriam, James is already in bed. Instead of rolling to the edge of the mattress, the way he usually does when Ellen lies down beside him, he presses himself against her, cups his hand affectionately over her stomach. It takes all of her willpower not to push him away. Only after she is certain he is sleeping does she lift his heavy arm and wriggle out from under it. The sound of his breathing, the smell of his body, the deep hollows of his nostrils: she experiences James piece by piece, part by part. She cannot force herself to assemble those parts. She cannot bear to view him whole. She does not love him.

She does not love him.

In the morning, Mom and Ketty come over with paper plates and cups, a big glass jar of instant coffee. "You're going to need these," Mom warns. "Everybody wants to see the inside of this house." She and Ketty explore the rooms, looking in closets, peering into cupboards, picking up Mary-Margaret's china knickknacks and putting them back in slightly different places. "So this is what she's so proud of," Mom says to Ellen, deliberately unimpressed.

Neighbors start to arrive: the Muellers, the Kaufmans, the Wenzels. They carry casseroles still hot from the oven, angel food cake, pork and beans, and their faces are bright with sympathy. They bring their children, who stare at Ellen, not knowing how to react to Teacher out of school. Ellen has heard them whisper to their friends that 512 Vinegar Hill is haunted. Sometimes they brag about having to walk past it on their way to school. At recess, they call Ellen *witch* just loudly enough that she can pretend she doesn't hear. But now they are silent, and Ellen can sense their disappointment as they look at the ordinary, everyday coffee table, the TV and couch, the familiar picture of the Last Supper hanging on the wall. Their parents' reaction is almost the same. They discuss the tornadoes, their effect on the local crops, the possibility of a long summer of storms. By lunchtime, everyone is eager to leave and they all get up together. They give Ellen instructions about reheating the casseroles. They say they will come by later for the pans. They ask Ellen to give their condolences to Fritz, who has come out of his room only twice today: once to use the bathroom, once to drag the TV from the living room into his bedroom.

We're sorry, we're so sorry, they say.

"She isn't dead yet," Ellen says.

Miriam quickly grabs Ellen by the arm and leads her to Mary-Margaret's chair. "You're tired," she says, "now you just rest." She and Ketty finish the good-byes while Mom sits on the couch across from Ellen and asks her does she want anything — another cup of coffee? A piece of pie? Ellen pinches a broken leaf off the philodendron on the end table. She's supposed to be at the hospital by two, when Mary-Margaret will be transferred to a private room. As if she's read Ellen's mind, Mom says, "I know it's hard but it's an opportunity. She never liked you or any of us. Now's your chance to make peace."

"She doesn't want peace," Ellen says.

"She'll remember how you cared for her at the hospital. She'll see how you did what's right."

"Whew!" Miriam says, falling into a chair. "That's the last of 'em for now." Her short legs dangle; the blunt toes of her shoes kiss. She selects a carrot-raisin cookie from a plate and nibbles on it thoughtfully. Early this morning, while Ellen was still in bed, Miriam pulled the living room drapes to let the sunlight in and propped the windows open with mildewed back issues of the *Catholic Digest*. She vacuumed and dusted, scoured the toilets and sinks. She even shamed the kids into cleaning their room.

"I understand," Miriam said when Ellen came into the kitchen for coffee, still in her nightgown, sleep in her eyes. She was dumping limp vegetables from the crisper into the trash. "You get a little behind on your housework, it all comes down like a landslide."

"You don't have to do this," Ellen said. *And it's not my housework*, she added silently. But it was a relief to let Miriam take charge, and she drank the coffee Miriam had made and tried to eat the bacon and eggs and pancakes Miriam set before her even though she wasn't hungry.

Now Miriam says, "Sputzie, you better get ready to go. Don't worry about the kids, we'll have a good time together."

"I sent them outside to play," Ketty says. "I brought along some trucks for Bertie. And Amy" — she shakes her head — "is *tanning*. Girls can be so foolish."

"Isn't she young to get started on all that?" Miriam says.

"Girls these days, they grow up fast," Mom says, and she looks at Ellen meaningfully. "They need a mother's close eye on them."

"I better tell them good-bye," Ellen says, and she escapes through the back door, squinting at the bright burst of sunlight. "Hello?" she calls, and Bert pops up from between the shrubs along the house. He's making tunnels for the trucks, probably damaging the shrub roots. When Ellen bends to kiss him, his face is peppered with fine grains of dirt. Amy is lying face down on a blanket. The straps of her bathing suit have been pulled around her shoulders; a bottle of coconut tanning lotion nestles in the grass. Where does she get the money for these things — the lotions and lipsticks, the magazines? Ellen can't believe she's stealing.

"I have to go to the hospital now," she says.

"To see Grandma," Bert says.

"To see Grandma."

"Why doesn't Grandpa go see her?"

"I don't know."

"I told you why," Amy says without lifting her head. "He says she's the Devil, that she kills babies."

"Does she eat them?" Bert says.

"Just the boys," Amy says. Even a month ago, this could have made Bert cry, but now he stares at her, thinking.

"You're lying," he says calmly, and he goes back to his trucks and the intricate maze of trails he has made for them. Ellen sits down on the blanket next to Amy. The air is thick with coconut, a good sweet smell. She plucks a piece of grass and flicks it against the bottom of Amy's foot until Amy rolls over, sits up.

"He said there were other kids besides Dad and Uncle. He said all women are devils. He said I am a devil."

"Amy," Ellen says.

"Don't believe me, then, I really don't care."

"It's not that I don't believe you, or that I do believe you," Ellen says. "Sweetheart, I'm just tired, that's all, and I have to go to the hospital now, so maybe it would be better if we talked about this later."

"You're always tired," Amy says.

"I know."

"What's wrong with you? Are you sick?"

Ellen stares out across the lawn, fighting the urge to lie down beside Amy on the blanket and not get up. There are so many things that she and Amy have to talk about, that she and James have to talk about, that she and her mother and sisters have to talk about, and she doesn't know where she will find the energy, now or later or any other time. Somehow, she has to pull herself together. She needs to create enough space within herself to think things through.

"Look," Amy says. "Just forget it. I made it all up about Grandpa."

"No, you didn't."

"He was mumbling some stuff, but I couldn't really hear it." She lies back down on the grass. "You better go," she says after a minute.

"I wish I didn't have to," Ellen says.

Amy takes the bottle of lotion, squirts it onto one slender leg. Tiny bees hover inches above her skin, searching for the sweet. Her earlobes are swollen and red; are they pierced? "It's not like I'm a little kid and you have to take care of me anymore."

At the hospital, Ellen gets Mary-Margaret's new room number from the front desk: 333. Easy to remember. She buys a yellow rose and a paperback at the gift shop before she goes upstairs. It's a relief to be moving through the cool, silent hallways. Undoubtedly the house will fill with a new round of visitors this afternoon. Ellen imagines the dining room table spread with food: congealed meats, sugary fruit breads, Ritz crackers, Jell-O salads. Her stomach churns. She finds a trash can and throws away the neat foil package of tuna casserole that Miriam tucked into her purse.

Mary-Margaret's room is plain and white, with two small windows, and a TV mounted high on the wall. Father Bork is standing beside the bed, and seated on the chair beneath the windows is a woman. For a moment, Ellen thinks it's Mary-Margaret, already sitting up. Then the woman turns toward the door, as if by instinct, as if she had caught a whiff of Ellen's scent, mouth open to taste the air. Salome blinks her beautiful eyes as if she doesn't quite remember who Ellen is. The bones in her face are fierce.

Father Bork comes over to greet Ellen, soft

white hands outstretched. "I understand you'll be staying here at the hospital," he whispers. His hands swallow Ellen's like gloves.

"Yes, Father."

"So good of you," he says. "Mary-May's sister wants to stay, but she seems a bit . . . confused. They both do, really, and I was reluctant to leave them alone."

"I haven't seen Auntie Salome in months," Ellen says. "I don't think she likes me."

"Well, I'm sure she'll forget about that now," Father Bork says. "One of the blessings of illness is that it draws people together." He smiles his calm, wise smile. She remembers his office, James nervously squeezing her hand. *The hearth and the home.* She keeps her eyes on the floor the way she did when she was a girl worrying that the nuns could read her mind.

"Mary-May," Father Bork says warmly, leading Ellen toward the bed. Mary-Margaret looks like a child's paper construction, gray with paste, wrinkled at the edges. IV tubes trail from her arm; another tube runs from her nose. On a portable stand behind her, a heart monitor flashes silently.

"Hi," Ellen says awkwardly.

"Look who brought you a rose! You always liked yellow flowers, just like your mama did."

He brings the rose to Mary-Margaret's face. Her eyes focus on Ellen; she swallows hard.

"Are you come to help?" she whispers.

"Yes," Ellen says.

"You?" Salome says. She rises stiffly. Sunlight cuts in through the blinds, dividing her face into savage shadows. She wears a housecoat that might have once been pink; now it's the color of an old bloodstain, and it hangs straight from her bony shoulders. A frayed black sweater is draped over the back of her neck, catlike, one long arm switching. "We won't be needing any help," she says.

"Come now," Father Bork says. "Ellen can make your sister more comfortable. You want her to be comfortable, don't you?"

Salome sits back down without answering, but she fixes Ellen with an angry stare.

"I have to leave now," Father Bork murmurs to Ellen, "but I'll give Mary-May Communion before I go." When he turns to prepare the Host, tears stream down Mary-Margaret's face.

"It's supposed to hurt," Salome tells her. "The pain is part of God's will."

Father Bork tries to feed Mary-Margaret the Host, but she bites her lips, shakes her head. He looks at Ellen; she doesn't understand either.

326

"She is dirty," Salome tells them. "She is unclean."

Father Bork puts the Host away. "Salome, my dear, may I speak to you in the hall?"

She allows him to take her arm. After they are gone, Ellen sits in Salome's chair, not knowing what to do. Mary-Margaret is taking short sharp breaths; she reaches for Ellen, her nails biting into Ellen's wrist. "It's my time," she says.

"But you'll be fine," Ellen says. "Doctor says you'll be home in a week."

"Go get Mama. I need Mama."

When Father Bork comes back into the room, he puts his lips to Ellen's ear. "I sent the sister to the chapel," he says, whispering again. "I hate to separate them, but if she's upsetting Mary-May, the nurse will make her leave."

"She wants her mother," Ellen says.

Mary-Margaret's eyes close; sweat shines on her forehead. Father Bork sighs deeply. "Her mother, rest her soul, filled Mary-May's head with girlish dreams, and after that she wasn't satisfied with anything. God blessed Mary-Margaret with a husband, two beautiful sons, a home —" He waves Mary-Margaret's life away with his hand. Ellen is aware of his smell; soap and talcum powder, like Bert after his bath. She flinches when he lowers his hand to her shoulder. "It's been hard for you, living with her," he says. "Your sisters are concerned. I understand you've been having doubts about your marriage."

Julia, Ellen thinks. Her face burns; she doesn't move.

"Sometimes God speaks to us through a tragedy, because that's the only way we'll listen. Perhaps this is God's way of showing you how much your family needs you. Families forget to say that sometimes; husbands forget." He smiles. "What you're doing here is a good thing, a Christian thing."

He pats her shoulder and leaves, his long skirt rustling. *Mind your own damn business.* That's what she should have told him — why didn't she? What has she got to lose? She imagines herself sitting by this bed for many years, growing thinner, grayer, brittle, the good Christian wife, the good Christian mother. Salome slips back into the room. "We don't need your help about anything," she says, her chin nodding sharply like the beak of a bird. She sits at the foot of Mary-Margaret's bed and begins to pray the Rosary.

By late afternoon, Mary-Margaret clutches her sides and wails with pain. The nurse has been in twice, an older woman with a kind, practical face. "I'll give her another sedative," she says on her second visit. "I don't know what else to do for her until Doctor stops by tonight."

"Can he come any sooner?" Ellen asks.

"There's no need," the nurse says. "Doctor was here just before you came."

"We don't need no doctor," Salome says. "Birth is a natural thing in a woman. It is death, you know, that's unnatural."

Ellen and the nurse exchange looks; the nurse shrugs and leaves. Salome opens her big black purse and takes out a bag of corn chips. She slits the plastic with a pin from her hair, puts a chip in her mouth, and sucks noisily. At home, they must be sitting down to dinner: Miriam, James, Amy and Bert, perhaps Fritz too, for by now he must be hungry. James will be quiet from having slept all day, his eyes glazed, his face still wrinkled from the dingy sheets Ellen hasn't washed in weeks. She sighs, opens the paperback she bought at the gift shop, but her mind spins the words in dizzy circles and she puts it back in her purse. Suddenly her chest feels heavy. She tries to breathe but can't. Anxiety builds in her throat like a taste, and she goes down the hall to the water fountain, where she swallows a pill, another, one more, then leans against the wall to wait for the feeling to pass. Her eyes close; she can sleep right here, and no one will notice because she is becoming invisible. Soon no one will be able to see her no matter how hard they try. When she opens her eyes she sees only her shoes many miles beneath her, and as she watches, even they disappear, front to back, as though they are being erased by a child's eraser. Father Bork is beside her; he grabs for her feet, catches only air. *What is happening to you?* he shouts.

Sacrifice is never easy, the aqua lady explains. Her aqua body fills the space where Ellen's body once stood.

And Amy says, *Women are devils. I am a devil.* Her eyes bulge red in her face; Ellen opens her mouth to scream.

The back of her shirt is cold with sweat. She gulps water, splashes it on her face, and her fingers seem huge to her, plump and sausage-pink. *I am going crazy,* she thinks. *This is how a crazy person feels.* She rinses her mouth, then walks unsteadily down the hall to Mary-Margaret's room. Dim evening light filters between the blinds, and Ellen squints, trying to see. Everything seems to be moving very slowly. She hears Mary-Margaret cry out, a low whistle of air, and she pats the wall for the light switch.

"Shut the door," Salome snaps. She holds her black sweater bundled in her arms, her body hunched around it as though Ellen might try to take it away.

"What's wrong?" Ellen says, and Salome smiles a strange triumphant smile. Mary-Margaret's gown is twisted up around her waist; her legs are bent awkwardly, her bony knees white as skulls. Ellen smooths her gown back into place, covers her with the sheet.

"Sh, sh," Salome says, rocking the sweater bundle, stroking it, tucking it around itself even more securely. Watching her, Ellen shakes with a sudden, sick feeling, recognizing the way she rocked her own children.

"What do you have there?" she breathes.

"Them two Ma killed," Salome says smugly. She tilts the bundle, showing Ellen its emptiness. "I was there the first time they was born, and I can tell you they're the same ones now."

Mary-Margaret begins to cry, the squalling voice of an infant.

"Nothing is there," Ellen says. "There are no babies."

"That's what Ma said. She fixed him good for what he done to Mary-May. But a man has a right to his wife under God's law." Salome stares into Ellen's face. "It is the will of God for babies to be born."

"There *are no babies*."

"The will of God ain't for everyone to see."

Amy's words rise like a knot in Ellen's throat. She turns to Mary-Margaret and realizes how very still she has become, her face milk white, her crying no more than a low, steady moan. "Wait here, just wait here," Ellen says, and she runs out of the room, fighting her way through the sharp angles of the corridors, bumping her hip on a cleaning cart, catching her foot on a wheelchair. By the time she returns with a nurse, Salome is gone. Mary-Margaret's face looks like it has been split in two and then put back together, one side lower than the other. The black sweater rests on her chest.

"She thinks she's had a baby," Ellen says thickly, but the nurse isn't really listening. She checks the heart monitor, hits a button, and the hallway outside the room comes to life with footsteps. "What she's had is some kind of seizure," she says. "I'm afraid you'll have to wait outside."

At the end of the hallway, Ellen leans against a vending machine, trying to catch her breath, trying to understand. What kind of woman would kill two newborn babies? But she already knows the answer: a desperate woman. A woman who was trapped. A woman who was driven to do something, anything, to change the way things were. *What might I be driven to?* Ellen thinks, licking salty perspiration from her upper lip. She does not want to know. She takes a deep breath and feels her own blood moving inside her, spreading sweet life through her body. Suddenly, it's as if Ann is with her in this cold gray hospital hall. At last, Ellen has found someone in her family who will understand what she must do, before it is too late, before her own rage grows into something she cannot control. Relief wells up in her, warmer than tears. When she tells her family she is leaving James, she will not be completely alone.

It is almost nine by the time she gets home. Miriam's car straddles the driveway, so she parks the car on the street and walks up the lawn, the night air cool and private against her skin, damp grass lapping her ankles. Inside, James and Miriam are watching TV with the children, and their heads could be the heads of any couple sitting side by side. They could be very much in love. They could be talking instead of watching TV, discussing the recent tornadoes, perhaps, or their next vacation, or the neighbors' children.

Marv and Sally Gray's son got another speeding ticket.

Does that make two or three?

Three, I think. Old Marv's got his hands full with that one.

Or maybe they aren't saying anything. Maybe they are watching the children, communicating only with pursed lips, a raised eyebrow. He slides low in his chair to poke her foot with his own; she pulls her foot away, edges it back, the children never suspecting their parents are involved in lives they do not yet understand. Ellen stands in the yard for a long time, watching them through the window the way she once stared through the windows of her sisters' dollhouse. She wonders where her own doll would have been placed had Daddy lived to carve it for her.

A quarter moon rises above the house, silver back arching, graceful as a fish. Somewhere down the street a dog barks. In the house, James gets up and turns off the TV, paces in front of the window, and Ellen knows she should go inside, but within those walls she is the piece that doesn't fit, the doll without a task. Here on the lawn with the sky stretching wide above her, the pinpoints of stars glowing billions of possibilities, she is whole and strong. Perhaps Mary-Margaret once stood beneath a night sky like this one, but she stood in one place so long that even Ann could not save her. For a moment, James stares out the window; Ellen's heart skips, even now, thinking he has seen her. But James sees nothing but darkness, and he turns out the light and pulls the drapes tightly closed.

By the time she lets herself into the house, everyone is asleep. She closes the door softly behind her, listening to the sound of Miriam's breathing, which reminds her of Mom and the sweet warm nights they slept together like spoons. She savors the memory of that closeness, something she cannot imagine she'll ever experience again. Then she creeps past the couch, down the hall toward the bathroom, closing the door before she turns on the light.

The pills fill the belly of the ballerina; Ellen unscrews her slender neck and tips them into the toilet. They float like water bugs, bumping noses. She flushes, wincing at the sound. Some of them do not go down, and she has to flush twice more before the last one disappears. Then she puts the head back on, careful so the ballerina's chin ends up pointing forward. She curves the soft folds of her skirt into her transparent hands before placing her, high out of sight, on the shelf. Mary-Margaret's doll.

She will tell James now, in the quiet darkness, the lamp beside the bed casting a rosy calm over what she must say. *I am afraid to go, but I am more afraid to stay. I have to take care of myself for a while.* James will be confused, coming slowly up out of his sleep, perhaps thinking this is all a dream until he feels Ellen's hand clasp his. Or maybe he will be angry; he will call her names, he will take off his ring and throw it at her feet. She turns off the light and goes out into the hallway, groping her way until her fingers brush the door to James's room at the end of the hall. The wood is cool beneath her hand; she moves her palm along its smooth surface. Only this piece of wood separates them. Ellen presses her forehead against it, feeling James breathing on the other side, content in his sleep, contained, complete, and she does not open the door because she knows that if she wakes him he will not be angry. He will not think it's a dream. *You're not going anywhere,* he will say, and he'll roll over onto his stomach with his head pushed deep into his pillow. Or worse, he will look at her as if she hasn't spoken, as if she isn't even there. And if that were to happen, she would not know what to do, because tonight, for the first time in months, she is certain that she *is* there, she *is* someone, a person whose life is of value, and if James failed to recognize that now, she would never be able to forgive him.

The children's voices register gradually; first Amy's whisper, then Bert's frustrated whine. A slender line of light winks beneath their bedroom door. Ellen turns away from James and slips into their room. They are playing cards on the floor, a flashlight glowing between them. When Ellen turns on the light, Bert sweeps up the cards defiantly and deals another hand, his small plump fingers amazingly agile.

"You want me to tuck you in?" she says, blinking against the brightness. Her eyes feel hot and sore, as if she has been crying, but when she puts her hands to her face, her cheeks are dry.

"I'm too old for that," Amy says.

"Me, too," Bert says quickly.

"Well, okay," Ellen says. "But I think you should get to bed soon. I'm driving to Schulesville early in the morning, and I'd like you to go with me."

"What for?" Amy says

"To pick out an apartment."

This gets their attention, but they don't say anything for a while.

"Will we live there?" Amy finally says.

"You and Bert and me."

"What about Dad?" Bert says.

"Not right now. Maybe someday."

Bert deals another hand. "Will he be angry?"

"He might be," Ellen says, "but not with you. I think he already knows that we can't go on living here. Grandma's going to need lots of quiet when she comes home."

"Who will take care of her?" Amy says

meanly. "Isn't that your job?"

Ellen holds her voice steady. "I've done the best I can, but it's hurting us all to be living here. We'll still visit as often as we can."

"Do we have to?" Bert says, just as Amy says, "I don't want to visit." They look old, sitting together, flipping the cards between them. They keep their bodies turned toward each other, away from Ellen, and she realizes they don't trust her any more than they trust James or his parents. It will take time before she is able to be their mother again, before she feels close to them the way she used to.

"Well," Ellen says. "I'm not really tired, so I guess I'll go for a walk."

"A walk?" Bert says. "In the dark?"

"Let me tuck you in first," Ellen says, and Bert drops the cards, suddenly young again, and hops up into his bed.

"What if you don't come back?" he says. "What if you die?"

"I'm not going to die," Ellen says, and she means it. Tonight she can't imagine not being alive in the world.

He looks at her suspiciously. "How do you know?"

"I can just feel it," Ellen says. "I am certain of it."

"But how can you be certain?"

"It's like with guardian angels," Amy says

338

to him. "You just have to know."

Ellen listens to Bert say his prayers, tucks the covers around him, and then she and Amy sit in silence until the sound of his breathing grows slow and deep. She watches Amy, the curve of her neck, the high cheekbones that hollow her face as if she were a woman Ellen's age.

"Do you want to walk with me?" Ellen whispers once she's sure Bert is asleep. "There's nothing to be afraid of."

"I won't be afraid," Amy says.

They follow the cracked gray sidewalk along Vinegar Hill, turn down toward the harbor, their feet making scraping sounds against the concrete. The business district is still out of power from the tornado, and the steeple of Saint Michael's is invisible tonight, the wide eye of the clock closed and dark. Ellen and Amy do not speak. They do not look at each other. But they reach the flat coin of the lake holding hands.